Secret Spirit Guardians of Santa Fe

by

C. A. Masterson

Secret Spirit Guardians of Santa Fe

Cover Art by *Debbie Taylor*

The Wild Rose Press, Inc.
PO Box 708
Adams Basin, NY 14410-0708
Visit us at www.thewildrosepress.com

Publishing History
First Fantasy Rose Edition, 2020
Trade Paperback ISBN 978-1-5092-3351-9
Digital ISBN 978-1-5092-3352-6

Published in the United States of America

The crack between worlds happened before I decided to move home to Santa Fe. Had the thought occurred to me, I'd probably have laughed, a little. Until the memory pushed through, a half-remembered nightmare hidden in an undercurrent of emotion, but always there, flowing beneath the surface of consciousness. Sometimes it's better if those feelings stay buried, where they can't pull you under.

After twenty-four years, here I was. Back in the City Different. Because sometimes, life makes hard choices for you.

Otherwise, I'd still be in San Diego, not in my aunt's house, trying hard to pretend I wasn't a stranger to my own family. For the last half hour, I'd tried to shake off the odd sensation after Zelda made an impromptu, awkward stop at the site of my childhood home, whatever that was about. No longer commenting on family social media posts from a distance, instead I was in the thick of things.

"How's Javi been?" I asked Zelda. My aunt had answered my offer to help prepare dinner by handing me a glass of wine and telling me to relax, she had it under control. I had no doubt. Despite driving me from the airport, she was as cool as a freshly picked jalapeno, and as likely to burn you.

"Wonderful. But you can ask him yourself at dinner." Her deep, distinctive voice was like smoke pouring across gravel.

"Cool, I can't wait." When I'd last spent time with my cousin, we'd been kids. Closer than most first cousins, we shared a family conspiracy, hoping none of our classmates would find out that we were not like any of them. No matter where we went, we didn't belong.

Praise for C. A. Masterson

The Pearl S. Buck Foundation awarded first place to her short literary story *CHRISTMAS EVE AT THE DINER ON RATHOLE STREET*. Her short literary story *ALL IS CALM, ALL IS BRIGHT* was awarded second place in the annual Pennwriters Short Story contest.

Dedication

For everyone who's ever felt out of place.
Your other-ness is what makes you amazing.

Chapter One

It's an ill wind that blows nobody good.

The crack between worlds happened before I decided to move home to Santa Fe. Had the thought occurred to me, I'd probably have laughed, a little. Until the memory pushed through, a half-remembered nightmare hidden in an undercurrent of emotion, but always there, flowing beneath the surface of consciousness. Sometimes it's better if those feelings stay buried, where they can't pull you under.

After twenty-four years, here I was. Back in the City Different. Because sometimes, life makes hard choices for you.

Otherwise, I'd still be in San Diego, not in my aunt's house, trying hard to pretend I wasn't a stranger to my own family. For the last half hour, I'd tried to shake off the odd sensation after Zelda made an impromptu, awkward stop at the site of my childhood home, whatever that was about. No longer commenting on family social media posts from a distance, instead I was in the thick of things.

"How's Javi been?" I asked Zelda. My aunt had answered my offer to help prepare dinner by handing me a glass of wine and telling me to relax, she had it under control. I had no doubt. Despite driving me from the airport, she was as cool as a freshly picked jalapeno, and as likely to burn you.

"Wonderful. But you can ask him yourself at dinner." Her deep, distinctive voice was like smoke pouring across gravel.

"Cool, I can't wait." When I'd last spent time with my cousin, we'd been kids. Closer than most first cousins, we shared a family conspiracy, hoping none of our classmates would find out that we were not like any of them. No matter where we went, we didn't belong.

Zelda's silver bracelets jingled as she briskly arranged vegetables around haddock fillets. "Phoebe will be excited to see you again."

"You still have her?"

"Of course. She's as old as you, which makes her barely middle-aged. Phoebe, dear," she called, "we have company."

A squawk sounded from the other room, where sunshine poured across the floor in a welcoming sea of light.

I'd always loved my aunt's house. From sunup to sundown, daylight flooded through the house's tall windows. The wood-framed stucco structure was a typical style for Santa Fe, not much different from the others in the neighborhood. What had stood out in my memory was the tall wooden fence that bordered the yard, painted a vivid shade of blue, with myriad crosses along the top of the front gate.

"Careful," Zelda said. "She's testy sometimes."

"Aren't we all?" I only half joked.

Before my aunt could answer, I made my way from the kitchen to the sunroom beside it. The glass enclosure looked out onto the back yard and faced the outdoor fireplace. On either side of the tall chimney, colorful painted angels decorated its white stucco surface.

The bird cage, as tall as me, occupied a corner. And as always, the door sat wide open so Phoebe could climb in if she wanted, which she almost never did unless she got hungry. A bamboo perch ran above the cage, between the two potted palm trees that provided shade. There Phoebe sat, eyeballing me. Sunlight caught the green and blue feathers, making their colors rich as jewels.

At my approach, the parrot bobbed its head and danced along the perch. Even a nip from Phoebe's curved beak hurt like hell, so I kept a few feet between us and cooed my greeting.

Pans rattled in the kitchen. "Be nice, Phoebe girl."

The bird gave no indication of recognizing me. I didn't know why I'd expected a different reaction. Because I'd taught it more than fifty words, over two decades earlier? Moving home shouldn't reduce me to childish notions.

So much for a reunion. I returned to the kitchen. "Sure I can't help with anything?"

"When do you start your new job?"

"Monday." Fluttering in my belly reminded me it was coming up fast. Another long adjustment period awaited me, learning a new job, getting to know all the quirks and qualities of my coworkers. After I'd been hired as the new reporter at the *Santa Fe Chronicle,* I'd read the online edition every day. The stories helped give me a sense about the writers. Glimmers of their personalities shone through in their word choices, the nearly undetectable spin they gave topics.

"That doesn't leave you much time for moving in."

Spooning a marinade over the dish, Zelda flicked up her gaze.

The look hit me like lightning. The cogs were turning in my aunt's head; I could practically see the rotation behind her eyes. If I didn't put her off track, Zelda would start commandeering my daily life.

I folded my arms and shifted toward the island, a not-too-subtle body language indicating my need for a barrier between us. "The two guys I hired to bring my stuff are supposed to arrive tomorrow morning. I don't have much, so they can get everything inside the apartment in a few hours. I prefer to take my time settling in." All taken care of, my subtext said. No need for Zelda to worry. She could divert those black eyes elsewhere.

On cue, Zelda flashed her Mona Lisa smile and glanced away. "Too bad I gave my extra furniture to Javi."

I watched my aunt with a mixture of wonder and frustration. All these years, and Zelda still pretended. Spoke with flawless Spanish enunciation, wore her long black hair in a bun at the back of her neck, decorated her house with painted ceramic geckos and metal sun faces, even named her son Javier to avoid question of our true nationality. My parents had committed the same sins of omission and pretense and expected us children to do the same.

Javi better show up soon. I needed him to provide a buffer, a distraction for my aunt so Zelda wouldn't probe too deeply into my life. "What part of town is his condo in?"

My aunt went on at length about Javi's place, how it was situated close to the fire station so my cousin could roll out of bed and arrive at work in five minutes. I kept my aunt talking as long as I could. Stalling. Just when I had to scrape the bottom of the barrel of my brain for conversational topics, Zelda turned to me with the strangest look.

"What is the real reason you've returned?" The way her entire body tensed, and her expectant expression, she already knew.

But I indulged her. "I'd thought about it for a long time. After Mom and Dad's accident, there was no reason to stay in California."

"So you decided to move back."

Zelda was obviously baiting me, which further aroused my curiosity.

"How could I refuse a request my mother made in her will?" I did the last thing I felt like doing. I smiled.

"What did she say?"

"That she thought I was ready to come home. But maybe you can explain the other part."

"What?"

Enough of this dancing around each other. "That I should move here in case you needed my help."

The house had gone so still, the silence was palpable. Not even Phoebe made a sound.

I arched my brows. "Any idea what she meant?" I startled when the back door burst open.

Javi stepped inside and came to an abrupt halt. "Mar!"

"Javier. Omigod, look at you." In person, he was larger than life.

He pulled me against his barrel chest, practically squeezing the breath from me, and rocked me in a bear hug. "About time you came home."

His shirt muffled my agreement.

Zelda set platters on the dining room table. "Let's eat."

He released me. "I'm starved."

We sat at the table, and Javi scooped food onto his plate and immediately shoveled it into his mouth. "Delicious, Ma."

Zelda wince-smiled. "How can you tell?"

His cheeks bulged as he grinned, then he frowned at his watch, his jaw working.

"Don't tell me," Zelda said with a sigh. "You have to leave soon."

"I gotta take advantage of my nights off. Hey, Mar, you should come with me to the pub. I'm supposed to meet up with Ray, but he won't mind a third wheel."

I took a sudden interest in my plate, though butterflies had killed my appetite. "Ray?" I tossed back my hair.

"Yeah, a good friend. Works at the same firehouse as me. You've probably seen him in the photos I post online."

"Maybe." Definitely. In every photo, Ray leapt out at me. His gaze reached into me as if we were face to face, as if he were silently trying to convey some urgency to me.

"If you're moving home for good, you might as well jump in with both feet." He dabbed the napkin over his grin.

He was right. "Sounds good. But we should help clean up first."

Zelda waved us away. "Go. Too many people in the kitchen make me nervous. And next time, you can cook for us."

Already, it was starting. The family hold. I was good with that, so long as it didn't become a stranglehold. "Only if you swear you have an iron stomach. But thanks again. It was really good to see you." I hugged my aunt. A squawk from Phoebe startled us apart.

"Marissa," the parrot called.

"She does remember me." A nervous laugh erupted. I turned to leave, ignoring the strange glare my aunt sent the bird.

"*Venganza!*" Phoebe screeched.

Icy fingers tickled my neck. "What?"

I searched my aunt's face, but Zelda's expression appeared suddenly…and forcibly…blank.

"Doesn't *venganza* mean—"

"Revenge," Zelda finished for me. "Was that one of the words you taught her?"

I shook my head, staring at the bird. What would a child know about revenge?

Phoebe gave me the fish-eye. "*Venganza!*"

The icy fingers slipped together and tightened around my throat.

Javi mock-scowled. He nudged my shoulder, and my breath eased. The simple action had unlocked my body from the frozen moment, and I wobbled. With a grin, I punched his shoulder.

"Crazy bird. See you, Ma." After a peck to his mother's cheek, he lurched out the door.

Zelda smoothed my hair. A simple gesture, but a motherly touch that made my heart ache. Zelda had the same thick hair as my mother, ebony as I'd remembered, with only a few glints of silver in my mother's shoulder-length strands. The same wide-set

7

eyes, almond-shaped, of an espresso brown. The same full mouth, usually quirked in a knowing smile. The same nose, nostrils curved in a natural flare.

All the same features as my mother. And me as well. Zelda differed in one respect: her ferocity. She was the eye of the hurricane, the stillness in the center of the chaos. My aunt's subdued intensity came across clear as a stick of dynamite dancing atop a sea of sparks. Zelda could go off without warning, and everyone in her path had better duck.

If only I could be more like my aunt. Except for a fierce curiosity, fierceness didn't seem to be part of my DNA.

"We'll speak soon," Zelda said. "Have fun. But do be careful."

Her warmth was reassuring, but the concern in her face made me second-guess my decision. "Always." I followed my cousin outside, the twilight sky deepening from yellow-pink to orange-red smears across the horizon.

****

The low lighting lent a cozy atmosphere to the Third Street Brewery. A popular pub, apparently, but not so packed that I grew claustrophobic. The number of people who greeted Javi with wide smiles and slaps to his back gave testament to his community standing. I only hoped I could eventually earn the same respect as my cousin. Their appraising looks seemed to give initial approval, but I stayed close behind Javi as the crowd made way for him.

Then he stopped abruptly. "Hey, man. Glad you're here." He swept an arm around my shoulder and scooped me forward. "You finally get to meet my cousin, Marissa. Mar, this is Ray."

The name vibrated through me, turning my muscles to stone but bristling every nerve to attention. As Javi's good friend, Ray featured heavily in my cousin's social media photos, usually with a beautiful woman or two draped around his neck. Beach-boy handsome, except that altar-boy smile hid a deep secret.

And now he was aiming that megawatt smile at me.

I managed to dredge up a pleasant persona. "Hey, Ray."

Ray's smile lit up his face like sunshine. "Hey yourself. Welcome back to Santa Fe."

Javi touched my shoulder. "I'm going for a beer. What do you want?"

"Whatever you're having." I watched my cousin shuffle through the crowd, then grinned at Ray, who still stared at me. "I guess Javi warned you I was coming."

"He did." Sheepish, Ray ducked his head. "I remember you. We were in the same kindergarten class."

A laugh burst out. "Oh, come on. You do not remember me from kindergarten."

"Sure, I do. You were the cute girl with long black hair and big brown eyes."

"Like half the girls in the class." That was the illusion my parents hoped for, anyway. Marissa Tahy, the girl who was just like everyone else. It worked well enough for the adults, but not the kids. It took all of two seconds for schoolmates to single me out as different.

Ray turned sly. "Yeah, but you had a tongue that could cut down anyone with one swipe."

I wrinkled my nose at him. "Was I mean to you? Sorry."

The wattage of his sunshine smile dimmed. "Guess I didn't make the same impression on you."

Javi returned and handed me a beer.

"I don't remember much from then." I tilted the bottle to my lips. The things I did remember, I wished I could forget.

"Not even outrunning most of the other kids? You were faster than everyone, racing around on your banana seat bike. It was purple and had those pom-pom things hanging from the handlebars. Usually they pointed straight back because you pedaled like the wind."

Never as fast as my brother Michael. I'd had to pedal hard just to keep him in sight.

Not a memory I wanted to share. "Sounds like the usual kid stuff."

To his credit, Ray let the subject drop, and instead engaged Javi in work talk.

I let my gaze wander and caught sight of a guy, only a glimpse, as he passed behind some people near the entrance. An aura of shadows surrounded him, but enough light fell across his face to outline his arresting features. An unforgettable face, but I couldn't place him. Another long-lost schoolmate? Doubtful. Something about him unsettled me. "Will you excuse me? I need to find the rest room."

"Course." Ray gestured. "They're that way."

As I walked away, the noise in the room washed together in a blur. So did the people. All but one. The man I'd glimpsed earlier stood watching me. He was so still, yet he didn't fit in with the scenery.

The same icy fingers reaching into my heart propelled an urge to run. I pushed open the rest room door and bumped into a woman leaving the bathroom.

"Sorry." My quick apology earned only a cursed response, so I took greater care on the way out.

Still unnerved, I was relieved to see the stranger had gone.

"Ready for another?" Javi asked.

"Not yet." I must have downed the last one too fast. My head buzzed, and a dull ache began to throb at my temples.

Movement in my peripheral vision made me turn. I froze. He was there again. Still watching me.

I wanted to look away but couldn't. The buzz in my head grew louder. Everything around me fell away. There was only me and him. Then he laughed, and the sound reached deep inside, rattling my bones. The longer he stared into my eyes, the more urgent it became for me to get away. I gripped the edge of the bar, wanting to push away, to run, but my muscles had turned to rusted iron, immovable.

The need to flee grew more intense when the man moved from the back of the bar toward me. He approached without discernible steps or obvious motion. Yet somehow, he closed the distance between us. My heart jumped into my throat. Adrenaline coursed through me, the pressure built until my skin wanted to explode.

I hoped Javi and Ray would notice my silent distress, but I couldn't make myself turn toward them. They were somewhere behind me, chatting up two girls.

The next moment, the guy vanished from sight again. I fought the urge to search for him and forced a few deep breaths to calm myself before facing my cousin.

"Javi, I'm sorry, but can we leave? I'm beat." I hated how shaky and weak I sounded and hoped he wouldn't see through my act.

"Already?" Javi gave me a pleading look, and a small nod toward the girl.

I held up a hand and backed away. "I can call a cab."

"I'll drive you." Ray set down his beer on the bar.

"No, don't trouble yourself." More quietly, I added, "I don't want to cramp your style."

He fished some money from his pocket and slipped it beneath the bottle. "I was about to leave anyway." He jerked his head toward the exit. "My truck's outside."

I sent Javi a *bail me out* glance, but he just grinned and curled closer to the woman.

Ray winked. "Come on, I won't let the monsters get you."

A tingle of electricity swept down my spine, and the joke doubled back on me. Monsters. For two decades, I'd been able to relegate them to cartoons, kid stuff. Here, they loomed all too real in the night.

Ray put on a great show of acting the gentleman, leading me through the bar, opening the door for me, then opening the truck door and waiting for me to climb in so he could close it nice and secure. The interior, though, was surprisingly tidy, the vinyl seats clean and no trash littering the floor.

He jumped in behind the wheel. "Where to?"

"The Old Culebra Inn. It's on Galisteo."

"Not far from the Plaza." A nod, and he fired up the engine. "Haven't found a place yet?"

"No." A silly lie. The apartment was vacant. I'd caught up with the landlord today to collect my keys, but sleeping there would have meant sleeping on the floor. Tonight, my weary bones needed a real bed. Why I couldn't just say that, I didn't know.

He grunted. His expression told me I hadn't quite convinced him.

"Funny," he said, concentrating a little too hard on the road ahead, "running into you again."

"Why?" Damn, I really needed to learn to keep my mouth shut. To stifle my reporter's reaction, always wanting to dig deeper. Know more. Sometimes it was better not to ask any question.

"You're the reason I became a firefighter."

I winced, as much in denial as confusion. "Me? Are you sure you don't mean Javi?"

"Yeah, we both did because of what happened to your family." He grew somber before adding, "Your brother Michael."

Hearing his name spoken was like a knife in my gut. I took a sudden interest in the landscape outside, though if someone asked for a description of it, I'd have to invent one. "You remember that night, too." I hated the catch in my voice.

"Hard to forget something so awful."

An understatement. "You're a firefighter?" I already knew the answer but said it to fill the empty air.

"Yes. You?" he asked.

"I'm the most recent addition to the staff of the *Santa Fe Chronicle*."

"A reporter." His smile was a mix of surprise and delight. "Guess we'll be running into one another on the job."

An occupational hazard. I ran into everyone at some point. "Guess so." Luckily, we'd arrived at the hotel. "You can let me out here."

He pulled the truck to the curb. "Want me to walk you up?"

I grabbed my handbag. "I'm good."

"Okay." His smile was lopsided. "Welcome home."

I glanced at the hotel. The entrance was brightly lit, and pretty enough, but not exactly home.

"Good night." I climbed out and hurried inside, glad when the door closed behind me, a barrier against any strangers and monsters cloaked by the thick darkness of the night.

****

In my room, I dropped my bag on the bed with an audible breath. The earthen tones of the room helped soothe my frazzled nerves, and the gas Kiva fireplace was a nice touch, but I was glad I'd only stay one night. Hotels brought back the unsettled feelings from my childhood. I had no need to relive those weeks after we ran away, the fear that at any moment the horror we'd escaped would find us again.

I crossed the room to the wide window. I don't know how long I stood there, staring out over the city. The lights dotting the darkness gave the city a peaceful appearance. If only some of that serenity would rub off on me.

Since stepping off the plane, I'd been too bristly, prickly as a cactus. Not like me at all. I hadn't treated Javi's friend very well. But old feelings died hard.

Yeah, I remembered Ray. Ray the Golden Boy. Even as kids, he could do no wrong. He did everything perfectly right, and I mean every little thing. No one was that good, that helpful, that sympathetic. People sometimes put up false fronts for reasons that had nothing to do with goodness or helpfulness or sympathy. I reacted now as I had then, the way I was brought up to react, by distrusting him.

I hadn't wanted the past to rear its ugly head. Not this fast, anyway. Stupid of me to think I could make a fresh start in a city where my roots were so deep. Of course, I was going to run into a few people outside of my family who vaguely recalled the girl I once was. If I didn't want them to think of me as little Marissa Tahy, I'd need to distance myself from that child. My journalism career would go a long way in achieving that, but I had to learn to do it on a personal level, too.

Before anyone else could let go of that perception, I needed to let go of the past.

And give Ray more slack. He had no clue what lurked beyond the city.

He'd find out in September, at Zozobra, when every person in Santa Fe invited it in.

With that cheerful thought, I changed into a tank top and drawstring pants, then climbed beneath the downy cover and rested my head against the plush pillow. As minutes ticked to hours, I willed myself to sleep, though my brain fought the slow descent.

The dream followed—both surreal and yet too real. Something in the shadows chased me while I tried to get away, but my feet moved too slowly, my body became sluggish as if I fought underwater. The harder I ran, the farther back I slipped. A deep rumbling rose behind me, roaring toward me like a tidal wave. My skin turned to ice when I realized it was a great swell of laughter. Whatever approached, I felt its hot breath closing in fast.

Heart racing, I pumped my legs faster and faster. The ground cracked beneath my feet and began to crumble. Rocks fell to dust. I scrambled for purchase but slipped down, down, down, too far below to reach the edge of the street. My arms and legs flailed uselessly. I screamed but the night thickened around me and smothered the sound. The rush of wind scraped my skin as I fell through nothingness.

"No!" With a start, I sat up in bed. My hair was damp against my fingers as I shoved it back from my face. My legs tangled in the sheet, until I kicked free of it. My heart pounded against my ribs and then in my throat. I inhaled as deeply as I could to stop my chest from heaving. The shaky breath did little to calm me, but the solidness of the mattress beneath my body helped. I must have cried out for real and roused myself from sleep. I was all right. It was only a dream.

To be certain, I switched on the light beside the bed. I wrapped my arms around my legs and pressed my mouth to my knees. Every tactile sensation helped ground me.

"Yeah, welcome home, Marissa."

I couldn't shake the feeling that the dream wasn't so much a dream as a warning.

Chapter Two

Over the weekend, I played hermit, not leaving the new apartment except to run to the grocery store for food, supplies, and the weekend edition of the *Santa Fe Chronicle*. With the cupboard only half bare, I set to work unpacking.

More than once, I stopped to simply take in the apartment. I'd rented the place after finding an online listing, viewing the photos of each room with a skeptical eye. Expecting to discover they'd been digitally tweaked to present a nicer-than-reality rental, I was pleasantly surprised when I entered. The whitewashed wood ceiling topped the white stucco walls, the orange-red Mexican tiles creating a warm flooring beneath. Slate blue wood framed the windows and doors. The narrow kitchen door opened onto a small stone patio large enough for an umbrella table, bordered by a tall wooden fence for privacy. I envisioned many evenings with my laptop or lazy afternoons with a book.

The built-in hutch at the far end of the kitchen, and the white-and-blue tile table attached to the wall, paired with a single blue chair, were a few reasons I needed so little furniture. The previous tenants had abandoned an oversized sectional sofa, which curved around a white stucco fireplace. The moving guys had set up my bed, and the bedroom closet was spacious enough that I didn't need a dresser. The bathroom's faded sage tile, edged with white and blue tile, seemed like a remnant of my childhood home. Though I remembered more patterns along the vanity top, edging the mirror, and inside the sink. At the time, I'd loved it, but I was glad the apartment wasn't an exact duplicate. My new place had enough similarity to the house I grew up in to make it resemble home, but enough differences that I didn't feel as if I'd moved into a living nightmare.

The location was less than ideal, situated a few streets over from my original address. At least I could avoid the burned-out lot on my daily drive to work, but I still wasn't crazy about living so close to Fort Marcy Park, which sat several blocks beyond the lot. But as fate would have it, this apartment was one of the few I could afford.

And I did love it. Already, it had become my sanctuary.

On Monday morning, an eerie red signaled the dawn—not a panoramic New Mexico sunrise as I'd expected when I peered outside. The very air was tinged red. A swirling haze of brick-colored dust blotted the view and pelted the window. Not the greatest timing for a dust storm, but thank goodness, it waited until after the movers had hauled my stuff into the apartment.

The thought of showing up on the first morning of a new job covered in a sheen of red dust made me cringe. The tan slacks I'd planned to wear were definitely out, but since I owned no red ones, I made do with brown. Hopefully, everyone else would be too busy dealing with their own mess to notice mine.

After filling my thermal travel mug with coffee, I

hurried outside to the rental car. The coating turned out to be only a dusting, less than I'd expected after the weird red-out earlier. With no broom to sweep it away, I bent to the door and blew on the handle to clear the messy stuff. The less I touched, the less chance I'd spread it all over myself. After managing to get inside the car without a smear, I breathed a sigh of relief. Maybe this day wouldn't start as a total disaster.

The wipers took care of the windshield, but I had to wait for the car's momentum to clear the rest of the windows. All the other vehicles I passed on the streets had smatterings of red, too, so the dust storm must have blanketed a good part of Santa Fe.

First day jitters shook me as I entered the double glass doors. *The Santa Fe Chronicle* arced across them in gold and red script.

"Good morning," I called to the girl at the front desk as I approached.

"Good if you don't mind dust." She put her smile on hold as she pressed a button and spoke into her headset. "Sorry about that. What can I do you for?"

"I'm not a fan of the red kind, either. Ugh." I set down my travel mug and brushed away another smear from my sleeve. "I'm Marissa Tahy, the new reporter. Mr. Weller said you'd have a packet for me?"

"Welcome, Ms. Tahy." She rummaged through folders as she spoke, then slid one across the counter.

"Oh, just Marissa, please."

"I'm Jill. Let me know if I can do anything for you."

I smiled my thanks, and then pointed to the hallway that led to the back. "This way, right?"

The phone rang on two lines at once. Jill nodded to

me, and I waved. Before I rounded the corner, she neatly answered one call long enough to put it on hold, and then smoothly grabbed the second.

Inside the large newsroom, about half of the desks scattered through the midsection were occupied. Offices lined the outer walls. Weller's, I recognized from the interview I'd flown in for two months ago. He was nowhere to be seen.

A slender blonde in a trendy navy blazer and matching skirt emerged from the break room, with three men close behind her. All carried steaming cups.

"I'm such a mess," the woman said, brushing at her lapel, then her sleeve.

A disheveled man laughed. "You? Never."

Tall and lean, another man appeared crisp in his pressed suit. "No one predicted the storm yesterday."

The third laughed. "Yeah, why don't you complain to the local TV stations? They won't think you're harassing them. Much."

The woman caught sight of me and swept her gaze from my toes to my head. "Look what the storm blew in."

I ignored the urge to check my clothes for errant dust splotches and approached with a forced friendly smile. "Hi. I'm Marissa."

The slick-haired guy shook my hand. "Yeah, we got the memo. Welcome aboard. I'm Mike." His fingers were icicles.

"Rich." One quick shake.

"Steve." He held a beat longer than necessary.

The blonde shook my hand last. "Ashley."

Her hot skin warmed mine, but for some reason, I shivered.

Mike sipped his coffee. "Bad timing for a dust storm."

"I was hoping not to look like a coal miner on my first day." Nothing like sharing a little crazy weather to provide an icebreaker for conversation, though Ashley's ice was slightly thicker to break through.

"We'd better go grab our seats." She sashayed away.

"Monday morning staff meeting." Mike gestured me ahead. "After you."

The others began to amble toward the conference room. I followed with travel mug in hand. Until I knew which desk to claim, I was forced to carry everything with me.

Weller sat at the end of the faux wood table, poring over the morning edition of the *Chronicle*. He didn't glance up once.

I pulled the electronic tablet from my messenger bag, then shoved the bag beneath a corner chair and sat, ready to absorb my new surroundings.

When the last reporter scrambled to the remaining empty spot, Weller slapped the tabletop. "We have lots to cover this morning so let's get right to it." He scanned the room and settled on me. "Good, you're here. Everyone, welcome Marissa Tahy to the staff. She comes to us from the *San Diego Examiner*." His silent stare prompted me.

I rose and addressed them. "I'm very excited to join such a prestigious staff, and I look forward to working with all of you." A formal nod, and I ended it. Seated, I was ready to get down to business. I adjusted the tablet on my lap, fingers poised over the electronic keyboard.

Weller took over. Only five minutes into the meeting, and already the air in the conference room had grown stuffy. Too many bodies packed into too tight a space made me yearn for the great outdoors. Too much coffee had made me jittery, but after unpacking all weekend, caffeine hadn't been optional. Not that it ever was.

"Planning ahead to next month." Weller's voice boomed. "The annual la Fiesta de Santa Fe runs September tenth and eleventh this year, with the usual burning of Zozobra the official kick-off that Thursday night of September ninth. This year's a bigger deal than usual, of course, being the centennial celebration." He scanned the faces surrounding him and landed on me. "Tahy. You just volunteered to cover it."

Unexpectedly struck dumb, I struggled for words. "I…" As the newbie reporter, I'd psyched myself up to garner brownie points by volunteering for anything— anything except the festival. "I have plans that weekend."

"You moved here two days ago, and already made plans for two months from now?"

"Yes. I'll be out of town." Where I wouldn't hear the townspeople chanting, "*Burn him! Burn him!*" with raised fists like the villagers chasing down Frankenstein. The Santa Fe monster waited bound by ropes, but those ties wouldn't hold him. The mere thought sent a shiver to my bones.

Weller cocked his jaw, his heavy-lidded stare saying he'd assessed me, and I'd come up short. "Weekend assignments happen on this newspaper. Staff rotates working events like this to keep things fair."

"It's not that. I'll work other weekends." Any other

weekend. "I just…" I held in my breath, the one that would unleash a litany of excuses, all of which would make me appear lazy, or worse, certifiably crazy.

His pursed lips resembled a duck's bill. "What? You don't want to be part of the biggest civic and cultural event of the city?" He spoke straight forward enough, but there was no mistaking the underlying taunt.

God, I hated bullies. The subtle ones most of all. "I don't mean that."

"Then what do you mean?" He leaned forward.

Those who had discreetly avoided looking at me gave up at that point. All eyes shifted to me.

I said, "Only that I had plans, nothing more." At this point, more like plans to make plans, but Weller didn't need to know that. I squared my shoulders. "If I have to, I'll change them."

"That would be lovely." The crisp words contrasted his gruff tone. "The next edition of the *Chronicle* will list you as the contact and direct any residents too squeamish to add their written troubles to the effigy themselves to drop them off with Jill at the front desk. The assignment also comes with an unofficial seat on the planning committee. You're the niece of Zelda Furtado, correct?"

"Yes."

"I'm sure your aunt would appreciate your company, if not your assistance. Even if the festival hasn't changed much since its inception, working on the committee would be a great way for you to re-acquaint yourself with current-day Santa Fe."

The committee? That was above and beyond my duties, and way out of my comfort zone. "I have been away a few years." Twenty-four, to be exact. No doubt the city had gone through some changes, but some things remained immutable. "I'll speak with Aunt Zelda." No promises for anything else. My aunt threw herself into the festival prep and planning with enough gusto for five people. Zelda was a dynamo, a one-woman event planning committee in and of herself.

"Good." Weller smacked the table, an unnecessary punctuation to his proclamation. "This festival brings in funds for a number of important local charities, and the more we highlight them in the coming month, the greater response we'll get from the public."

Monetary response, he meant, which in this case was a good thing. A crucial thing. Funding projects that would benefit the needy. The nods of my fellow journalists affirmed it. And wasn't that why I'd wanted to become a reporter? To bring truth to people, to give shape and depth and context to meaningful events in the world? To be part of something worthwhile, something bigger than myself?

My nod was less certain than the others. "Of course."

Even as I said it, I couldn't imagine bringing myself to actually do it. But if I couldn't be part of this, why was I even here?

A grunt, and Weller adjusted his reading glasses and scowled at the crumpled paper he held. "Keep me apprised so we can adjust our focus accordingly. Next. Political coverage. What's on the horizon, Fisher?" He peered over the glasses on the bridge of his nose at the handsome man at the other end of the oval table.

The collective attention of those in the room shifted to Mike Fisher, who looked ready to run for office himself, with his dimples and Kennedy good looks. His un-ironed cotton shirt beneath his blazer lent a sharp appearance despite the wrinkles. His tone was matter of fact but intense as he expounded on the stories he currently had lined up. The former mayor's legal scandal. The current mayor's hang-up with city council. His discussions with the police chief about budget and staffing. Fisher shone in the spotlight, a real TV anchor wannabe, complete with the perfect tan and too-bright teeth.

The guy knew his stuff, I had to give him that. And I still had a lot to learn about how Santa Fe operated, so I took plenty of notes while he talked, and each reporter after. Despite my impatience to get straight to the heart of my work and go out on assignment, I managed to live through the standard first-day red tape. Juanita from IT schooled me in digital etiquette and procedure, and Bernard from HR ran through the paperwork.

At five o'clock, when Mike Fisher announced it was time to head to the bar at Hotel la Fonda, I breathed a sigh of relief. Workday one, done.

Now to get the real scoop on Weller and the *Chronicle* in general.

****

The moment I walked into the Hotel la Fonda, an inkling of déjà vu struck me, which made no sense. I couldn't have been here before. My parents would never have taken a child into a bar.

I trailed behind the others to a table, and the server, a boy who barely looked of legal age, took our orders.

Huddled over his beer, Fisher eyed me like a suspect. "Don't make the mistake of assuming you dodged a bullet this morning. Weller will dog you twice

25

as much now that he thinks you're trying to shirk weekend duties."

If he was hoping for a wimpy gasp or a more dramatic panic attack, my cool shrug must have disappointed him. "I wasn't. I actually did have plans." Or would have had some, eventually.

"Hopefully nothing too important."

"My job takes priority. I know I have to work hard to get up to speed with the rest of you." No time like the present. I plumbed my colleagues for the next half hour, until Ashley Stirling called time out.

Ashley settled her startlingly blue gaze on me. "Enough about work. What's your story?"

Finally, someone who hadn't heard about my family's sad history. "Pretty boring. I was born here, we moved to San Diego when I was five. I wanted to move back." I waited a beat for any rebuttal.

Ashley's smile widened, and she pointed a glossy red nail at me. "Marissa Tahy. I thought I knew that name."

I braced myself for another onslaught of the past. "Pardon?"

Her smile appeared more genuine. "My family lived on the next block over from yours. My maiden name was Martin."

I shook my head, not wanting it to be true. "Martin." No. No. How could I have missed it?

"I was in the same grade as your brother Michael. Oh." Pressing her perfectly manicured fingernails to her chest, Ashley batted her sad doe eyes at me. "Such a beautiful boy he was. I can still see those big, dark eyes... He used to ride his bike past my house every night and give me the sweetest smile." She gave an

26

exaggerated sigh.

"Did he." I wished Ashley had pretended not to remember. Alcohol wasn't to blame. The girl had been spoiled then, and apparently hadn't outgrown her entitled attitude. Ashley Martin had had a crush on Michael, and when her best efforts to befriend me failed, Ashley took every opportunity to make my life miserable.

I made a show of checking the time on my cell. "I better head home. I can't live out of boxes forever." I left a twenty on the table—more than my share—and said goodnight. Ashley's farewell rose above the murmured responses as I walked away.

Outside, it wasn't the evening air that refreshed my senses so much as escaping the atmosphere of the bar. The odd familiarity of the surroundings was oppressive and would haunt me until I figured it out.

Once back in my apartment, I ignored the boxes. Instead, I opened a bottle of wine and the laptop. After exchanging my business suit for comfy clothes, I climbed into bed. Enough back issues of the *Chronicle* were waiting online to keep me busy for a few nights. The rest, I'd access through the library.

I gave a light huff. "Me, not work weekends? I wish." All I did was work. When I wasn't working out. Which reminded me… I did a quick search and located the gym where Javi took mixed martial arts sessions, according to his online posts. No wonder he was a member. The facility offered an array of equipment and sessions. I was more of a cross trainer type, but I entered the contact number into my cell and promised myself to visit the place soon. Losing myself in a workout kept worries from burrowing too deep in my bones. Until I found my rhythm between job and home again, I'd need someplace to physically vent, clean the stickiness of stress from my psyche.

I stretched an arm to ease the soreness, and my shoulder ached.

Yeah, after all the unpacking and work drama, it might be a good time to check out that gym tomorrow, right after I called Aunt Zelda about joining the festival planning committee. I added a reminder to my phone.

At the specter of my aunt, I topped off my wine glass and returned to scanning the *Chronicle* back issues on its web site.

****

Light poured from the Hotel la Fonda's windows and doors, a warm sight in the cool darkness. I stood outside, my bare feet rooted to the cold street. I shivered and realized I was wearing the same tank top and drawstring pants I'd dressed in for bed. Had I walked back to the bar in my sleep? My rental car wasn't in sight, only some old-timey vehicles. Funny, but I didn't remember any mention of an antique auto show in town.

By contrast, the la Fonda appeared newer than it had earlier. Without intending to, I had drifted through the entrance. The people inside the smoke-filled bar might be character actors in a period play, dating about the same era as the autos. A group of five men sat at a table sharing a pitcher of beer. A few of them looked familiar, but I couldn't sort through the haze in my mind to identify them.

As I stood nearby, their casual conversation became complaints. Women trouble, money woes, worries about the future. I knew I shouldn't be listening but was unable to move away. No one took notice. They just kept refilling their mugs with beer. The more they drank, the more they complained.

"I know what we can do." The sandy-haired man jabbed his finger on the table. "Write it down."

The others exchanged confused glances. "Write what down?"

"Everything." He dug a notepad from inside his jacket and began tearing out pages and dealing them like a hand of cards. "Your worries, troubles, whatever is currently bothering you in your life. Jot it all on there."

A few bent to scribble right away. One raised his hands and shrugged, but then gave in and began to write in earnest like the others, cigarettes between their fingers.

I waved away the blue cloud. "Number one should be your addiction to tobacco. You guys smoke like fiends."

They continued as if I'd said nothing. As if I weren't there. One by one, they sat back.

"Now what?" one man asked. With his high cheekbones, strong nose, and slash of a mouth, he was unmistakably Native American. And unnervingly familiar, but the memory simply wouldn't break through.

The sandy-haired man crumpled his list and set it in the ashtray. "Add yours."

I glanced around the bar. Every other table had an ashtray at its center. "Where the hell am I?" Restaurants didn't allow smokers inside.

The last of them tossed his paper into the ashtray. The sandy-haired man struck a match and touched it to the edge of the pile of paper. Flames crackled and climbed.

The bartender froze to watch, and not a hair of his handlebar mustache moved until the papers crumbled into black ash. "No more of that," he called, while he continued drying a glass with a white towel.

"There." The sandy-haired man grinned. "Your troubles are all gone."

"Up in smoke?" The Native American man's laugh mocked them.

"Exactly." The sandy-haired man sounded triumphant.

"I can see the headline now," the man with wire-rimmed glasses said, and swept his fingers across the air. "Bill Shuster turns magician, rids the town of trouble."

Shuster. I knew that name. William Shuster, Jr. had initiated the burning of people's written woes and founded the Zozobra festival. He'd died in the 1960s, I thought. But sitting there, he looked plenty healthy—and young.

Another man raised his mug. "I'll drink to that." His blond hair and blue eyes were strikingly similar to Ray's.

The man with wire-rimmed glasses exhaled. "This is only a temporary solution. Troubles won't stay away because we burned a few of them."

Shuster perked up. "We'll do it again next year, then." Beer sloshed out of his mug when he thrust it to the center of the table.

The others met his cheers and gulped their drinks.

So that's why the bar appeared newer. Why their clothes appeared out of date. I was watching a scene from the 1920s. Why? Was I supposed to stop them? Talk them out of staging the first burning of Old Man Gloom? But no, that would be another two or three years later. The next few, as I recalled, would take place in Shuster's back yard.

But why was I here?

"I'm dreaming." I tried to move, fearful I'd be stranded there, in another time.

I heard my own voice, almost as well as I heard my heart pounding. The room began to dim, the lights slowly fading until only darkness remained. My eyes were still open, and I held still as a stone, but the scene around me shifted, a slow transition like stage props being moved by an unseen force.

Then I was standing in my bedroom. Sweat dampened my top. I shivered from the chill.

"So weird." So very weird that I couldn't tell anyone about what happened.

Chapter Three

The next morning, no sooner had I set my takeout coffee on the desk than Weller called out, "Domestic scuffle on Twelfth Street. Tahy, go find out what you can."

"Right." Twelfth should be easy to find. I hoped. Good thing my rental car had a GPS.

Weller saved me from embarrassment. "Bill, go grab some shots."

Bill Larson slung his photographer's bag over his shoulder. "I'll drive, Tahy."

"Thanks." The rental got me around, but I preferred the familiarity of my own vehicle. On the ride to the site, I asked Bill if he could recommend a reliable used car lot.

"There's a slew of them out along Yuma Drive."

"Okay, thanks." Not exactly a recommendation, but better than nothing, I supposed.

A pickup cut in front of his auto, a faded blue blur across the windshield.

"Whoa." Bill jerked the steering wheel to the right, missing the truck's bumper by inches.

Heart lodged in my throat, I gripped the door panel, bracing against the impact of my head against the window. He gained control of the car again, but my heart still pumped crazily. "That was close."

"Too close. And I've been having too many close

calls like that lately."

I glanced over at him. "Really? That's strange."

"The people around here are generally laid back, but these past few months, I've been out on more assignments than I care to cover—accidents, domestic disputes, robberies, fires, you name it. It's like there's something in the water."

"Or in the air." I said it without meaning to. My thoughts strayed to Old Man Gloom. His grimacing figure loomed above the city. His breath tainted the breeze.

"What?" Bill shot me a look.

"Nothing, just thinking out loud. Not very clearly, but—" It was time to shift the conversation back to the real issue. "Why do you think it's happening? Has something changed in Santa Fe this year?"

He shrugged. "Like what?"

"I don't know. I'm grasping at straws, but is anything political going on that might cause such a widespread discontent?" I couldn't help glancing left and right, bracing for the next near miss.

"No, the local politics have stayed pretty mellow for a few years. The governor's a little flaky sometimes, but most people only react with a groan."

"What about gang activity?"

He spurted a chuckle. "In Santa Fe? No."

I smiled an apology. "I've been away a long time."

He arched his brows. "There were gangs when you lived here?"

I didn't appreciate his snide tone but kept my voice pleasant. "Not beyond the playground, as far as I knew. I'm just kicking ideas around."

Traffic slowed to a crawl ahead of us, forcing him

to brake. I was glad I hadn't relaxed my grip on the door.

"We'll never get there like this."

He jerked the steering wheel, forcing me to brace my knee against the door. He sped down a side street and back to the main drag ahead of the cars jammed behind them.

He slapped the steering wheel. "Ha. He got his due."

I looked behind the car. The blue truck sat sideways across the roadway, its hood crumpled and steam pouring out. "Guess so."

"Better get some photos." He jammed on the brakes again.

Bracing again, I hoped I could get through this assignment without getting whiplash. I climbed out and jogged behind Bill to the accident site.

The truck driver argued with a dazed-looking woman. "You better have enough insurance to cover this, lady."

"Me?" she yelled, her finger close to his face. "You rammed that hunk of junk into me."

Clicking away, the photographer made a half-arc around them. A siren wailed in the distance, growing louder. A police car pulled to a halt, and a uniformed man leapt out, a little too eager to intervene. When he asked both their names, I typed them into my cell.

The argument expanded into a three-way with the cop. *This could take all day.* "Got what you need, Bill?"

"In a sec," he snapped.

"The cars won't get any more damaged."

He glared. "What's your point?"

His sudden irritation took me by surprise. I kept

my voice even and hopefully rational. "We're supposed to head to Twelfth Street for the domestic dispute. And you must have shot three dozen photos already."

"That's the beauty of digital. I just delete the ones I don't need."

Or wasted a lot of time on poorly composed shots. There was something antagonistic about the way he circled the scene, though, like he wanted to provoke them. Like he wanted to join in the argument. The truck driver had given us a fright earlier.

"Shouldn't we get going?" The other scene wouldn't put itself on hold for us, but I didn't dare point that out.

"Yeah, fine." He strode away toward his car.

I walked double my usual pace to catch up. I jumped in as the engine roared to life, racing higher with each pump of his foot. I was pulling the seat belt across when he veered sharply into traffic. I considered making a joke about my insurance not kicking in for a few weeks, but the grim set of his jaw changed my mind. All I wanted was to finish this assignment and get out of this damn car.

Great intro to the city. Not exactly the Santa Fe I remembered, but nothing ever stayed the same, did it? Every city suffered from the same discontent these days, didn't it?

The more I tried to placate myself, the less the excuses made sense. Bill's 'something in the water' statement covered it better. I wondered if he always acted so irritated by everything, or had something affected him, too?

Either way, I'd better learn to keep my mouth shut. I couldn't afford a bad rep that would follow me no matter how hard I played nice to counter it. I stayed quiet the rest of the ride, and Bill seemed to forget I sat beside him even after we reached the address Weller had provided. The houses lining Twelfth sat close to one another, too tightly packed for my comfort. A dozen people gathered outside, and all of them strained to see and hear what was going on inside the home in question. The door was ajar, an officer positioned in the entryway. The wide front window allowed a view of the couple. The woman gestured wildly at the man, and a cop stood between them.

Bill wasted no time capturing the scene with his digital camera, so I plastered on a pleasant smile and introduced myself to the nearest pair of onlookers. The first question hadn't left my mouth before people volunteered information. I took down names of witnesses, and as many facts as I could. The two police, one man, one woman, emerged from the home and headed for the squad car. I excused myself and hurried to question them.

The partners couldn't agree whether the husband or wife was at fault, so another argument erupted.

Officer Susan Worth grimaced. "He punched her."

Officer Ted Jumper smirked. "She provoked him. Just like last time."

Grabbing the opening, I asked, "You've been called here before?"

Officer Worth shook her head sadly. "A few times."

"They're on our list of regulars." Jumper glanced at the residence, distaste plain on his face.

"The list is growing by the day." Worth absently laid a hand on her holstered weapon.

I jotted the offenders' names, Terry and Jim Sutter, married four years, no children. "Have you taken either one into custody?"

Worth and Jumper exchanged wary glances, and he said, "Neither will press charges. Until one of them takes that step, our hands are tied."

Still taking notes, I nodded. "Sad. There's nothing the department can do proactively. Require domestic abuse classes or something?"

Both officers glared at me.

"Like we don't do enough." Jumper waved me off and turned to leave.

"I'm sorry, I—"

"Sure you are," sneered Worth, and followed her partner.

"Wait. Can I get some statistics about the city's cases?"

"Call the precinct." Jumper threw open the car door. "We're done here."

At a chuckle from behind, I turned.

Bill scrolled through the shots in his viewfinder. "Do you always make friends so easily?"

My face went hot. "Normally. But this place isn't exactly normal, it would seem." I clamped my jaw shut, went to the front door, and knocked. No response, other than a dog's yapping. They'd closed the front window curtains, too.

A second knock got an answer. "Screw off!" Terry Sutter screeched.

A shrug, and Bill headed toward his car.

"Okay then." Guess I was done here as well.

As I followed Bill back to his car, my cell chimed. Weller's name showed in the display. "Hello?"

"Are you on your way back yet?" His gruff voice scraped through the phone.

Bill threw open the door and climbed inside.

I did the same. "We are now. We should be at the newsroom in ten minutes."

"Get over to Santa Fe High School," Weller barked. "Someone called in a threat, and they're on lock down."

Oh God. "When did this happen?"

"Go find out." Click.

I let the harshness roll off me and buckled my seat belt. "Weller wants us at the high school."

"When?" he shot back.

"Five minutes ago."

He sent me a sickly smile. "Funny."

"Threats to kids aren't."

His vehicle screeched as he pulled a U-turn in the street. "Deets, please."

"All I know is someone called in a threat."

"Shooter? Bomb?" he prompted.

"I guess we'll find out."

"You didn't ask what kind?"

What was this guy's problem? Weller hadn't been in a mood for interrogation. "I will when we get there." As many questions as I could think of. "There haven't been any similar incidents in town this year, have there?"

His sigh had a tinge of exasperation. "Not in Santa Fe, but Albuquerque has had a few."

Every city was prone to school attacks, and once one occurred, sometimes a slew followed. "Could be a copycat."

"We'll find out."

"Thank goodness for zoom lenses."

"Aw, are you worried about me?"

I sweetened my tone. "Of course. If I lose you on my first real assignment, the other photographers will think I'm a jinx and won't want to work with me."

"So thoughtful of you," he muttered.

"Just trying to lighten things up." Heavy situations tended to weigh on journalists a long time. "We might be stuck there awhile."

That brought another wince. "No doubt."

Our approach was hindered by an officer directing traffic away from the campus. After we showed our press cards, he let us pass. "Stay behind the line."

The line turned out to be a few black-and-whites parked end to end, with scattered uniforms waiting beside them. Engineers adjusted the mobile satellite on a local television news van, and the young reporter finger-combed his hair with one hand, mic at the ready in the other.

Bill stopped well back from them, and far away from the front entrance. "In case we need to scram in a hurry. I don't want to get blocked in."

"Good thinking." The very air hummed with danger, the electricity in the atmosphere dancing along my nerves as I climbed out.

Already, another car with reporters snaked down the lane toward us.

There was no gunfire or telltale smoke, or noise of any kind. State and local officers appeared on edge but controlled. After flashing my ID a second time, I peppered them with questions.

"What time did the call come in?" I asked no one in particular.

A state police officer answered, "Close to nine. All the students were already in class."

"What was the threat?" I directed the inquiry to a local officer.

The same state policeman answered again. "A possible shooter."

I guessed he must be taking point on the case, so I continued my queries to him. "Have you spotted anyone who might have a weapon?"

His narrowed gaze focused on the school. "Not so far, but the school's on lockdown."

"What's the procedure from here?"

"We have a tactical team inside performing a room-by-room search. So far, no weapons have been found. The teachers followed protocol and locked the kids in the classrooms."

Great. "And you weren't able to trace the call?"

"We have people working on that."

I hoped for a prank, though the caller would soon learn the stiff penalty was no joke.

Another forty-five minutes, and the investigating team signaled the all-clear. When Bill and I wrapped up, I was more than ready to head back to the *Chronicle.*

Then, along the main road to the school entrance, among the group of people, I saw him, the stranger from the bar who gave me the willies. With his back to the sun, I couldn't make out his features clearly even though he stood facing me.

Was he responsible for this? Or did he know something? Only one way to find out. "I'll be right back," I told Bill and headed straight for the man. "Hello?"

The man ducked behind the others, then I caught sight of him slipping around the corner of an adjacent building.

I'd written enough crime articles to know not to give him any advantage. Keeping a steady pace, I gave the structure a wider berth. Tall trees shaded the outer wall, but along the grassy knoll leading to a sports field, there was no one.

"Sonofabitch," I whispered. Disappeared again.

What had I expected? That he'd accept an invitation to coffee and answer all my questions?

Every time the stranger appeared, more questions cropped up, but I suspected I wouldn't like the answers.

****

I returned to the high school the following day to speak with the principal, and to catch up with the boy chosen by the event planning committee to receive a scholarship funded by profits made at the festival.

A policeman halted me at the front entrance. "Are you a parent?"

"A reporter. I'm with the *Santa Fe Chronicle*. I was here yesterday, in fact."

No reaction. So much for pleasantries.

"ID," he droned.

I fished it out. "Good to see the school's bolstering security. Everything quiet today?"

He examined my press card and license then handed both back to me. "So far."

I flashed my reporter's smile, and hoped I appeared non-threatening. "Great." I stood still while he searched my handbag and the camera bag, then gestured me on.

I was signing in at the main office when Principal Monica Henley hurried in.

"Ms. Tahy, you're here."

"Hi. You ready for me?"

"Give me two seconds." She breezed into the adjacent office and closed the door.

Two seconds became two minutes, then ten. The door popped open, and a slightly more haggard Principal Henley smoothed her long hair. "Come on in."

No, *sorry for the wait*? I wouldn't invite more trouble. "Thanks for making time to see me." Hot on her heels, I closed the door behind me. "How are things going today?"

"Better than yesterday."

No mistaking the sarcasm in Henley's tone. "Chief Smith says he has no new leads. The call came from a burner phone purchased in Albuquerque."

"Yes, they're working on tracing it to a buyer. I'm confident we'll know soon."

I wasn't so confident, but I nodded. "No students have come forward with information?"

"No."

"Are they generally cooperative in such situations?"

Her gaze turned sharp as obsidian knives. "We typically don't have 'such situations' here, Ms. Tahy."

I nodded. "I understand."

Hands sprawled atop the desk, Henley stared at her blotter. "However, I will admit that this past month has proven more of a challenge than usual."

"More than the normal end of the school year restlessness? How so?"

"More arguments. More students serving detention." She spoke slowly, seeming to choose each word deliberately.

"So, general civil disobedience?" I ventured. Henley clearly didn't want to share everything she knew. While I respected her protectiveness of her students, I also needed to learn what was going on.

Her smile was tight and brief. "As you said, end of the school year restlessness. We have it under control."

"Certainly." I wouldn't undermine Henley's confidence, and I wasn't out for blood. Only the truth.

Henley lifted the phone receiver. "Yes. Could you send Luis to my office? Thank you."

So, interview one had concluded, apparently. "I appreciate you allowing me to speak with Luis."

"His parents gave their approval. He's still seventeen, you know." Henley stood.

I stayed in my seat. "Making his accomplishments even more impressive." And I got the underlying message that the boy was, in fact, still a boy. A minor. I'd tread lightly.

A soft knock, and the principal rounded the desk and let Luis in. "Enter."

The teen glanced nervously at me as he shuffled into the office. A wiry kid, he was all legs and arms, about my height.

I rose and extended my hand. "Hi, Luis. I'm Marissa from the *Chronicle*. Thanks for letting me interview you."

He glanced at Henley, then shook my hand. "I have to be at practice soon."

"Sure, we'll make it quick. I already have your background. Take a seat?" I nodded to the one beside me.

He dragged it a few inches farther from mine, then

sat. "I don't have a background." He sounded defensive.

"We all do." I made light of the fact. Well, I tried. "I looked up public information, like your birth date, the usual boring stuff. But I'm hoping you'll share your personal story for our readers."

He averted his gaze. "I'm boring, too."

"Oh, come on. A track star, science club president, and I love that you're on the school newspaper, too. Do you enjoy journalism?"

His shoulders hunched. "Not as much as medicine."

I relaxed at the small opening he'd given me. "What do you plan to major in?"

"I'm going to be a neurosurgeon."

"Wow. That's impressive. You have an exciting future ahead."

The boy visibly relaxed. With more encouragement, I gleaned a few more facts. After he graduated next year, Luis Valdez would be the first in his family to go to college. His father had been laid off two years earlier, his mother worked two jobs but barely made enough money to pay for rent and groceries, so they appreciated the small scholarship awarded by the festival planning committee. Especially since a year ago, his older brother ran off a month before his eighteenth birthday. No one had been able to locate him.

"I'm so sorry." His poor parents really needed any good news. "The festival planning committee looks forward to presenting you with the award on the evening of Zozobra."

With a nearly indiscernible flinch, Luis narrowed

his eyes. "As soon as I graduate, I'm going to make a lot of money and live far away."

I covered my surprise. "What about your family?"

"They can visit me. Sometimes." His jaw hardened. "I'll be busy with work."

I didn't want to put him on the defensive again, so looked at my notes as I asked, "But Santa Fe's your hometown. Won't you miss it?"

He raised his chin. "Why should I?"

I realized I'd furrowed my brow and corrected it to a neutral expression. "Right. You'll have a new life. You'll be someone important." Someone else. I'd tried that myself. I'd warn him that the effort would be wasted, but I bet he wouldn't listen. It was one of those things a person had to find out for himself. Or herself.

He tapped the arms of his chair. "Are we done? I don't want to be late for practice."

"Do you have time for a photo? The light's better outside. How about near the track?"

He frowned out the window. "I guess."

Hopefully, I could coax a smile from him. "Great. This shouldn't take long." I thanked the principal again and handed her a business card. "Please let me know if you learn anything?"

Henley placed the card on her desk blotter. "Of course."

This school was a hotbed of subliminal messages. I hurried to catch up to Luis, who really, really didn't want to keep his coach waiting, or really, really, couldn't wait to ditch me. Once we were outside, I found out why he was a track star. I struggled to keep up with his long strides.

I positioned him near the track, with the school

45

building in the background. He barely smiled when I prompted him. A quick check of the digital image, and I said, "Great."

With a wave, he jogged off before I could thank him.

"Bye," I murmured, and headed back to the car.

At the newsroom, I downloaded the photos to the computer. On the screen, the boy's face appeared more than sad, more than teenage impatience. His features were drawn tight, and instead of the glowing confidence of a young man headed toward a promising future, an emptiness filled his eyes. In short, he looked haunted.

Why, I wondered? And was that why Luis wanted to leave so badly?

Those weren't questions I could ask him.

Chapter Four

At the smooth pebbles beneath my bare feet, I found myself moving along a dark street. Not walking, exactly, but sliding along an invisible stream flowing into someone's back yard.

Five men sat in a circle around a small fire. The glow illuminated their faces, and as I drew closer, I recognized them as the same five I'd seen at the la Fonda. Again, I was struck by the uncanny resemblance of the blond-haired man to Ray White.

The newspaper man E. Dana Johnson settled his elbows against his knees. "Let's hear it. What's the big surprise you promised?"

Bill Shuster leapt up. "Give me one minute."

The others laughed as Shuster ran inside the back door, but their joking quieted when he returned carrying a crudely crafted doll. "I came up with a better rite to rid ourselves of our troubles. We write them all down, like we did before, but then put them inside the puppet, and burn the whole damn thing."

"A doll?" one of them asked with a chuckle.

"Why not? There are plenty of similar practices in cultures around the world. This is just a vehicle to keep everything we write in one neat package." Shuster held the burlap figure in his hand like an offering. The faceless effigy barely resembled a person.

"True," the Native American man said. "Many

cultures hold the same sort of ceremony at some meaningful time each year."

One man snapped his fingers. "Like New Year's."

"Exactly." Shuster perched on a chair. "Let's test it right now. Did you bring your lists?"

Each man pulled a folded paper from his pocket.

"Here, I'll show you where to put them." Shuster opened a flap on the front of the doll, inserted his sheet, and handed it to Johnson.

Johnson shoved his paper inside and passed the effigy to the Native American man. Once they had each added their written troubles to the figure, the person beside Shuster gave the doll back to him.

Shuster fastened the bulging figure to a metal rod. "Now, our troubles will burn," he said, and laid the rod atop the rocks encircling the fire.

The flames ate away at the fabric, tan burlap charring to black ash.

"I admit, there is a certain satisfaction in witnessing this," said the Ray White twin.

"Revenge of the woe-begotten." Shuster shook his fist at the burning figure. "*Venganza!*"

The night breeze swirled around me in a spiral cage and chilled my skin. The wind died down as quickly as it had kicked up.

Shuster went on. "We should make our ritual a regular event. Not only among ourselves, but for all of Santa Fe."

The Ray lookalike nodded. "Not a bad idea."

"Ours should be different, though," Shuster said. "Meaningful to Santa Fe. Maybe as part of la Fiesta de Santa Fe."

"That event has become fairly dull," Johnson

agreed.

"Yeah," said Ray's doppelganger. "I don't think they've changed one part of the event since the first one in 1712."

"The whole thing's so predictable," said Johnson. "The past few years, I've struggled to make the coverage sound new. People accuse me of using the same articles over and over."

"Then we all agree a change is in order. Let's get everyone in on this." Shuster pointed to the smoldering doll. "Have a night dedicated to burning the troubles of everyone in Santa Fe. City of Holy Faith, eh?"

"I bet people would love that," said Johnson. "But we'll need a bigger puppet."

Shuster grinned. "I'll get right on it."

"We need to come up with a name, something snazzy to separate it from the fiesta." Johnson snapped his fingers. "Zozobra."

The Native American man startled and sat straighter.

"Huh?" Shuster cocked his head in question.

"I came across the word a few weeks ago, while I was doing some research. Zozobra stuck in my head because the definition means anguish, gloom, or the gloomy one." Excited, Johnson inched to the edge of his seat. "Hey, that can be the name of the puppet—Old Man Gloom."

Alarmed, the Native American man shook his head. "Don't put a name on the doll that you burn."

"Why not?" asked Ray's lookalike.

"You have no idea what you're messing with. Unless proper rituals are followed, you could create trouble in the spirit world."

Johnson waved him away. "That's nuts. People will eat this up, and they'll cheer when Old Man Gloom burns."

"Last time, our little ceremony only created a temporary disturbance in the spirit world, a ripple like a pebble dropped in the water that eventually spread too thin and faded away. But this…" He shook his head again. "If you name the effigy, you'll stir up more trouble than you can deal with. Mark my words." He turned and looked directly at me when he said the last warning.

The chill that hit me this time had nothing to do with the night breeze. The Native American man was the only one who'd acknowledged my presence. Somehow, he could see me when the others couldn't.

Shuster winked at him. "You can protect us then. Your grandfather was a Sioux medicine man, right?"

Mouth set in a grim line, the Native American man sat silent.

Shuster stood and waved his hand near the man's head. "I name you master of ceremonies. Judge Sparkio Illumino. You'll pronounce judgment and keep the prisoner in line while the public metes out his punishment."

As Shuster spoke, a young Native American woman approached from the distance. She was almost painfully beautiful as she walked—no, her feet didn't move—she glided up behind the Sioux man. Each cheek bore a painted red dot. She was radiant in her white buckskin dress, and her glossy black hair had a bluish sheen.

I'd never seen anything like the fantastic embroidery that decorated her dress, but my soul quivered at their sacred designs. When I caught sight of a star wrought in shimmering black beads, I couldn't look away for several moments.

The woman rested a hand on the Sioux man's shoulder and murmured something to him. He bowed his head in acknowledgement. When she turned to me, I was electrified in place. An energy hummed across my skin, sparked my flesh to life, and danced along my bones. Despite her serene expression, her eyes were impossibly black and sparkled with immense power.

"Yes, my grandfather is a medicine man," the Sioux man said finally. "I'll ask him what to do, *Ptesan-Wi*."

Ptesan-Wi. I hadn't heard that name since childhood. Now I couldn't quite place it.

The young woman gave a nod, and I understood the man spoke to her, not to his friends. She glided to me, turned over my hand and dropped a white and gold feather onto my palm.

The Native American man afforded her such reverence, I understood this must be some sort of gift. I silently thanked her, then she circled the group of men and departed. Light burst above the peaks of the Sangre de Cristo Mountains beyond the city. Scorching fingers of light surged across the black sky, then vanished. A nod to me, and *Ptesan-Wi* glided toward the horizon, illuminated by flashes of brilliance.

When I turned back to the men, I startled. The Native American man's face loomed close to mine, as large as Old Man Gloom's enormous head.

"*Ptesan-Wi* has chosen you," he said.

Me? I wanted to ask. To argue. To decline, though it would do no good. My role in this had been cast long before I'd set foot in Santa Fe again.

A curtain of darkness fell. My eyes were open, but I could see nothing, although the feather felt heavy in my hand.

I was beginning to understand. Naming the puppet—that's when the real trouble began. In doing so, the men conjured a spirit from the mountains. In christening the effigy, they had set in motion a chain of events that would grow more powerful each time they laid their troubles upon it. Unlike their ancestors, they offered nothing to the spirit in return. Later, they would learn they had no control over Old Man Gloom.

Somewhere far-off, an eagle screeched. Veins of lightning split the dark sky with blazing light. The peaks of the Sangre de Cristo Mountains glowed red.

My spirit grew heavy and weighed me down like a wet cloak. Fear urged me to run, to put Santa Fe far behind me. I was neither sleeping nor awake, but I'd return to my life soon enough. The choice I made in this moment would follow me forever.

Yet there really was no choice. Too many had already suffered. I had been chosen.

The decision shed the weight from me. Lightened, I turned and walked toward the lightning.

Chapter Five

In the morning, the same red dust spread across the city. Overnight, the landscape became a swath of red, including the SUV I'd driven home from the dealer's last night. I was glad I hadn't shopped for a new vehicle. This one was used, already beat up so I wouldn't have to worry as much about other drivers and their states of mind.

The SUV outside had seen better days, but its dull blue paint ranked as the least of my concerns. All I'd demanded from the salesman was reliable transportation, and the fact that its size was slightly larger than a car lent me peace of mind. I didn't bother clearing away the dust except for the windows, so it wouldn't block my view.

After I arrived at work, I passed Mike Fisher's desk. "Morning. Some crazy dust storms lately, huh?"

Across the aisle, Ashley rose from her chair and brushed at the elbow of her jacket sleeve. "They're a pain in my ass. This is the second blazer ruined by the damn dust. Wait till you try getting the red stains out." She headed toward the break room, hips swishing.

"Do dust storms always happen so frequently this time of year? Or did I just move here at the wrong time?" The image of the Sangre de Cristo Mountains burned bright in my mind. The crimson that tinged the range was alpenglow—an optical illusion. The hilltops weren't actually red and had nothing to do with the translation from Spanish, Blood of Christ. That was just the name given the mountain peaks by overly religious settlers, just as Santa Fe meant Holy Faith.

Still, it bothered me that the dust storms blew from the direction of those peaks.

Mike tapped his fingers on his desktop. "No, I can't remember the last time we had this many dust storms, and especially not red." He flipped through screens on his electronic tablet.

My cue to leave. "Interesting. I'll have to ask my aunt about it. She's kind of an unofficial historian." Oh no. Zelda. I'd forgotten to call my aunt about the festival planning committee. Weller wouldn't be happy with me.

My aunt, on the other hand, would be ecstatic to learn of my involvement. At my desk, I booted up the laptop, checked voice mail, email, anything to delay the call. Might as well get it over with. My fingers moved in slow motion over the phone's keypad. I closed my eyes and set a smile on my face when it began to ring. My aunt would hear the dismay in my voice otherwise.

On the third ring came the distinctive answer. A deep, "Hello?"

"Good morning, Aunt Zelda."

"Oh, Marissa, it's you. I should have known it was, but you threw me, calling from work. Is everything all right?"

Zelda must have checked the caller ID and seen the newspaper's name rather than mine. But this call involved official business, and I intended to keep it that way. "Yes, fine. I hope I'm not waking you."

"Don't be silly, sweetheart. I've been up since five

thirty, as usual. Are you sure everything's all right?"

Zelda was fishing for trouble. I was about to make my aunt's day.

"Everything's great. In fact, I've been assigned to cover the festival in September, so I have some questions for you."

"You were? How wonderful."

The feigned surprise didn't fool me. I had a feeling my aunt had put Weller up to the assignment.

"I need to get up to speed on all the event details. I wondered if we could meet for lunch?"

"I'd love to, dear. And tomorrow night's the next planning committee meeting, so this is perfect timing."

I could almost hear the *what took you so long to call* in Zelda's voice. "Perfect." What little enthusiasm I'd mustered had drained away, and I found it more difficult to maintain the fake smile.

"Are you free for lunch today?" Zelda asked.

"Unless something pops up. Where do you want to meet?"

"Tia Maria's is one of my favorites."

"Sounds great. How's noon?"

"Eleven would be better." When I didn't respond immediately, she sniffed. "Unless you want to wait for a table. I'm only thinking of you."

Zelda understood that I was a reluctant participant, so I'd have to work twice as hard to meet my aunt's expectations. "See you at eleven at Tia Maria's."

****

West San Francisco Street bustled with traffic. I should have understood that to mean the restaurant would be busy, as well.

Zelda was waiting for me inside the foyer. "Hurry,

dear, or they'll give our table away." She signaled the hostess, who then guided us through the crowded aisle to a small table for two.

Bustling was an understatement. Boisterous was more accurate, given the fact about a quarter of the customers had brought along their kids, who ran back and forth to a bookshelf overflowing with children's books. The din of conversation ratcheted up a notch above usual. Servers spoke more loudly to be heard above the noise, and silverware clacked noisily. A woman at the next table bumped her chair into mine repeatedly and chattered nonstop. I had to lean closer to my aunt to hear her deep voice. She skirted some of my questions with vague answers or polite smiles that suggested that, having been away so long, I couldn't possibly understand.

I understood some things all too well. "Aunt Zelda, if I'm going to be part of the planning committee, I need to know certain things. If only for my own use. Of course, I won't write anything detrimental about the festival or the committee members, or—"

Zelda held up her hand. "All right. But not now."

"Why not?" That was the whole point of our meeting.

"As I said, the next planning committee meeting is tomorrow night. You are coming, correct?"

So she knew I'd been drafted. "Yes."

"Arrive early, bring all your little questions…"

"Little questions?" I held in a laugh. "What if I have big ones?"

Even Zelda's expression was condescending. "We begin planning a year in advance, dear. You're coming on board at practically the last minute."

"It's only July," I pointed out. "And if I am to be of any use, I need to get up to speed." Why hadn't the *Chronicle* assigned another journalist before now? That question would have to wait for a later date.

The look my aunt gave me reminded me of when I was five and had done something naughty. I wouldn't be relegated to that again. "Is it going to be a problem that we're related? Because I can work with another committee member if you'd be more comfortable."

Disbelief shone in her wide eyes. "It's not my comfort I'm worried about."

I bit the inside of my lip. If I tried to hold in my frustration much longer, I might draw blood. "I'm trying to do my job, but you seem intent on throwing road-blocks in my path."

The hard gleam in Zelda's eye reminded me of the parrot. The bird's screeched warning of revenge, *Venganza!* If it weren't for Shuster echoing the same thing in my vision, I'd wonder if Phoebe hadn't been referring to working with Zelda.

I met my aunt's look with equal determination. "One way or the other, I'm going to learn all I can about what happens before, during, and after the festival."

Visibly softening, Zelda reached across the table and squeezed my hand. "That's what worries me most."

I withdrew my hands to my lap. "I'm a big girl now. I'm fairly sure I can handle whatever duties the committee requires of me."

Studying me, my aunt dabbed the napkin to her pursed lips. "Come for dinner tomorrow. I'll tell you what I know. Then if you still want to attend the meeting, we can go together."

I should have felt more triumphant rather than wary, but she knew the meeting wasn't optional. Until the dawn following Zozobra, it was part of my job.

"Thank you." I had the feeling I was thanking my aunt for turning the tables on me.

****

The city conspired to keep me from reaching my aunt's house on time. Every traffic light turned red at my approach. Wayward pedestrians paid no attention to the signals and walked in front of my car, forcing me to jam on the brakes, and then they had the gall to grimace at me as if it were my fault. All day, everyone I'd run into was either preoccupied or in a bad mood.

By the time I finally reached Zelda's house, my mood had plummeted, too. A brief knock, and I pushed through the back door. The scent of barbecue brisket teased my senses, but not enough to overpower the need to vent. "Since when did Santa Fe turn into New York City? Everyone's so rude and awful." I pressed the bottle of wine I'd brought into her hands and sent a look of warning Phoebe's way before I dropped my handbag on the bar chair at the island. I couldn't handle any mystical predictions from the parrot tonight. The bird ruffled its feathers but settled on its perch.

Zelda pressed her lips tight as I spoke, then said, "Hello to you, too. How was my day? Fine, thank you for asking." She examined the label on the bottle. "Mm, thank you very much. This will go nicely with dinner."

"Which smells wonderful. And I'm sorry for the outburst. Today's been a bear."

She drew a bottle opener from the kitchen drawer and fastened it to the cork. "Every person you meet has troubles. And they deal with their problems in their own

58

way. Some lash out, some turn inward. We must respect each one and offer kindness in return."

With each twist, the metal arms of the opener lifted higher until the cork was free, and the small silver man silently declared *Hallelujah.* I wanted to join that chorus.

"When did you start working for a greeting card company?" The same sort of memes appeared on social media every day. Good reminders, but not everyone carried them through in real life.

Zelda waved in the direction of the lettuce, carrots, cucumber, onions, and celery spread by the cutting board. "You can chop the salad."

"All right." Putting a knife in my hands might not be the best idea my aunt had.

"Don't sound so put out. Working with your hands is a good release." Zelda smirked. "And I'll pour you a glass of wine."

"Much better incentive." I washed my hands and set to work. The repetitive motion at the chopping board did help ease the tension. Not as much as the wine.

Zelda bustled in and out of the kitchen. "Javi may pop in. He wasn't sure if he could make it. His team has been quite busy, he said."

"Yes, there's been an uptick in crime, too." At my aunt's skeptical look, I added, "So my colleagues tell me." The last thing I wanted was a lecture from Zelda about how Santa Fe was the most wonderful town in America. It wasn't living up to the glowing recommendations in the travel articles. For me, the city's reputation had tarnished long ago. If my mother hadn't requested in her will that I return, painful memories might have kept me away much longer.

Time to change the subject anyway. "Can you walk me through what the committee will expect of me? Other than taking notes and spinning committee business into newspaper pieces people will actually read?"

"Residents love to read about the festival preparation." Zelda perfectly imitated a stern schoolmarm. Taking a long sip of wine, she appeared thoughtful. "As liaison, that will be your most important task, officially. Apprising everyone of the preparations through the *Chronicle*, and of course encouraging more people to participate. This event has raised a great deal of money for local charities over the years, and certain organizations depend on these funds. Particularly this year, which marks the centennial celebration. We must double all our efforts."

Just my luck to return on the one hundredth anniversary of the first Zozobra. Too bad the committee didn't plan to re-enact that first burning of Old Man Gloom, a hand-crafted effigy no bigger than a Barbie doll that a small group of friends roasted in someone's back yard.

No such luck. From the videos I'd watched online, the effigy towered over the city, forty-nine feet of gloom. And tens of thousands of people gathered to watch. I could only imagine what a hundred-year event would entail.

I wiped my hands on a towel and reached for my handbag. "I should be taking notes."

"No need. The others will tell you this again tonight, and we'll give you a packet of all the pertinent statistics and information. This year's edition goes into more historical detail. We spent extra on the glossy covers. Make sure you don't lose it."

I tried not to bristle at the insult. "Of course, I won't lose it."

She braced her hands on the island and tapped a nail. "I'm speaking off the record, but what I'm going to tell you is critical. It goes to the very heart of Zozobra."

I held back a chuckle. The way Zelda sounded, I was about to join the Knights Templar or something. "Sure you don't want me to take notes?"

Zelda pressed her finger to her temple. "You must keep this foremost in your mind."

One thing for certain, I wouldn't forget Zelda's performance. "Okay. Shoot."

"Right up until the Thursday when the festival takes place, people will show up at the newspaper and at the warehouse, though we'll have moved the various parts of the effigy to the staging area by then." Zelda dropped her voice deeper than usual, the personification of doom. She moved her hand slowly through the air, fingers arched, sharp nails ready to shred. "They'll bring their slips of paper with their troubles written down, and it's our job—all of us—to make certain that those papers are sealed inside Old Man Gloom." She scraped her long fingernails in a circle around an imaginary throng of people.

The over-dramatization nearly made me laugh again, but the mention of the effigy's name sent a chill over me. "I get it, that's the whole reason for Zozobra."

"Precisely, dear. And if we don't follow through for every single person, then we fail at our responsibility."

"Right." I spoke with authority so Zelda would lay off the theatrics. It seemed a long shot.

"What we do next is equally fundamental in its importance. I cannot stress it enough."

Apparently. "Okay." The chuckle I held back gurgled in my throat.

Zelda briskly left the room.

I waited, uncertain whether I'd offended her, or something had happened that I'd somehow missed—a feeling I probably should get used to. My aunt was treating me like an outsider. And a child.

I sing-songed my voice and called, "Aunt Zelda? Is everything all right?" I lifted the glass, then set it down. No more wine until I'd eaten, or else I might let loose with some flip comment, and my aunt would throw me off the committee before I'd attended one meeting.

Zelda stalked back into the kitchen and stopped at the island directly opposite me. I had the sense everything my aunt was doing was part performance, and all for effect. She stared at me like some sideshow hypnotist.

"You," she said pointedly, "are responsible for monitoring the contributions. Every single one of them."

What the... We'd already covered all this. "Got it." Hopefully, we could move on.

"You must ensure that everyone writes their name on the list."

"Isn't that a violation of their privacy?"

"It is committee policy. For every donation, we give one of these." Zelda held up a small ceramic star, shiny and...black.

Not beaded, as on *Ptesan-Wi*'s buckskin dress, but

just as striking. I reached out, and she handed the star over. At closer inspection, the glossy finish had a pebbled feel, surprisingly, like the smooth skin of a toad. I almost expected a pulse of life beneath my touch. I couldn't take my eyes off the ornament, though my aunt continued her instructions.

"Make absolutely certain that every donor takes one and hangs this on the outside of their home. No matter if they live in a mansion or a shack, an apartment or an RV."

After I set the star atop the island, my aunt's words sunk in. "You mean a mobile home?" Hopefully, I didn't have to chase down every recreational vehicle passing through town.

She waved sharply. "Mobile home, tree house, whatever place they call home. I don't care if it's a basement in their parents' house, they can still hang this on the window. However they choose to do it, it must be hung." Zelda's glare intensified. "Do you understand?"

I spoke with equal intensity. "I absolutely understand. They hand in their troubles, we give them a star."

My aunt pursed her lips and narrowed her eyes. "You understand the procedure. What you fail to understand is the importance."

"Do I need to take a blood oath?" I didn't expect Zelda to appreciate the joke. "It's simple enough. The more black stars that hang around the neighborhoods, the more people will see them and want to get on board with the festival."

"It's really not so simple as that."

Oy. I gulped the wine for liquid courage. "It's a

great marketing idea. Except...black? Seriously?" I braced for an explosion, but it didn't come.

Zelda flashed her signature Mona Lisa smile. "There is a reason for everything."

A memory sprang to life, of Michael banging on the window of our burning home, his mouth open in a scream. My stomach churned. No, not everything had a purpose.

"Maybe. But is it a good reason?" I lifted the star, which had surprising heft to it. Heavier than ordinary ceramic, but the substance was beside the point. "Because while this may appear classy or unique in its own vampirish way, this star's not necessarily attractive." I tried to make it sound like a joke, but my aunt obviously didn't find it funny. "And a black ornament might not even be visible on a house." How would a small black star stand out on any large structure? Whatever marketing genius crafted this concept should be fired.

Zelda heaved a long sigh which contrasted the sizzle in her eyes. "Perhaps you were right. Perhaps someone else at the *Chronicle* should handle this duty. One of the other reporters. Someone not related to me."

"That won't be necessary. I'm a professional. I have no problem working with family."

"You either follow my rules and respect them or bow out."

I nodded slowly. Bow out? Sure, and blow a new job straight to hell, not to mention create a rift between what little family I had left. "I will be the best damn *Chronicle* liaison your committee has ever had, Mrs. Furtado."

Our stares could have put a noontime showdown in

the Old West to shame. Neither of us moved when Javi came through the back door.

"Hey, I made it. Dinner smells delicious. Do you want me to stir the barbecue, Ma?"

Without breaking eye contact with me, Zelda arched a brow. "I will take care of it." She tilted her head to receive his kiss to her cheek.

"Am I interrupting?" He laughed nervously. "Want me to leave?"

I glanced away first. "Don't you dare."

Zelda's heels clipped the tile on her way to the back patio.

Javi scrunched up his face. "I better grab a beer then." He turned to the fridge, fished one out, and twisted off the cap. "What's up with you two?"

"The festival planning committee. I'm the *Chronicle* liaison." I hated the defeat in my tone.

Javi sucked air through his teeth.

"Yeah." I forced a grin. "I risk bringing shame on our family's heads, and failure means banishment—from the family, from Santa Fe, possibly all of New Mexico."

"Failure's tantamount to sacrilege. Not an option, Mar." He raised his bottle in cheers.

We laughed, and the stress left me. "Thank God you showed up when you did. I think she must have gotten contacts fitted with lasers or something. My eyes are singed from her burning stare." To be certain she wasn't giving me the evil eye right now, I glanced through the window set in the back door. Zelda stood at the stainless-steel grill, tending to dinner.

"Laser contacts. You're too funny." Javi leaned his elbows on the island. "You should come to MMA sessions with me. You're going to need an effective stress reliever."

I nodded. "I was checking out that gym on the web. Their yoga and spin classes look like the right level for me."

He blew raspberries. "Those aren't going to do squat. MMA is what you need."

"I really don't need to get beat up." Any more than I already was verbally. "Thanks anyway."

"You have to try it at least once. Ray's a great instructor."

"Sunshine boy?" The words slipped out.

Javi mock-scowled. "He's a good guy. Lay off."

Committee work had already turned me bitchy. "Sorry. It's been a rough week."

He turned wistful. "For everyone, I hear."

Being around him always lifted my spirits. "How do you always stay so damn cheerful? I may have to nickname you Sunshine the Second."

Javi sobered and turned the bottle in his fingers. "Watching people lose everything they own in a fire makes me appreciate all I have. Getting to pull someone alive from a death trap is a real blessing. A gift, not just for them, but for me, too."

Now I wasn't merely a bitch, I was a selfish one. "I shouldn't have whined to you. Sorry."

His grin held no judgment. "Come to MMA. You won't whine anymore."

"Except about my bruises." I laughed.

He glanced at me askance. "You can't be the girl who used to outrun me and fly past me on your bike like a super girl."

I didn't mind so much when Javi dredged up the

memory. "The good old days, huh?" My smile turned crooked and my vision misty.

Javi didn't seem to notice. "These days are pretty good, too."

I took a long look at him. "When did you get so sweet?"

The creak of the door signaled Zelda's return, but she kept walking. "Ten minutes till dinner. I'll get the festival packet for you."

"I'd better finish this salad fast." I busied myself. I didn't need another strike against me.

Zelda swept past and returned with the promised packet. "Carry this with you." She pressed something cold and hard into my palm. "At all times."

I glanced down. "The star?"

"At all times," Zelda repeated, and gave my hand a squeeze.

"Who is *Ptesan-Wi*?" The question burst from me from some dark place in my subconscious. I had no idea what made the name come to me. In a flash, I recalled the gorgeous beading on White Buffalo Woman's dress, and how the black beads, like the star, shimmered even in the darkness.

"What?" Zelda looked like I'd hit her with a stun gun.

Javi waved. "Grandfather Tahy used to yammer on about *Ptesan-Wi*. She is White Buffalo Woman." He snorted like it was the craziest thing he'd ever heard.

I knew better. "Yes, White Buffalo Woman," I repeated, the dream rushing up, looming in my vision much like the Sioux man had done. Oh God, that's why the Native American man looked so familiar. Though I'd never met him, I recognized family.

"An old Indian legend," said Zelda.

My great grandfather had been somewhat of a legend, too. Adults shushed other kids when they teased Michael and me about our crazy Sioux relative, the old man who walked in the spirit world more often than the real one. Most people gossiped that he was a drunk, a fool, a raving lunatic. He claimed to commune with mythological figures, to seek advice from them. He told everyone that he himself was a shapeshifter, a holy man—though few still believed in such things. He'd been the butt of jokes and abuse that had flowed over onto my brother and me.

Zelda turned to Javi. "Do you need another beer?"

He sloshed the liquid in his bottle. "No, I'm good."

"How was your day?" my aunt asked him, pointedly ignoring me.

I took the hint. I wasn't supposed to ask about the star, so I merely listened while Javi and Zelda discussed dinner, how their days went, the casual family talk that I missed so much. A pang in my heart reminded me that no matter how difficult relatives were, they were still family. And family should be treasured, no matter how great the temptation to strangle them.

Chapter Six

"At a church?" I tried not to gape as I followed
Zelda inside the enormous tan structure with twin
towers. A stained-glass medallion glowed in jewel
colors above the arched entrance.

Before passing within, her cocked brow was
enough to silence me. "Not any church. This is the
Cathedral Basilica of Saint Francis of Assisi."

Did a cathedral hold more sacred power than any
other religious meeting place? I wondered as she
crossed the vestibule and dipped her fingers into the
small well on the wall and made the sign of the cross.

I lingered a few paces behind. "Should I…" I
gestured to the holy water.

"Couldn't hurt." Her lips curled like a cat's.
"Unless you're a demon." She tugged her scarf over her
head and proceeded into the church.

I resisted the urge to scowl. "Funny." But she'd
still managed to make me feel like a five-year-old
again.

Zelda genuflected in the aisle, then continued to
follow it to the altar, where she veered to the left. A
short hallway was dark except for the light from an
open doorway, leading into a small room where three
men and one woman crowded around a card table.
Instead of game pieces, they guarded note pads like
poker hands. Conversation ebbed when we entered.

"*Hola*," my aunt called, her smile cherubic. She set her handbag in front of the only empty chair. "This is the new liaison from the *Chronicle*, Marissa Tahy. She's also my niece."

Nice afterthought. My aunt needed lessons in giving the warm fuzzies.

After claiming her seat opposite the other woman, Zelda gestured to the others. "Marissa, meet Tomas Gomez, Mrs. Trisha Brock, George Blake. and Peter River."

I nodded at each as she introduced them. "A pleasure to meet you."

Awkwardness set in as I remained standing, then George Blake leapt up. "There must be another chair around here somewhere." With three long strides, he was out in the hallway. Some rattling and a thud later, he carried in a metal folding chair, then set it near Zelda's.

My aunt's graciousness thinned, but she scooted over an inch, then an inch more. To her right, Tomas Gomez did the same, which set off a chain reaction of shuffling. Despite the flurry of movement, there was still not enough room for one more at their table. Only a meager corner was left to me. Clearly, I'd disrupted the established seating arrangement.

"Please, don't bother. I'm fine here." I plopped down and forced a grin, feeling every bit the child at the adult gathering.

Zelda inhaled deeply. "Let's get started, shall we?"

I kept my head down and took notes. Plenty of them, even when it wasn't necessary. Each person exhibited the same level of dedication, however, and I made it a point to never joke about any aspect of festival preparations. These people were dead serious about their duties. I might as well not have been there at all, until the end of the meeting, when my aunt mentioned she'd briefed me earlier.

I waited for some acknowledgement, but Mr. Gomez only said, "All right. Guess that's it." Which set them all into motion again, carrying chairs from the room, and Mr. Blake collapsing the folding table.

"Nice of the pastor to let you use this space, but aren't there other places with permanent seating?" I joked. "The library? A bar?"

Zelda's icy glare shut me up. "We cannot conduct business in a rowdy environment."

Which one, the library? I let that question die in my head. "Of course." But a margarita would have gone a long way toward making these meetings bearable.

I withheld a sigh. The next several months were going to last an eternity. My pulse raced like a caged animal, all the pent-up frustration begging for release. I texted Javi.

—*I need to check out those MMA sessions*—

His response arrived within seconds.

—*Saturday morning. Be there at 8 sharp*—

Eight? I groaned inwardly. Can't even sleep in. Saturday mornings were for luxuriating in bed, hanging out in pj's reading, embracing my inner sloth until errands demanded my attention. I texted back.

—*Sounds good*—

I needed a kick in the pants, though these jabs would be literal. But this time, I'd kick back. The thought brought a grin as I exited beneath the archway. Dusk had given way to darkness, and the evening air held an unusual chill.

Shadows stretched down the side of the cathedral and formed a sharp angle, the delineation so clear, it could have been a triangular door. The thickness of that angular darkness heightened the illusion. That, and the fact I sensed a presence within, palpable enough to capture my attention.

Except, there was no one there. I was sure of it.

I fumbled in my bag for my keys, panic mounting when they weren't in their usual spot. I always slipped them into the side, right pocket at the front for easy access. Had they fallen out in the meeting room? The idea of approaching those shadows, even skirting past them, gave me the willies.

I was being silly. Without keys, I couldn't get home. Yet I couldn't force myself forward.

My feet became rooted when hushed whispers sounded. Not loud enough to hear the words, but they were talking about me. I sent a disapproving look in that direction, thinking my eyes would clear and I'd make out the figures of some committee members, possibly casting disdainful looks my way. But the longer I stood there, the more evident it became that no one was there. No one I could see, anyway. The whispering, I heard fine. Too well, in fact. Then it repeated one word in a long, sibilant hush.

My name. I could swear it. Someone's sick idea of a joke? A sudden chill swept over me. I backed away. Habit made me dip my hand into my jacket pocket. My keys. I closed my fingers around them and pivoted on my heel. The streetlight slanted an anemic light across the parking lot, the darkness less malevolent the farther I walked from the cathedral.

Scrambling inside the vehicle, I cursed at the

engine for turning over once too often. With a roar, it caught, and I slammed the gear into drive.

"Aunt Zelda's going to hear about this tomorrow. If any committee member objects to me so much, that's their problem. They'll have to learn to deal with me. End of story. I have no intention of putting up with such harassment."

I spoke aloud to scare away the memory of those whispers. Much as I tried to convince myself it was a committee member acting badly, none of what happened added up. No one on the committee would behave that way. No one would deliberately try to frighten me. No person, anyway.

Too wound up to head straight home, I drove through town. The lights of a crafts store still shone, so I parked and went inside to browse. A shelf held boxes prettily decorated in floral designs with encouraging phrases like *follow your heart*. I found one to hold the Zozobra papers people would contribute, plus sturdy enough to carry the black stars.

Before leaving for work in the morning, I filled the box with the ornaments and schlepped the heavy container to my SUV. At the *Chronicle*, I parked to the side of the front entrance and hefted it inside so I could hand it off to Jill, the receptionist.

"Morning," she called cheerily. Overhead lights gave her dark hair a brilliant sheen and spotlighted the oversized *Chronicle* logo on the wall behind the semicircle desk.

I tried not to puff as I lugged the box toward her. "Hi. You've probably forgotten me, but I'm Marissa Tahy."

"Yeah, the new reporter. I remember." She glanced

at the box. "That for me?"

"Sorry to burden you with another job."

"Not my first rodeo, hon. Oo, this is heavy." She grunted as she slid the box closer and opened it. She held up a star and examined it. "These are new."

Oh joy, no one had told her. "Yes, but the committee stressed—about a thousand times—to be certain to give one to every person who hands over their troubles. Please be sure to tell them to hang the star on their home."

"Gotcha." She tapped the empty space on the counter. "I'll print up a sign to sit right next to a sample one, to remind myself and the donors."

I wanted to hug her. "Thank you. You will save the committee from collectively having a cow."

On the way through the corridor that led to my desk, some old photos hanging on the wall caught my attention. A closer look, and I recognized Bill Shuster and his friends, all the men from the group who'd been at the Hotel la Fonda bar and in Shuster's back yard. I read the caption aloud: "E. Dana Johnson, editor. 1926."

My jaw gaped. *1926?*

"There you are, Tahy." Ashley oozed attitude as she approached me in the hallway. "I thought maybe you were playing hooky today. What's got you stumped?"

Leave it to Ashley to snap me out of the funk and back to harsh reality. I almost preferred the funk. "Just checking out these old photos."

She came to a stop like a hyped-up racehorse and scanned the pictures. "They've probably hung there since 1926."

More than a century. I was awestruck.

"Do we have digital copies?" I wondered aloud.

"Doubtful. But Marian in layout could scan it if you need it in digital. She's great at restoring old photos."

"Thanks." I heard the surprise in my voice and hoped she wouldn't take offense.

Her huff was more disappointment than sarcasm. "No problem. We're all on the same team, right?"

I liked to think so, but some days, I couldn't be certain. To keep the peace, I said, "Absolutely."

But I had no official reason for wanting copies of the photos, so resolved to return later with my cell to snap my own digital images. Poor substitutes were better than nothing.

****

When my cell buzzed with a text at 7:00 on Saturday morning, I groaned. "Not the *Chronicle*, please."

I blew a breath of relief when I read Javi's message:

—Don't forget, 8 a.m.—

Forget? I'd stressed about the mixed martial arts session for days and had been awake since six. Showered and dressed except for my running shoes, I was eager to get there. And get the session over with.

—On my way—

I was tired of wrestling with my demons, and with no holy water to battle them, I was ready to unleash myself on an opponent.

If I wanted to stand any sort of chance, I'd have to pay homage to the coffee gods. At a stop at a café I found along the way, I filled a travel mug with one order to keep it warm and drank from the carry-out cup. Afterward, I'd need the boost just as much.

Inside the facility, I caught up with Javi and Ray, who stood together on the sidelines. The oversized mats on the floor gave me zero confidence. I suspected that I'd end up there more often than I cared to think about. "Honestly, I have only a vague idea of what mixed martial arts even is."

With the patience of a saint, Ray maintained the image of cool and calm. "It's all about staying in motion and taking opportunities when they open."

"Sure we're not talking about careers?" Not funny.

"Same concept. Keep your body moving but focus on your opponent. When he jabs, you duck. When he lowers his defense, you strike."

"Sucker punch him? Isn't that bad sportsmanship?"

"Don't think of it that way. MMA is about advantage and leverage and power."

"I'm not going to have to spar with a guy for real, am I?" I scanned the dozen or so people. Three pretty females mixed with the mostly male bunch. One sent me a glare as she sipped her water bottle.

Ray took no notice. "Sometimes you will. More men than women sign up for this class."

"I'll get my ass whipped." My face flushed at the phrase. Not the image I wanted in his head.

He visibly erased a grin. "Not if you use leverage and advantage. He might have bulk and power, but you're smaller and you'll be quicker."

I winced. "I guess the thought of getting beat up is a good incentive to move fast."

"No one plays too rough here. Tell you what, we can pair up today."

Another phrase that brought a blush. "But you're the instructor." I didn't want to appear to be a special case, a teacher's pet.

He didn't hold back his grin this time. It was wide and smug. "I'm great at multitasking. And I promise not to whip your ass."

I waited for it, the unspoken *unless you want me to* but to his credit, he left it hanging there between us, a silent Cheshire Cat whose smile said it all. "Thanks. I think."

Hands rested on his hips as he gave a kingly survey of the room. "One session, and I bet you fall in love."

The words pinched my insides alive. I raised my eyebrows.

He blanched. "With MMA, I mean."

Yes, it was going so well already. "Just keep in mind that I'm a beginner. The lowest level beginner you've probably ever had."

"Not for long. We'll get you up to speed in no time."

His confidence was not contagious. "Let's not exaggerate."

The intense way he stared at me, some internal debate was going on in his head. A single nod tipped me off that he'd decided.

"Bet you dinner," he said.

Taken aback, I blinked. Talk about making the stakes personal. "You don't need to." I'm pretty sure I blushed like a schoolgirl, but I didn't know what else to say.

"I have to." His cheeriness sounded strained. "You'd say no otherwise. Wouldn't you?" He ducked his head, but a challenge lit the blue flame in his eyes.

God, he was serious. And I was dumbstruck, my instincts whispering, *no, don't*. "You're Javi's coworker. His friend." A potentially bad combination. I didn't relish the thought of being a topic of conversation between them.

Ray widened his eyes. "Guess you better beat me, then."

I flared mine back at him. "Except the playing field's tilted in your favor."

"I'll level it out." His gaze wandered to Javi, who chatted up a girl beside the bench halfway across the room.

Had Javi put him up to this? "How?" I asked. "Tie one hand behind your back?"

He shook his head once. "That wouldn't be enough."

I formed an O with my mouth in mock awe. "Sorry, I can't, then. I'm too frightened."

"I'm not bragging. It's true. But I give you my word not to use my advantages of superior skill and knowledge against you."

Breathy and soft, I asked, "Then how are you going to teach me anything?"

A laugh, and he scratched his chin. "You're not leaving me much wiggle room, are you?"

"Not an inch." About as much as he'd left me.

"Then I've already taught you Lesson One. That's the spirit, Marissa."

If I was going to have any hope of besting him, I had to get my game on. "I'll show you spirit, Sunshine. Let's go."

He grasped his chest and moaned, though it sounded more like a chuckle. "You're killing me."

"Soon," I promised, and hoped it wasn't in vain. "Very soon." No match is worthy until the opponents tossed around some trash talk, I told myself.

But the moment we stepped onto the mat and circled one another I knew I was doomed to embarrassment. In about three seconds, he proved me right and flipped me.

I scrambled to my feet. "I'm not that easy, Sunshine."

"No worthwhile victory ever is." He lunged at me and wound his leg around mine. With a jerk and a twist, he flipped me onto the mat, then pinned his body on top of mine.

His heavy breath puffed warm against my face. "I'm pretty sure I've won."

I wriggled but he held fast. "I thought you weren't going to use your superior skill against me?"

He scrunched his mouth to one side. "I…may have exaggerated."

I groaned and let my muscles turn to jelly.

He turned serious. "Hey, the stakes were too high. I couldn't lose."

The stakes were probably always high for him. "Let me up." I pushed and managed to raise my wrists.

He pressed them back to the mat. "First, is six o'clock good for you?"

"Tonight?" I croaked, ready to argue for at least a week. Maybe a year.

"Yes. Do you need more than seven hours to get ready?"

Wise ass. I should have included more lead time as a condition, but too late now. "Depends. Where are you taking me?"

"Somewhere nice but skip the little black dress. A little black top will do fine." Smugness had loosened his grip, and he relaxed atop me.

Now was my chance. "Got it." I pushed at his shoulders, angled my leg, and twisted upward.

He slammed backward onto the mat. "Nice. We'll make a killer out of you yet."

The words turned my bones into icicles. A shudder stole the pleasure from the moment, and I brushed at nonexistent dust on my legs. "No, you won't." I hadn't intended to sound so hard and cold.

"Easy. Just an expression." He bounced to his feet and headed for the two students sparring nearby, calling out instructions to them.

Javi caught my eye. Seeing his obvious disappointment, I turned, walked to the bench and grabbed my coffee so I wouldn't have to look at either of them.

****

I took the long way home, down Canyon Road. Still as many little art shops as I remembered. I used to love strolling along, Mama's hand in mine, looking at the sculptures, paintings, woodwork, jewelry, and other pieces, each unique and amazing. Spying an empty parking spot, I pulled over and got out. The morning sunshine already sizzled.

"Sunshine," I muttered. I needed a different nickname for Ray. The thought of having dinner with him, alone, stole my appetite. What the hell had I done? Something told me it would only lead to trouble. If tonight went well, he'd ask me out again. If it went terrible, which it very well could, Javi would accuse me of mistreating his friend.

I strolled along, hardly noticing the beautiful crafts around me, too caught up in worrying. My last date with a guy had been a disaster. I'd ignored the standard advice about getting involved with a coworker. Jacob reminded me a lot of Ray, all cute and charming and funny, the blue-eyed blond every other girl drooled over. Our time together was easy and relaxed. Until he wanted to have sex on our second date. Nothing cute about him, then. He turned ugly fast. Apparently, rejection baffled him because he kept showing up at my apartment. When I finally threatened to call the police, he punched through the glass in my door. If his bleeding hand hadn't forced him to the ER...I still wonder what would have happened. It was a relief to get away from San Diego and from him. Monsters came in such pretty packages.

Ray was very pretty. *He's not Jacob.*

At that moment, I passed a jewelry shop, and a silver necklace stopped me cold. The small pendant dangling from the delicate chain was formed in the nearly identical shape of the birthmark on my hip—a three-pronged flame. My breath caught.

The girl behind the counter jerked her head toward me. "Everything all right?" A silver stud gleamed from one nostril, and tattoo sleeves decorated both forearms.

"Yes, sorry. Do you know anything about this?" I held up the necklace.

She frowned thoughtfully. "Like what?"

"Who's the artist? Someone local?"

Sandals scuffed the floor as she shuffled over and looked more closely. "No idea. All I know is, it costs seventy-five dollars."

"Yeah." That much I knew. A bit steep, but the

coincidence was too great to pass up buying the jewelry.

As soon as I got back in the car, I fastened the chain around my neck. The silver flame lay just below the hollow of my throat, the perfect length.

I laughed at myself. "Yes, Marissa. Fate drew you here." My smile turned wry. I'd have to keep telling myself that so I wouldn't complain when I didn't have enough money to buy groceries.

A growl from my belly reminded me that I'd only wolfed down a yogurt for breakfast, and the workout had increased my appetite. My fridge held a few apples and more yogurt, and the pantry held little more than crackers and cereal. In the distance, the church bells rang out through the square. I drove toward town, ready to splurge on lunch, and stumbled across the Fortress, a restaurant my coworkers had sung high praises about, so I climbed from the car again. Jammed, from what I could tell, but I went inside anyway. Yep, absolutely jammed. Damn, the food smelled delicious, too. I sighed.

A waitress bustled by. "If you're alone, you're in luck. A seat opened up there." She balanced three plates as she gestured.

"Thanks."

"Be right there."

Lunch did not disappoint. I savored every bite of the Mediterranean salad, so amazing it made me wish I'd been hired as the *Chronicle*'s food critic. Or glad I hadn't been... I'd stuffed myself to the gills. What I needed now was a walk.

I left a hefty tip and headed down the street. Through the window of one shop, I spied the cutest black top. Mixed feelings warred within me. Ray had suggested a black top as an alternate to a little black dress, so I was inclined to wear another color. Except this one called to me.

In answer, I entered the shop and made a beeline for the wall, where a rack held the shirt in various sizes. After finding a Small, I held it up against myself and turned to the narrow full-length mirror set into the posts.

A salesgirl approached. "You would look so cool in that."

I wrinkled my nose. "I don't know."

"If you want to try it on, the dressing booths are right there."

A row of curtained stalls lined the back wall.

"I probably should." I shushed the tiny nag in my head telling me to stop spending so much money, I had bills due. *Hey, I hardly ever indulge in shopping except when I need to. And today, I need to.* The one black shirt I owned was old and wouldn't do the job of wowing Ray. And for some reason, I wanted to knock him off his feet without having to physically assault him.

After slipping it on, I had no doubt I was buying the top. The fit flattered my figure, and the style was chic and classic. Exactly the competitive edge I needed. "You're going down, Mr. White."

I changed into my boring shirt and flung open the curtain. The woman browsing at a nearby rack looked up.

Ashley Stirling's striking blue eyes pierced mine. "Marissa. I didn't expect to see you here."

"I wasn't expecting to be here."

Her smile turned sly as she glanced at the top I held. "Oo, let's see what you have."

I stood there dumbly as she snatched the top from my hands and held it up.

"I love it. This would be perfect with my new jeans. Are you buying it?"

"If I can get it to the cashier." I opened my palm.

Her expression froze for a beat, and she splayed her fingers, letting the shirt fall across my wrist.

I felt terrible for acting so rude. Something about her always agitated me, and I reacted badly every time. All I wanted was to get away from her.

When the shirt kept sliding down, I grabbed it mid-air. "Have a nice day." I strode toward the register.

"Oh, there they are," Ashley said.

I didn't take the bait. I knew she'd sashay over to the row of tops and select one to mirror my purchase. I wasn't going to let Ashley reduce me to that timid kindergarten girl again. I bought the damn blouse.

And as I drove off, I resolved to have a good time. It was only a date, for God's sake. If Ray and I didn't hit it off, no big deal. We could remain friends, and Javi would get over it.

Before heading home, I ran errands—the grocery store then the liquor store to replace the six-pack of the beer that Ray drank. Him or some other visitor, I told myself.

I ran an assessing eye across the apartment. Not exactly impressive, and my domestic skills left much to be admired. Still, it was home for now, and the sofa sat on a Navajo print rug that I loved. Perfect, because I watched the Kiva fireplace opposite more often than the small television mounted beside it. Nothing extravagant. Furniture might be sparse, but my favorite prints hung on the walls. Mostly, I loved the light, and the way rays of sunshine angled through the tall windows most of the day gave the whole place a homey feel. I didn't need shelves full of bric-a-brac or tons of furniture.

While cleaning, I wondered what shape my black boots were in. The snug pair of jeans, my new necklace, and silver bangle bracelets would make a wicked outfit. I abandoned the vacuum to rummage through the closet and held up a boot in triumph. A little dull, but I could put a shine on them. I dragged them out and set them in the kitchen, then returned to cleaning.

The boots caught my eye time and again, until I was compelled to switch off the vacuum and search the cabinet for boot polish. Nothing. I was fairly certain I'd tossed the dried-out tin before moving. Wood polish would do for now.

My arms had begun to ache by the time I was satisfied with the sheen on the black leather, but then I couldn't wait to see how everything looked together. One glance at my dirty clothes sent me heading for the shower. I took extra care to lather and shave. I wanted to look my best. To put on a better face than the one I'd worn this morning.

Not that Ray was special to me. But I'd been rough on him. I owed him a chance to redeem himself. And surely there was more beneath that pretty-boy surface, just waiting to be explored. Who knew? I might find the real Ray hidden like a treasure chest.

The jeans took some convincing to get on, a sign that I needed to get back to working out, but the black top went on like a silken breeze. My silver jewelry added the perfect touch, the necklace glinting in the V opening.

The girl looking back at me in the mirror was barely recognizable. Not bad, I thought. The little pretender wasn't quite a swan, but then I'd never intended to be one. Or anything else I wasn't.

I tugged the blouse outside the jeans. Tucking it in made me look like I was trying too hard. And I wouldn't do that anymore. Any guy I dated would have to accept the real Marissa, or I'd just have to forget him.

The muffled chime of my cell sounded from the bed. I dug it out from my bag and grinned. *Ray.* "Hey." At the scream of sirens, I imagined him in the center of some terrible scene, and sobered quick. "Are you—"

"Marissa," Ray practically shouted. "We're on our way to a fire. A big one. Might be there a long time."

My every nerve stood on end as he spoke. "Oh God. Be careful."

The reception broke up, and I thought he said he'd call later. Then the line went dead. A bad feeling crept over me.

For a moment, I stared at the phone. Why hadn't I asked where the blaze was? Then I dialed Weller. "There's a fire, I'm not sure where—"

"Over on Galisteo."

Galisteo? The hotel where I spent my first night was on that street.

Weller grumbled, "Stirling's already on the scene."

So fast? Damn. "Okay. Let me know if anything else comes up." Had Weller assigned the story to her? Or had Ashley found out and volunteered?

Galisteo was across town, only blocks from the

plaza. I could drive there in fifteen minutes. Hang out. Make sure Ray and Javi were all right.

But firefighters hated gawkers. People who gathered around disasters like vultures clogged up the intersections and roadways, making it more difficult for emergency crews to do their jobs.

I rose and paced aimlessly. Staying home would drive me crazy, wondering all night. Maybe I should go out alone. I didn't dress up often.

I wouldn't have a good time knowing my cousin and Ray were out battling a big fire. I undressed and hung the top carefully in the closet, separate so it wouldn't wrinkle. A tank top and some sweats would do. A cup of Chai would be just the thing to help me relax. After gathering what I needed in the kitchen, it didn't take long to brew. With my tea in hand I returned to my room and took out my laptop. Hopefully, it would keep my mind occupied.

My tea cup emptied, I settled on the bed with my laptop, ready to continue researching old newspaper editions on the Internet, while the local news droned in the background. I searched the online news, hoping it might provide an update on the fire.

An old article about Zozobra popped up. The first photo I ran across stunned me. Someone who looked like a much younger version of my aunt was captioned, listing the names of the committee members, but gave her name as Zelda Chin.

Zelda was unmistakable. She looked young, and though she couldn't have been any older than twenty at most in 1964, her eyes always gave the impression of her being a wise old soul.

The smiles on the faces of the committee members

were stiff as they stood in front of the tall figure of Old Man Gloom, hanging behind them. Ready to be burned at the festival that night, the effigy's head drooped, so the figure appeared to be glaring down at the group with a mocking sneer. The newspaper piece gave all the relevant statistics, and on the surface everything about the event appeared to be a success, but the faces in the photo said otherwise. There was a weariness about them that looked very much like defeat. Maybe their success that year had been hard won, but why?

I jotted a note to remind myself to ask Zelda about the 1964 Zozobra. Either something had gone wrong that year, or else it had posed a great challenge to my aunt to keep a disaster from occurring.

More searching unearthed random photos from previous festivals and years after, but none from either the festival the immediate year before or following. A coincidence? Maybe. The committee's record-keeping was spotty and disorganized.

Why hadn't previous liaisons taken that task upon themselves? Seemed a no-brainer, to me. Unless one or more committee members had discouraged it. If the messy record-keeping was intentional there must be a reason.

Either way, I had to find out. The best way to go about it was to assign the story to myself. If anyone put up a fuss, I'd argue the effort would yield more public interest. It was a marketing tactic to raise more funds. No one argued with money. They were all about profit for the charities. Or so they claimed.

Zelda, I suspected, had another purpose.

Chapter Seven

A strange sleep locked me in its hold. Fully conscious that I lay in bed, I was unable to move. My eyes were closed, yet I saw everything. Unable to even look away from the fire that sprang up in front of me and split the darkness. I found myself in the same nightmare I dreaded, of my five-year-old self standing on the Mission Road curb, helpless as I watched my house burn down, my brother trapped inside.

Yet this time was different. The outline of the boy in the window was taller, the figure familiar. In one terrible instant, I saw my brother. And finally, I heard him, clear as if he stood beside me, as if no fire roared around him.

"We must protect them, Marissa."

I heard him but didn't understand what he meant. Protect who?

Then he changed. He grew taller—a man stood there, not Michael anymore.

Now it was Ray who banged on the glass, yelling at me. Warning me to run.

Terror scorched my senses. "No!" I ran toward the burning house, but the heat forced me back. "Ray, jump!"

He pounded his fist against the window. "Get out of here, Marissa. Hurry!"

Tears streamed down my face. I reached out

toward him. "Not without you."

He punched the glass. It splintered, shards raining down among the smoke. The fire roared, an angry beast lunging for Ray, all power and snarling flame. Ray dove through the window, fire biting at his heels.

"Ray." I lurched toward him. Heat rolled over me. A sea of hot waves pushed me back. I dove into the strong current of superheated air, but it slowed my movements. I was too late to get to Ray and cushion his landing.

He curled his back as he fell, but there was nothing below him to break his fall but the sparse grass. He hit the ground and tumbled away from the house. On impact, his breath left him in a rush. Each time he rolled, he moaned, his arms flailing. It seemed like forever, but when I caught up to him, we were only a few yards back. Not far enough.

"Don't try to get up." I cradled his head in my lap.

"Get away," he said in a huff, and curled into himself like a trapped animal.

I gulped back the hurt. "I'm going to help you." I stroked his hair, hoping to soothe him.

He went still but grimaced up at me. "Get away from him."

"Who?"

Face pinched in pain, he twisted and turned. "Old Man Gloom. He's coming for you."

He must have hit his head hard. Tenderly, I parted strands of hair, searching for cuts or bumps, but found none.

A loud groan split the night, echoing from inside the burning house. Creaks and crashes sounded, room after room collapsing in on itself. The fire would consume everything soon, then sweep hungrily toward us.

I had to get him far away from here. "Can you get up? I'll help you walk."

"No. No, Marissa." Eyes glazed and wild, he punched the air. "Go!"

A heavy shadow crawled over us, blocking the blaze. I turned, my movements heavy and slow as underwater. The smoke billowing up from the fire had thickened into dark grey, its edges creeping closer to neighboring houses on either side. The center turned black. From within, a familiar shape emerged.

"Old Man Gloom," I whispered, then scrambled to tug Ray away. "Hurry. Let's go!" My grip slipped on his shirt, so I looped my arms around his chest. His boots might have been roller skates, unable to find purchase on the gritty soil.

Terror locked my muscles as the forty-foot effigy stomped toward us. Leering at us. Laughing.

"No. This is a dream. A dream!" The scream tore from my throat, a raw and primal sound. I wanted to break free of this nightmare. But I was trapped.

Old Man Gloom bent his head lower. Closer. His red lips opened to reveal jagged teeth, ready to devour me.

In that moment between wakefulness and sleep, when the two states of consciousness shifted from one to the other, the two faces began to merge—the young man who'd been following me, the one the shadows loved so much, and the face I hated more than anyone's: Old Man Gloom.

In that instant, when one face superimposed upon the other, I saw the truth. They were one in the same.

There was no mistaking the jagged brows, the too-red lips quirked between a smile and a snarl, the almond-shaped eyes, wide set and black enough to make you feel as if you were staring into an abyss.

Even while I slept, that truth shocked me. Enough of a shock to snap me awake, gasping, my head reeling. *No.* My world turned topsy-turvy, nightmares blurred with reality. Until now, I could pass off the similarities as the remnants of a nightmare come back to haunt me. Not anymore.

The last vestige of sleep was instantly gone, but I grasped the bed covers tighter to convince myself I was no longer dreaming. The cool air against my sweat-drenched skin and my audible gasp both helped to ground me in my surroundings.

Yet I couldn't shake the image fixed in my mind. Old Man Gloom had the same features, the same laugh as the young man I'd encountered in the pub on my first night back in Santa Fe.

And the man in the bar...I knew where I'd seen him, years ago. Back then, he'd been an old man, desperate to cling to this world. A few weeks ago, when I'd returned to Santa Fe, he'd looked mid-twenties, at most.

If the dream was true, and the two were both Old Man Gloom...

"He's getting younger instead of older," I whispered. But how? If the dream were real, it could only mean one thing—he'd cast off everyone else's troubles and refused to carry their burdens for them. Suggesting what? He intended not to burn during Zozobra. He had something terrible planned.

Which meant that I had to devise a plan for

something more terrible. For that, I'd need help from my family. I'd rather dance the tango with Old Man Gloom on burning coals—almost, anyway.

Another thought struck me. "Ray." He was in trouble.

A desperate search for my cell phone felt like an eternity. I found it buried under the covers behind the laptop. Panicked, I fumbled to turn it on and called Ray. The number rang and rang, then went to voice mail. "Ugh! Sorry," I said to the recording. "Hey, I'm just checking in. Please call me so I know you're okay."

The cold lump in my gut told me he wasn't. I tried Javi next. His cell went to voice mail, too. "Hey, please call me. I'm freaking out."

My thoughts straightened enough to remind me to check the time. Five thirty. Too early for local news reports. But Zelda said she woke up at that hour. Given the circumstances, my aunt would forgive a frantic phone call.

On the second ring, Zelda answered. "Marissa?" Alarm tightened her voice.

"Sorry to call so early. The fire…is…is Javi all right?" I squeezed my eyes shut. *And Ray?*

"He will be."

God. I hadn't really considered Javi might be injured. Before I could ask, Zelda went on.

"They treated him for smoke inhalation, thankfully only a very slight case. You should be proud of him. He was hurt trying to save his friend Ray."

Trying to? Breathing suddenly felt like inhaling broken glass. "What happened to Ray?" My coiled nerves sprang loose. I leapt up and paced.

"He was trapped. The ceiling caved in. Javi

dragged him out. The ambulance took him to Santa Fe General."

Trapped? Too much like my dream. "But he's alive? He's going to be all right?"

"Ray had some burns, but nothing life threatening, thank goodness."

I couldn't shake the ominous feeling that Ray was still in danger. "Javi's home now? He's fine?"

"Yes. He's fine." Zelda's clipped words conveyed her disappointment that I had asked about his health last. "He's resting. Don't disturb him."

"No, I won't." I had other things to worry about besides my aunt's feelings. "That's a relief."

Zelda sighed. "I'd better let you go. I have things to do. I'm sure you do, too."

If Zelda was fishing for information about my relationship with Ray, I wouldn't confirm her suspicion. There was nothing to confirm anyway. "Sorry again for calling so early."

After ending the call, I rubbed my eyes. The horror of my dream had leached into the real world. The image of the two faces merging, Old Man Gloom and the guy I'd seen around the city, was still all too vivid.

And disturbing. That much had been all too real.

****

Hospital visiting hours didn't begin until ten o'clock. I filled the time by staying in motion: I showered, cleaned the kitchen, and ran the vacuum. My knees bobbed when I sat at my laptop, so I moved it to the kitchen to stand at the counter while I scanned the web and read emails. By nine, I was ready to jump out of my skin, so I drove to Santa Fe General. For a few minutes, I sat in my car outside the building. People entered and exited, so I decided to wait inside. When I checked in with the receptionist, she searched the computer for Ray's room—number 209. I thanked her and wandered to the waiting area, but my nerves were wound too tight to sit. I pretended to watch the wall-mounted flat-screen TV but kept an eye on the hallways. When the last person left and I was the sole occupant, I straightened my spine, squared my shoulders, and made my way to the elevator, then on to the second floor. 209 was adjacent to the nurses' station, but the woman behind the counter sat facing the wall, engrossed in the computer. I allowed only a beat of hesitation before slipping inside.

Both beds were occupied. In the nearest one, gauzy wrappings covered the man's head. My breath hitched. My pulse paused. I forced my gaze to the second bed and released a breath. *Ray*. Awake, he stared out the window. Both arms were blistered and red, but his expression didn't appear to register pain. More like consternation so intense that I hesitated to disturb him.

I paused at the curtain dividing the beds. "Hey. Are you up for a visitor?"

He turned toward me as if coming out of a dream, almost seemed not to know where he was. For a moment, he narrowed his eyes. Only when I smiled did he break free of whatever hold he was under.

He struggled to sit up and immediately winced in pain.

I crossed the remaining space with light steps. "No, don't get up. I can't stay long anyway."

His gaze flicked to mine, disgust dulling his eyes. An exhale, and he settled back against the pillow as if it held shards of glass.

No use asking him how he felt. Obviously, he felt shitty. Lost for words, I said, "I'm so sorry."

"Not your fault." He sounded as distant as he looked.

Or the fault was entirely mine, if my dream was any indication. I couldn't bear to see blame in his face, too, so looked away. "I could have kidnapped you, turned off your phone…" Some joke.

Our planned date was obviously the last thing on his mind. He stared at the ceiling as if at images only he could see.

I knew I shouldn't have come, but there was no way I could have stayed away. "What's wrong?"

"Nothing. Except there's a chance I'm going crazy."

Join the club, Sunshine. "What makes you say that?"

The glaze in his eyes was like a reflection of the fire. "I heard someone calling to me. Inside the flames." He spoke in a whisper, and I had to lean forward to hear.

His gaze pinballed, panic blazing in his eyes. "The other guys signaled they'd gotten everyone out, that every person had been accounted for. But…" His expression hardened, and his scowl set in stone as he dropped his gaze to his arms.

I finished for him. "But you heard a voice."

He searched my face before answering. "Yes. Not just a voice. I can't even explain what it sounded like. It had no real sound. When I followed it, I couldn't find anyone." He shook his head, and bitterness pulled his grin sideways. "I told you. *Loco.*"

Hardly. But if I simply told him he was wrong, I'd

never convince him. "Did it sort of sound like a whisper?"

He sent me a look that warned me not to play the condescending friend.

I met it with my own expression that warned him not to bullshit me. "Did it?"

"Kind of." He sounded wary. "But the weird thing was, it was calling me. My name."

Old Man Gloom. He'd targeted Ray, too. Because of me? Without meaning to, I eased away from the bed.

His smile soured. "See, I knew you'd think I was crazy."

"No. I don't." But now I could never go on a date with him. If Old Man Gloom harmed Ray because of me, I'd never forgive myself. "I should go." I turned.

"What, did you just remember an urgent appointment?" he sneered.

Sarcasm was so unbecoming on him. I was both glad to note it, and sorry, mostly because I'd caused that, too. "No, you need your rest."

He glared out the window. "I haven't been sleeping anyway." Then I noticed how dark the circles under his eyes were, like he'd been punched.

The poor guy must have been torturing himself all night. "Can't they give you something?"

"No." He laid his head back on the pillow and stared at the ceiling. "I don't want it."

Because he was afraid of what would come for him? I wanted to tell him that I could relate, but instead I bit my lip.

His expression cooled. "Thanks for stopping by. I appreciate it."

I nearly said I'd check in again, but I couldn't do

that. And I wouldn't make false promises.

He visibly steeled himself as he lifted the remote and switched on the TV, but a hint of another wince etched lines in his face. "There's a good show coming on I want to watch."

My cue to leave. He was trying to make it easy on me. "Take care of yourself."

He glanced pointedly at his arms. "I don't have much choice. Will I see you at MMA?" He shrugged. "In a few weeks, I can coach from the sidelines, at least."

The hope in his voice made my heart ache. I couldn't let him see my hesitation, so I grinned. "It's really not my thing."

The light left his face. "Yeah, sure. I get it. You take care of yourself, too."

It killed me not to take his hand, tell him how sorry I was. He stared at the television on the wall as if I were already gone.

"Okay." It came out in a breath. I hurried out of the room before I did anything stupid. Like go back to him, hold his hand, and tell him he was anything but crazy.

On the way to the car, a hushed chuckle resonated through the air.

"Leave him alone, Old Man." The laughter changed to a long breath, a powerful whoosh that swept out toward the mountains.

Chapter Eight

On Monday morning, the weekly staff meeting started in the usual way. Weller's coffee mug hit the tabletop like a gavel, and conversation dropped off. Either Weller'd had a hell of a weekend, or work was starting to get to him. Frown lines around his eyes and mouth deepened, and his face looked twice as puffy, as if he'd drank too much.

He cleared his throat. "A few new items are on the agenda. Tahy." He barked my name.

I snapped to attention. "Yes?"

"Get over to the Valdez residence. Cops are there now. I want you to speak to the two officers, and to the parents about the boy. He didn't come home last night."

"Luis disappeared?" The kid had the brightest future of anyone in Santa Fe. The thought hit me like a gong. *And so had the farthest to fall.* "I'll go now." I paused in case he argued.

Weller waved me away. "Go. I want something up on our web site this morning before the damn TV news airs the story."

A nod, and I was out of there.

As Weller had said, a squad car sat in front of the Valdez home. I waited for the police to end their interview and exit the residence before I approached them. The house held no black star that I could see, and it added to my growing sense of unease.

The two officers gave terse, factual responses to my questions.

A stark contrast to the scattered answers of Mr. and Mrs. Valdez, who were understandably agitated. I framed my inquiries as simply as I could to keep from further upsetting them, all the while taking mental stock of the surroundings. Their home looked a mess, and it had taken longer than a day or two for that mess to accumulate. From what I gathered, the family had been under a great deal of strain for some time.

"I just want my boy home safe." Mrs. Valdez appeared not to notice the tears trickling down her face.

Her husband grunted. "We both do." He looked angry—at her, at me, at the world.

To defuse any possible argument brewing between them, I nodded. "I understand."

He snorted. "You reporters are all the same. How could you possibly understand? Have you ever lost a child?"

A brother, I wanted to say. Not in the same way, but this story wasn't about me. "I'm very sorry. Luis is a great kid. I'm sure he'll turn up."

"I feel so much better now," Mrs. Valdez sneered.

I skimmed past the sarcasm. "Did Luis leave a note? Or any sort of communication?"

"What's that supposed to mean?" Mr. Valdez snapped.

I pressed on more softly but no less diligently. "Did he give any indication that he planned to leave? Maybe on social media? Or his cell phone?"

"Who said he planned to leave?" Mrs. Valdez turned to her husband with wild eyes. "Someone might have kidnapped him."

I forced an apologetic smile. "Sorry, I know this is difficult."

Mr. Valdez inched to the edge of the sofa, poised to pounce. "Do you know something that we don't?"

"No, of course not. How could I?" Wrong move, to put up a defense.

Mrs. Valdez regarded me differently. "You're the same reporter who wrote the feature about Luis, aren't you?"

I kept a calm demeanor but set my recorder atop my bag and readied to bolt, if necessary. "That's not relevant—"

"She is." Mr. Valdez jabbed a finger at me. "You wrote something about our boy wanting to leave Santa Fe."

"It was a direct quote." I'd softened what the teen had said by putting his statement on the same level as other high schoolers who dream of getting away from their hometown.

"Luis would never have said that." Mrs. Valdez's jaw trembled. "And now he's gone."

This was getting me nowhere. I gathered my things and rose. "If you think of anything helpful, please let me know." I held out a business card.

The couple glared at it. Their anger boiled below the surface but threatened to burst forth. I didn't want to be around when they exploded. I left the card on the coffee table and let myself out. At least my visit gave them a new target for their anger, and they might not tear each other apart later.

When I wrote the article back at my desk, I glossed over their combative natures and focused on their parental concern. The sidebar would display the police number to call with any information on the boy's whereabouts. After I submitted the piece to the editor, frustration hit me at not being able to do more. All my high-minded journalistic integrity amounted to squat when someone was in danger. Information was a useful tool in many situations but in this one fell short of filling anyone's needs.

****

The day had been grueling for everyone at the *Chronicle*. Apparently after my abrupt departure, the city erupted. There was a shouting match at a restaurant. Two auto accidents attributed to road rage. A cyclist rammed his mountain bike into a hiker who wouldn't share the trail. And those were only the reported incidents.

The stress had taken a toll on us all.

After pounding out a political piece, Mike Fisher leaned back in his chair and stretched. "I need a beer. Anyone else?"

"Oh, yeah. I'm all over that." Her makeup fresh as if she'd arrived minutes ago, Ashley logged off her laptop and shoved it into the stylish bag.

Others chimed in their agreement, and the exodus began from the newsroom, the regular pilgrimage to the bar.

Ashley slung her bag over her shoulder. "Aren't you coming?"

"Maybe after I finish up," I lied.

Ashley fixed her gaze on me. "Oh, please. You finished before any of us, as usual. You must need a drink after today's craziness."

Was the girl psychic? Or a little too focused on me? "You're right." I tempered my defiance with a

102

pleasant expression. "I do need a drink." A few clicks and taps later, I'd shut down the laptop and slid it into my utilitarian black messenger bag.

Outside, Ashley climbed into her shiny white sports car, and me into my beat-up SUV. Shifting into reverse, the gears ground, and my face flamed. My embarrassment was wasted, as Ashley had already sped off.

Once I reached the parking lot of the bar, I ignored the empty spots near the entrance and opted for one farther away.

Every seat was occupied by the time I went inside. I veered toward the bar.

"Hey Tahy," one of the guys called. "We saved you a seat."

Very funny. I shot a wry grin over my shoulder, then saw that Bill had pulled a chair between his and Ashley's. Oh, joy. "Be right there."

I signaled the bartender. "Beer, please? The bottle's fine." I dragged myself to the table and forced a smile as I squeezed between them.

They shared the easy banter of coworkers who'd worked together for years and knew the others' families and personal histories. I offered a comment here and there, but each time only further spotlighted me as an outsider. I tossed back the beer and readied an excuse to leave.

Bill called to the server, "Another round here."

Ashley swung her head toward me. "I guess you're all settled in at the *Chronicle*."

Another keen observation? "Yes, I guess so."

"Javi Furtado's your cousin, isn't he? Did he help you move into your place?"

"Yes, and no, respectively. I didn't bring much from California."

Bill hooted. "Ashley has the hots for the firefighter."

A *tsk*, and Ashley limply slapped at his arm. But didn't argue. "I'm grateful to every person who serves the community." She swigged her beer. "And I can't help it if he's hot."

Low murmurs circled the tabled.

With some difficulty, I plastered a grin on my face. "And what does your husband do, Ashley?"

Her expression soured. "Besides cheat on me?" she practically spat.

My bravado deflated. "Oh." Leave it to me to hit the woman's sore spot. Another strike against me. "Sorry. I didn't know."

Ashley waved dismissively. "How could you?"

Right, we were hardly friends. And I didn't engage in break room gossip.

Mike nudged his elbow against Ashley's. "You'll clean up in the divorce."

Ashley raised her beer. "I'll drink to that." Her hard eyes focused on something across the room as she tilted the bottle to her perfect lips.

I guessed perfection wasn't all it was cracked up to be. Must be exhausting for beautiful people like her, not to mention disappointing, to maintain the façade for so little reward.

Ashley looked the image of innocence. "I'm not really a horrible bitch, you know."

"Neither am I." I'd meet her halfway.

Ashley begrudgingly grinned and raised her bottle. "Cheers to that."

I touched my bottle to hers with a clink. "To letting go of misconceptions."

Ashley's face became porcelain hard. "To honesty."

"And integrity," I countered, trying not to grit my teeth.

Her fingertips turned white as her grip tightened around the beer. "And letting go of the past, for *chri'sakes*." She shivered, as if shaking off a bad vibe.

I huffed at her theatrics. "Oh, I'm an expert in that area. If you want pointers, let me know." A reality check might do her some good.

She set her bottle on the table with a clunk. "Seriously. You still hold it against me that I liked your big brother in like, fourth grade."

Third, but I wouldn't quibble. "Why would I?"

"Good question." Ashley tossed her blonde hair back with a shake of her head.

The curl of disgust in Ashley's lip signaled I was the one, despite all my bravado, who couldn't get over the past.

I took a breath and affected a humble tone. "That was a difficult time in my life, to say the least. I hope you'll understand if I'm reluctant to talk about it."

"My present life's no picnic either. So cut me a freaking break."

A truce might not be out of the question. "Deal."

The slightest flinch in her wide eyes gave away her mistrust, but Ashley extended her hand. "Deal."

From the way she said it, a tentative one, at best. For now, I would take it. I shook the girl's hand, and we returned to drinking, no less awkward than before.

By the time our little group split up, each of us

heading in a different direction toward home, I took pride in the fact none of us had succumbed to the tendrils of negative energy winding its way through the people of Santa Fe, feeling for any dank, deep place to take root.

The constant struggle, though, was exhausting. And there were two and a half months left before the festival.

Chapter Nine

Somewhere between stepping out of my shoes and climbing into bed, my reality shifted. My bedroom slipped away, and darkness surrounded me, encircled by a border of mist. I knew I was standing because cold ground pebbled beneath my bare feet. I knew my eyes were open because I blinked, but still could see nothing.

A pinpoint of brilliant light appeared, far-off but getting nearer. Instead of going to meet it, I waited to see who might be carrying such a light. I wasn't at all sure I wanted to know, and the closer the light came, the more apprehensive I became. The approaching glow acted like a magnet on me—simultaneously pulling me toward it and pushing me away.

Slowly, the form of a woman took shape within the light. Long blonde hair flowed in the night. She was beautiful or would have been if not for the fire. Where her eyes should have been, flames licked through the sockets. Fire danced inside her skull, filling it, spilling out of her ears, her nose, her mouth.

She stood close enough that I recognized her.

"Ashley?"

Her lips were wide open, as if set in a permanent scream of horror, but she made no sound. Only the fire's crackle and pop broke the silence.

I reached out, wanting to help her, to ease her distress, but had no idea how. The most I could do was say, "I'm sorry." Nothing about her changed, so I doubted she even heard me.

From behind me, a different glow signaled another's approach. Radiant in her white buckskin dress, *Ptesan-Wi* floated up beside me. I dared not look her in the eye again, so bowed my head. After a moment, she glided toward Ashley. Whether Ashley was aware of White Buffalo Woman, I couldn't tell. She appeared to be consumed, body and mind, by the flames within her.

Ptesan-Wi's hands shook as she raised them and spoke in what sounded like Sioux. In one hand, she held a black star, the very same as those Zelda had given me. Then *Ptesan-Wi* pressed the star to Ashley's forehead.

No! I lurched toward her. The distance between us closed as I stepped toward *Ptesan-Wi*. As if fitting a figure within a mold, my body snapped inside hers. My hands wore hers like shimmering gloves, flesh that was not flesh. I saw through White Buffalo Woman's eyes. We were separate but moved as one. Our combined touch absorbed the white-hot heat emanating from Ashley. Her anguish, anger, despair, the pain she'd swallowed and kept inside, though the storm of emotions grew worse the longer she denied them. *Ptesan-Wi* was drawing them out like an infection from a wound. As they flowed from Ashley, each arrow of pain struck me. The divorce. Her husband's betrayal. His lies. The loneliness. All the hurt Ashley had suffered and pretended none of it touched her, she'd carried like burning coals that scorched her soul. The lava of her pain sizzled over my skin, *Ptesan-Wi*'s skin, leaving boiling bubbles of acid in its wake. The current held me in its thrall, unable to move. The infallible strength of *Ptesan-Wi* kept me upright. I stood locked in her frame.

The stream sputtered and finally eased, the flow beginning to ebb. I waited for the end, for relief for all three of us. I let myself float, suspended within White Buffalo Woman, her light and goodness re-energizing me.

Then another wave poured out of Ashley, more powerful than the others because of how long she'd hidden it away, though the wound had never healed. A child's anguish. Confusion. Loss of loved ones. I braced against the new current of pain.

I understood who she'd mourned: her mother, but also my brother. That grief rolled over me, a crushing weight that stole my breath. If not for *Ptesan-Wi*'s spirit encasing me, I'd have slid to the ground. At the point of exhaustion, when I thought I could take no more, the flow trickled to an end.

The flames likewise died away, leaving only the glow of *Ptesan-Wi*'s spirit to light the darkness.

Ashley's features solidified with flesh and became whole. Her mouth was closed, no longer a mute cry of anguish. Her blue eyes held surprise, then recognition, as she looked through *Ptesan-Wi* to me. I couldn't answer the questions they held but was comforted by her more peaceful appearance. Not quite Zen but getting there.

Ashley was pulled backward by some unseen force. Distance grew between us. She soon faded from sight. I no longer worried for her welfare.

The illumination enshrouding me faded, and I knew that *Ptesan-Wi* was leaving, too. Darkness greedily crowded around me, except for a small but powerful light that shone from my hand. I opened my palm. Within a cushion of brilliance, the black star held the darkness at bay. Its obsidian pulsed, lifelike and radiating energy. The other stars were reminiscent of this one, but also very little like it. Sometimes, though, a little was enough to guide you home.

Chapter Ten

In the morning, I kept my nose in my computer, hoping to avoid Ashley. The vision from the previous night lingered in the forefront of my mind, all too vivid.

I could feel her gaze heavy on me throughout the morning. Finally, she perched on the side of my desk. "I'm going for coffee. Want some? You've been at it all morning without a break."

Offering me coffee? "I'll grab some in a bit. I want to finish up while it's fresh in my mind." When she rose, I felt my shoulders slump in relief.

But she didn't leave. She crept toward me, slow as a cat approaching water. "You know what's fresh in my mind? The strange dream I had last night."

"About what?" I hoped I didn't sound as paranoid to her as I did to my own ears.

Stopping in front of me, she rested her hands on the desktop and studied me. "You were in it. And a lady I felt like I should recognize, but I didn't."

I made a sound, a noncommittal *hm*, hoping she'd drop it, yet I didn't want to discourage her either. Did she recall *Ptesan-Wi*? Why else would White Buffalo Woman be familiar to her?

"I can't explain what happened, really," she said, "except that I had the worst fever, but by the end, I felt so much better."

"That's all that counts." I gave her a thin, brief

smile. A hint to go away.

But she didn't take it. "Strange as it was, it was incredibly realistic."

"Dreams are weird like that."

"Yet they also oddly strike at the truth." A small smile curved her mouth. "I woke up with a sense of calm that I haven't felt in a long time."

"Great." Whatever other realm experience we'd shared must have actually healed her. I wished I could explain it to her, but I wouldn't know where to begin.

"Another funny thing." She absently touched her forehead. "Those black star ornaments for the festival were in my dream, too."

She remembered. I sputtered, "Really?"

Moving with greater purpose, she went back to her desk and took something from her purse. "We still have them at the front desk, right?"

"The stars? Yes, for the people who contribute their troubles to burn in the effigy."

With a pert smile, she held up a folded paper. Or multiple papers, judging by the thickness. Probably a collection of all her troubles.

I didn't bother to hide my surprise. "You wrote yours down?"

Her grin looked sheepish. "As the saying goes, there's a first time for everything. I'll be back."

I felt like I should cheer her on, make some show of encouragement, but Ashley's triumph needed no validation from me. Nor could I share my relief that she intended to trade her contribution for a black star that would protect her home. One less resident to worry about, at least. If there were only some way to blanket the protection across the entire city, I'd sleep easier.

I managed to get through the day without any disasters. Only a feeling of unease followed me like a ghost, straight out the back door at the end of the day.

The sun was dipping toward the horizon, casting distorted shadows that stretched like fingers, reaching out. The weight of a stare made me turn, searching for anyone looking my way, but the only other people in the parking lot were heading for their own cars.

Ashley sauntered outside like a runway model. "Anything wrong?"

"I thought I'd forgotten something. It'll come to me at home." I sent her a grin, which faded at hearing a distant, low hum and a series of clicks interspersed with shrieks, like an internal timer ticking down. To what, I was afraid to guess.

Ashley waved in my general direction. "I have to run."

No sooner had she said the words, an image flashed through my head of the strange young man. His sly smile taunted me.

Pinpricks hit me like a full quiver of flame-tipped arrows. "Ashley, wait." I had to stop her. The star couldn't shield her from the man. And until Old Man Gloom burned, Ashley's troubles would remain her problem.

But she'd already climbed in her car. The roar of the engine momentarily drowned out the eerie sounds, then she was gone. I pulled out my cell to call her but held myself in check. What was I going to say to her? Don't go out tonight? Stay away from strange men? She'd think I'd gone off the deep end.

To hide a sudden shudder, I hopped in my SUV. Turning the ignition, I closed my eyes and whispered prayers. It also helped mute the noise, but in my mind, their presence was palpable.

And a bad omen. I pressed my foot to the gas pedal, but there was no outrunning what those sounds would bring.

****

As dusk deepened into night, the source of the noise took shape in my mind. The chorus from Hell took many forms, their small size a poor indication of their power, especially when they joined together. In a pack, they flew from the Sangre de Cristo Mountains toward Santa Fe. They swarmed street by street, and flitted from house to house, condo to apartment, either searching or taking inventory. Their passing registered on my skin like insects, alighting for only an instant. The black star hanging outside my door repelled them, a cosmic citronella but more effective on these nasty pests. *Thank you, Zelda.*

The invisible attack lasted only minutes but left a shadowy smear across my consciousness. Long after they'd followed whatever scent they tracked out of town again, I lay in bed, unable to quiet my mind. Even when sleep overcame me, I had no rest. I fell into a nightmare I knew too well.

My mother and father were smiling down at me, encouraging me to draw a picture of whatever troubled me. Together, they said, we would place our worries inside the giant puppet. They promised that when the fire consumed Old Man Gloom, our troubles would vanish. But when we entered the warehouse where the giant puppet waited, a cold wind whipped up. I shivered. My feet refused to budge. My parents led me forward, one on each side. I wanted to cry out, to run far away, but my father held my arm fast. He inserted his folded paper into the puppet's side and urged me to be brave. So, I stepped forward. The paper trembled in my hand while I slipped the drawing into Old Man Gloom. His huge head flopped to face me. He stared at me with an evil grin and whispered, *"Venganza."* Spanish for revenge. I yelped and leapt backward. My parents laughed and assured me everything was fine and that the workers had moved the effigy.

But at Zozobra that night, when the fire dancers twirled their lit batons around the giant puppet standing so tall that his head scraped the sky, Old Man Gloom whispered it again. Louder. Grittier. And when the master of ceremonies touched their torches to the huge puppet, and fire greedily climbed his robes, Old Man Gloom's agonized screams horrified me almost as much as the angry faces of the people who cheered for him to burn. He suffered terrible pain at the people's hands. My aunt Zelda stood watching with an intense expression, and I had the sense she was overseeing Old Man Gloom's destruction for a darker, deeper reason.

The wind kicked up. Embers drifted through the city, and in my mind's eye, I saw our house catch fire, I saw my brother Michael inside, trapped and afraid. We ran to our home but were powerless to stop it. We lost everything, but the most devastating loss was my brother. Later, I told my parents what Old Man Gloom had said, but grief blocked their senses, and they didn't hear me. They held a hasty memorial service for Michael, and then we packed up what little we had left into the car and said goodbye to Zelda and Javi. I locked my arms around my cousin and cried, but my father pried us apart. We drove for days and days. I still couldn't remember exactly how many, only that my legs kept going numb, and my mind.

After we arrived in San Diego, I begged my parents to go back. I hated that awful motel room we first stayed in. I could tell that my parents hated it, too, but they barely spoke to one another. After two weeks at the motel, my parents told me they'd found a new house, one I would love. But I hated that, too. It never felt like home, and my parents had become empty shells who couldn't love each other or me. I pleaded every day to return to our real home. Home to Santa Fe, where we belonged. The only place I ever felt like I belonged.

And yet it had taken me years to move back here. Years after college, after creating a semi-successful career as a journalist. Years to build up my strengths, both personal and professional. My parents' deaths nearly robbed me of that, but my mother's request that I move home to Santa Fe bolstered me. Only then did I feel compelled to return. Though I was still not strong enough to trust my heart. The fire that killed my brother had scorched any life from it, crushed it so there was no room left for anything besides a steady *beat, beat, beat* that kept me moving forward. But here I was, again living in Santa Fe. The city of my birth, but not the city I once knew.

Returning? So much had depended on chance. If I hadn't mentioned to an editor my wish to someday move back to Santa Fe, and if his friend at another newspaper hadn't mentioned that the *Chronicle* had an opening, I likely wouldn't have heard about the job. I wouldn't have emailed my resume, Weller wouldn't have responded, and I wouldn't have flown in for the day to interview.

I rose before dawn, before the hint of pale-yellow light rimming the horizon flooded the city with healing rays. They never lasted long because the brighter the sunshine, the darker the shadows. And the sun always set again, bringing the darkness and evil that hid within.

That suspicion grew stronger every day. Weller assigned every available reporter to crime scenes: a convenience store break-in, a church arson, a home invasion. He sent me to cover an overnight vandalism along Canyon Road. My heart broke to see the smashed ceramics, cracked sculptures, toppled metalworks. All those pieces of art crafted so lovingly—days or months-worth of work destroyed in less than an hour. So senseless, yet the pattern was becoming clear.

Outwardly, Santa Fe appeared the same peaceful arts community depicted in the travel brochures, but the closer the festival drew, the more agitated people became. It had taken its toll on my colleagues, too, but I couldn't say a thing. I was the newbie. Even though the strange occurrences multiplied like insects—parasites waiting for the right moment to strike in full force. Their bourgeoning numbers formed a kind of invisible mass—imperceptible to everyone but me.

Me and, I suspected, to my aunt.

****

With the regal surety of a princess, Ashley entered the newsroom. I had the feeling if I pried open her smiling Cheshire cat lips, a canary would fly out.

At the thought, I choked back a giggle. "Morning."

"It's a beautiful morning." She flourished her hand through the air, then grabbed the mug from atop her desk. "I'm going for coffee. Want me to get you some?"

Another offer to fetch me a beverage? To keep myself from falling out of my chair, I leapt from it. "Why don't I come with you?" I said, more out of curiosity than a need for a third refill.

Her smile never wavered as she puttered around the break room, draining the last of the java into our two cups, then actually making a new pot. I'd never witnessed her doing that before, either. She was beginning to freak me out.

"You're in a good mood," I observed wryly.

"I am, in fact." She offered me the sugar.

Preferring my coffee strong and black, I declined. "Did you win the lottery or something?"

She wrinkled her nose. "Better. I have decided to move on with my life."

"Good for you." Then I remembered the awful feeling that had come over me as I watched her drive off after work the day before. I tried to sound casual, but my nerves had coiled, ready to spring. "So, did you meet someone?"

"Mm hmm." Her smile widened as she sipped.

I no longer found it amusing. "You had a date, I take it?"

"I saw him last night. He's like no one I've ever met," she said softly, almost trance-like.

I quelled the shiver threatening to overtake me. "How do you mean?"

"I can't explain it, except that I've never been so drawn to anyone before. Like it's fate." She wrapped her polished red nails around the cup.

Oh, God. "He has you under his spell, huh?" *Not funny, Mar.* Though hopefully the subliminal message would penetrate her doe-eyed haze.

"That dream changed me." She spoke with renewed energy. "It opened doors in my mind. Or something." She laughed at her own inarticulateness.

"The dream?"

"I'm not usually one for mystical, woo woo stuff. But yes, the dream unlocked something inside me. I'm freer."

About as free as a fawn leaving its mother's side for the first time and heading straight into the path of tractor trailers on the busy interstate. She didn't stand a chance. I kept that thought to myself.

"But…" *Say something intelligent.* "You also don't want to leap too fast. Take a good look before you leap into something new." Now I sounded ridiculous, spouting platitudes. "You know what they say about rebound relationships."

Thoughtful, she tilted her head. "He's not like that. We have such a strong connection. Like he knows what I'm going to say before I even know myself."

"After one date?" I tried to make it sound like a joke, but I was not laughing.

Switchblade quick, she snapped her gaze to me. "I'm not going to hold myself back from what I want anymore." She pivoted and glided away.

I caught up with her. "I'm not saying you should…" Except she should run in the opposite direction. "Taking a step back isn't a bad idea, though. Go slow. There's no rush, right?"

After rounding her desk, she glared at me. "He makes me feel alive. And I need that right now."

I understood her need for more in her life. My skin burned at remembering the flow of pain and acidic emotions gushing from her. "I just want you to be safe." Feeling alive and staying alive were two distinctly separate things.

She flashed a smile so thin it was almost transparent. "I'm fine. Except I have work to do."

I saw myself through her eyes—standing at her desk, badgering her. Crossing the line of professionalism. "Yes. Me, too."

Despite the terrible urge to find out more about Ashley's mystery man, I forced myself to back away and return to my chair. I went through the motions of checking email, opening some documents on my laptop, but my focus kept traveling back to Ashley. She appeared to function normally, but the faraway look never left her eyes.

If I'd asked her what he looked like, would she be able to describe him? Something told me she wouldn't. In my heart of hearts, I knew that Zozobra's younger self had targeted Ashley. He would feed off her many troubles, and she'd be defenseless against his power. From the way she talked, she already was.

My hand fisted against the keyboard. Why did I always manage to screw things up? The one good thing I'd accomplished within the vision—helping Ashley heal—had become the very thing that was permitting Ashley to make a terrible mistake.

I had to protect her somehow, but she wouldn't make it easy. Whatever truce we'd forged had turned fragile. Zozobra's tainted spirit had wrapped around hers, and already she was receding into the gaping wound of his hungry mouth.

Keeping myself and Ashley, too, out from between those blood-red lips would be the trick. One I had no clue how to pull off.

Chapter Eleven

By the time I reached my aunt's house after work, my frustration had ratcheted up to near panic. I burst through the back door and found her sitting on the wicker loveseat in the sunroom. "I need help."

Glancing up from the newspaper, Zelda merely cocked a brow.

I took the action as a request for more specifics. She already knew I was a mess in general. "Right, you need context." Where to begin? "My colleague's in danger. I think."

Phoebe danced along her perch, but thankfully didn't join the conversation.

Zelda looked down her nose at the *Chronicle*. An odd time to notice, but my aunt never wore reading glasses, though she had to be in her early seventies.

"You *think*?" she asked, scanning the article I'd written.

I heard the unspoken *since when* in her voice. It only served to bolster my stubbornness. "Yes. But you already know that more than my colleague are in danger, don't you?"

"Now is not the time." She folded the newspaper, set it on the table, and rose.

I blocked her path to the kitchen. "Now is absolutely the time."

Zelda shot me a glare as Javi came in the back

door, then skirted around me to embrace him. "Hello, sweetheart."

"Hi, Ma." Oblivious, he kissed his mother and glanced to me over her shoulder. "Hey, Mar. I didn't expect to see you."

No smile today, which was not like him. "I surprised your mom, too. What's up?"

Silent as a ghost, she glided out of the kitchen.

He got a beer from the fridge, then plopped wearily onto a chair at the kitchen island and sprawled his legs in front. "I'm worried about Ray."

"He's out of the hospital, right?" I should have called to check on him but didn't dare risk it. Any personal connections I'd made since moving home seemed to put people in danger.

"Yeah, he's home." Javi absently tapped a finger against the tabletop.

I went to the cabinet, pulled out a glass, and filled it with water. "And he's doing better?"

"No. It's nothing physical. He has a few scars from the burns, but it goes deeper. He's… I don't know. Different."

There was no way to avoid this conversation. I sat adjacent to him. "Different how?"

Deeply troubled, he kept his gaze lowered. "He won't talk about it. But he keeps to himself. He's always serious."

And now so was Javi. "The accident probably traumatized him. He'll bounce back in time." What a cheap saying, like I'd recited it from a greeting card. And it obviously did nothing to help Javi's mood. His somber expression hadn't changed for one second.

"I don't know. It changed him," he murmured, as if

123

at a funeral. "The other night, I finally got him to go out, and all he did, all night long, was look around. The more I talked to him, the more distracted he was. He was spooked about something. I asked him if he was waiting for someone."

I stiffened. "Was he?" For a girl? Had he given up on me so fast?

"He wouldn't answer me. Then he left." The furrow in his brow deepened. "Very abruptly."

How shallow of me, to make this about me and not Ray. If Javi was that worried, something must be terribly wrong. "Keep checking up on him."

"That's the other weird thing. He ignores most of my calls. He never did that before." He stared at me but seemed to look right through me.

Or he saw me too well. How much did my cousin know? "What do you think is going on?"

"The way he acts, it's almost like someone's threatened him. And he keeps me at bay because he's afraid they'll get to him, and I'll get caught up in it."

"He didn't say that," I supplied in hopes it was true. But had Ray heard more than his name in the fire?

"No," Javi said, "but that's my gut feeling."

Why hadn't Old Man Gloom left Ray alone? I hadn't gone near the guy in weeks.

"He was pretty down." Javi swung his gaze to me. "I bet you could cheer him up." For the first time since he'd walked in, some of the defeat left his voice.

"I doubt it." I sipped my glass, glad I'd opted for water, though I could've used something strong.

"Go see him. As a favor to me."

While I shared Javi's concern, I'd only worsen the situation. "I shouldn't."

He slapped his hand against his knee. "What do you have against him?" Anger flushed his cheeks, tightened his mouth.

I tried to lighten the mood. "Nothing. He's cute. He's nice. A little vanilla, but nice."

"Vanilla?" Javi's laugh held no humor. "Yeah, a little. But he's a really good guy, Mar. And aren't you supposed to be past your bad boy phase?"

I tsk'd. "Javi." My poor judgment of men had caused some problems in the past, one of the reasons I was more cautious these days.

"Please, Mar. I don't know what else to do." Worry etched lines in my cousin's face.

How could I say no? "Okay." I'd talk to him. Let him know he wasn't crazy. And find out why Old Man Gloom had targeted him. "One time."

Rushing into the kitchen, Zelda scooted past us. "I have some errands to run."

"Now?" Silly to ask, as she carried her purse and held her keys.

"There's no time like the present." She was out the back door and gone like lightning.

"My thought exactly." Javi sent me a toothy grin.

A sigh of defeat, and I caved. "I'll call as soon as I get home."

"Why not now?" He drew out his cell, tapped a few keystrokes, then handed the phone to me.

Sure, no pressure. "This is a bad idea," I told him even as I held the cell to my ear and the call rang through.

A gruff man answered. "Who is this?"

"My name's Marissa, I'm Javi Furtado's cousin. Sorry, I think I dialed the wrong number." I scowled at

Javi.

My cousin furrowed his brow and mouthed, "What?"

Through the phone, the man asked, "Who were you calling for?"

"Ray White."

"Oh. I'm his grandfather, Rusty."

Rusty White? Interesting name. "I see." I wasn't any less confused. "So, is Ray there?"

"He's boxing in the garage." The way he said it, I should have already known.

"Don't disturb him, then. But I need to speak with him. Do you think it would be all right to stop over?" I nearly slapped myself in the head. A stupid idea just became ridiculous. The last thing I wanted to do was actually confront him.

"Sure, come on over. He'll be out there awhile. Usually is."

"Good. Thank you." I ended the call and handed the phone back to Javi, then stood.

Javi rose in tandem with me. "He lives over on Old Santa Fe Trail. The pink house. You can't miss it."

If I went now, I could put it behind me and be done with it.

He squeezed my shoulder. "I owe you one."

"A big one," I grumbled, and grabbed my handbag on the way out.

****

After some mental cheerleading, I drove to the Old Santa Fe Trail address Javi provided. The houses were more spread out there than in my neighborhood, so it didn't take me long to find Ray's place. Sure enough, there it was. The pink house. More of a dusty-rose colored stucco, but maybe the two house lights on either side of the front entrance didn't throw off enough light through the pierced designs in the hammered copper. Mostly, the place struck me as flat. Flat front, flat roof, like someone had plastered a giant rectangle out of stucco, carved some windows and a doorway into it, and called it a house. In short, it looked pretty much like every other building in Santa Fe. Framed in aqua wood, the front door looked inviting with the painted ceramic sun smiling down at me.

The front windows were dark, but a muted glow shone from the back. The gravel driveway curved around to the rear, where light flooded out of the open garage doors. The fluorescent lighting overhead bathed Ray in brightness.

Drawn as if by a beacon, I followed the stone pathway along the side and under a roofed rear entrance. The pounding noise grew louder, Ray pummeling the bag.

I stopped for a moment, distracted by another light at the far end of the yard. A tall adobe fence, topped with trailing greenery, bordered the back yard. A wooden loveseat sat in front of a white outdoor fireplace, and a short distance beyond that sat a smaller version of Ray's house. Lights flickered in the darkened windows, a sign that someone was inside watching television.

A tenant? Javi hadn't mentioned it, but then again, we hadn't discussed Ray's personal business. And I had my own business to conduct.

Just do it. At least I hadn't interrupted dinner.

Though he was covered in sweat, there was an effortlessness about Ray's movements. Precise as a machine, he pumped out anger, yet somehow rather than releasing it, he kept producing more. Frustration. Pain. Anger. The stream seemed relentless.

My pulse whirred higher, too, as I approached. The sound of my footsteps was lost in the noise. I stood just outside the open garage, watching him. So focused on the bag, his gloves pounding the bag, sending it spinning. Sweat dampened his hair, trickled down his face. Where he'd been burned, the skin on his arms had dried to a ripe red.

I cleared my throat, but he kept punching. He winced with each jab but didn't look like he'd tire out anytime soon. "Ray?"

No response.

"Ray!"

At the moment he caught the bag in his gloves to still its swing, he jerked his head toward me, eyes glazed. At first, he seemed not to recognize me.

"Hey, it's Marissa. Sorry to intrude." I inched closer.

"I know who you are." He grabbed a white towel and scrubbed his face. "What are you doing here?"

I ventured nearer, step by easy step. "Just wanted to say hi. See how you were doing."

"I'm fine." He tossed the towel away harder than necessary.

"Maybe not great though." I trained my gaze on his face to avoid looking at his arms.

"Look, I know Javi sent you. Tell him I'm fine. You did your duty."

I crossed my arms. "I won't lie to him. So you better prove how fine you are."

"I'm busy right now." He went back to punching

the bag.

Stubborn fool. I walked up and stopped beside him. "I know what's going on," I yelled over the noise.

He stopped hitting the bag but wouldn't look me in the eye. "Whatever you think you know, you're wrong. Just go."

Tempting. He was giving me the easy way out again. I wouldn't take it. "You're not crazy, Ray."

"Did you become a psychiatrist in the last few weeks?" he sneered.

"No. But he's following me, too."

He glanced at me side-long but whacked the bag hard. "I don't know what you're talking about."

"Old Man Gloom."

He stopped then, and assessed me head to toe.

"I was freaked out, too. Now I'm pissed. And I want to do something about it. What about you?"

I was finally able to fully assess him, too. He appeared a stripped-down version of the man I'd dubbed Sunshine. No suave smile, no carefree Golden Boy.

He affected a smirk, a half-hearted attempt that didn't fool me. The bare bones Ray who stood before me looked fearful.

"Is this some sort of joke?" Bitterness dragged his voice lower.

"Is it a joke when someone whispers your name in a burning building? Or outside your home? Or anywhere you go at night?"

He listened without reacting, without moving at all. He stood with wide, glazed eyes, only the rise and fall of his chest registering his breath.

"Isn't that what's been going on with you? Because

that's what's happening to me."

He cocked a brow. "Old Man Gloom. The figure they burn at the festival."

"It's more than some puppet made of wood and fabric. Something inside that thing has come to life." I realized how ridiculous I sounded but went on. "I heard him the night Michael died. I think Old Man Gloom killed my brother in that fire." There, I'd said it, the suspicion I hadn't even dared to acknowledge thinking before.

When he furrowed his brows, he dropped whatever wall he'd put up between us and actually joined the conversation. "Michael?"

"Yes." Suddenly weary, I heaved a breath. "I need a beer."

"Me, too. Come inside." The fight had left him, and he sounded weary.

"You're really going to need one after you hear what I have to say next." I trailed him to the back of his house.

He threw open sliding glass doors and stepped aside.

Off-white stucco walls reflected the light from the kitchen, located just beside the dining room where we entered. The warm, honey-colored wood ceiling ran the length of the open space, lined by long wooden beams. A chocolate leather sofa in front of another white stucco fireplace made the living room cozy. At the far side of the room, the plank flooring was interrupted by a stucco divider, graduated like steps. Probably where Ray's bedroom was.

A flush heated my face, and I ducked my head.

Brushing past me, Ray didn't appear to notice. He

pulled two beers from the fridge and handed me one. We leaned against the sink and, without looking at each other, I told him the most important part.

"The night you were injured in the fire, I had a dream. About you, me, and Old Man Gloom."

He huffed. "Kind of a funky threesome. But dreams can be weird like that."

Exactly what I'd said to Ashley, so I knew he understood. "This was more than a dream. It was more like a…" I couldn't quite express the idea in words. "Like your soul was sending a message to mine."

"What," he asked wryly, "did my soul tell yours?"

I expelled a long breath. "That the guy I've seen around Santa Fe since the first night I came home…" *Say it, dammit.* "That guy is Old Man Gloom."

He choked on his beer and dragged his hand across his mouth. "What?" he rasped.

"I told you, it's crazy. But in my dream, you were inside my old house the night it burned down. Instead of Michael, you were banging on the window, yelling to me." I hung my head. "I never told anyone before, but that night, when I was five, I knew my brother was trying to tell me something. I couldn't make out what he was saying, and it's haunted me ever since."

Ray stared at nothing, said nothing.

Yeah, it was a lot to take in. Voicing my thoughts and dreams, I had to admit that I'd sounded loony. But I believed it, more than ever, now.

And God, it felt good to unload my soul, to finally tell someone else about what really happened that night.

After a few moments that lasted forever, Ray took a breath. "Okay. Here's the thing. The night you had the dream, we were supposed to go out. You weren't crazy about the idea."

"Hey, I bought a new shirt and new necklace. I am not one to idly shop."

"I guilted you into agreeing." He held up a hand when I started to argue. "Hear me out. When you fell asleep, you had that in the back of your mind. And since you've come home, you've obviously had to face a lot of hard issues from your past. Everything collided in your head, and that's why you dreamed that dream."

The entire time he spewed those lame excuses, I couldn't stop shaking my head. "No. That guy gave me the creeps the first night I saw him. The first night I was home. And every time I see him, he gets creepier."

"Maybe he's a secret admirer." He tilted the beer against his mouth.

"Funny." Mr. Chivalrous was giving me another escape hatch and practically shoving me through it. "Have you ever followed a girl, from a distance, and disappeared when she tried to approach you?"

"I'm not a creep." He sipped, then swallowed hard. "You're not going after the guy, are you?"

"I haven't." I gave him a canny look. "Yet."

"Don't, Marissa. He could be mentally ill."

"I know exactly what he is. Evil." A vengeful spirit, but I wouldn't give Ray any more reason to call 911.

"All the more reason to stay far away."

Interesting that Ray didn't argue the point. From the look he gave me, he knew more than he was admitting.

"How can I when he keeps following me? It has to mean something, him showing up now. It's the centennial anniversary of Zozobra. Old Man Gloom has carried everyone else's problems for a hundred years. I think he's tired of it."

"Marissa." He didn't bother to chide me, but he didn't need to.

"And he's planning on doing something to change it." When Ray sighed, I turned to him. "He already is. He's sending his…minions, or whatever they are, to stir up more trouble. And the red dust? That always means a rough day for everyone in Santa Fe." My jaw dropped when he screwed up his face. "You don't believe me."

He pulled his lips inside his mouth and searched my face. "Tell me one thing. Did Javi put you up to this?"

With a huff, I flailed my hand, then set it against my hip. "Do you think your boxing gloves will fit me?"

"What? Is that how you answer my question?"

"Yeah. Either that, or I punch you in the face. Because goddammit, Ray, I just told you something I've been carrying around inside me for twenty-four years without telling another person. Not one…single…freaking…soul." I poked into his chest so hard my finger slipped against his sweaty t-shirt. "And you accuse me of—"

"All right, all right." He caught my wrist. "You have to admit, this is all pretty bizarre."

I jerked from his grasp. "You think this is the norm for me? In the beginning, I was as freaked out as you are."

He gave me the once-over. "So, what changed?"

My fists had clenched, and I consciously stretched my fingers. "The high school boy I interviewed disappeared, and I feel responsible."

"You can't blame yourself for that. Kids run away

sometimes."

Not willing to give myself that break, I shook my head. "I'm tired of being terrorized. I want it to stop."

"And you think you can stop it? Stop him? Some evil…man?"

It struck me again that he sounded like he was trying hard to convince himself rather than me.

I settled against the counter beside him again. "I'm going to damn well try. What about you?"

He moved his head as if to shake it, but he didn't even commit to that much. "I have no idea."

At least he was honest. "Neither do I, but I'm not giving up until I find a way."

From the hard look in his eye, I could tell he was at least considering the idea.

A yell from the back yard startled us.

"What was that?" I slammed the beer bottle onto the counter.

He ran for the door. "Pop." He was outside in a heartbeat.

I rushed after him, a blur of an outline in the darkness. The scent of smoke teased the air and pumped my adrenaline higher. *Please, no.*

Chapter Twelve

I scrambled to catch up to Ray, who had already crossed the dark yard and pushed inside the door to the small cottage. He disappeared for a moment and then emerged with a small fire extinguisher. "Wait outside."

"I want to help." Smoke was billowing along the interior ceiling from somewhere down the hallway, the dark grey an ominous contrast to the white adobe walls. I clutched the straps of my handbag. Why had I grabbed it before following Ray? Such a stupid thing to do.

"Go. Call 911." He called, "Pop?" and then pulled the front of his t-shirt up over his mouth before rushing through the kitchen.

My feet rooted to the floor as I strained to hear any response. The grandfather coughed, and hoarsely called, "Ray."

He's alive. But now they were both in danger. I felt inside my handbag for my cell, but it wasn't there. It must have fallen out somewhere along the way. I waved away the smoke and scanned the wall for a phone. *Come on, come on...there.* I'd nearly missed it because it sat beside the fridge, partially hidden in the shadows.

I hurried over and dialed 911. "Hurry. There's a fire."

Shouts came from the back of the cottage. The spray of the fire extinguisher sounded in bursts.

"Address?" the emergency dispatcher asked.

Ohgodohgod. My brain fumbled the house number. "Old Santa Fe Trail, Ray White's place. The pink house. The little building in the back is burning. His grandfather..." A wave of thick smoke rolled in. Choking, I coughed but my throat stung. "Hurry."

I hung up and ducked my head low. "Ray?" The smoke was thickening. I raised my arm across my mouth.

A hoarse cough. "Told you...get out of here." Shuffling footsteps, maybe dragging a weight. He must be carrying his grandfather.

My head grew light and my chest grew heavy. If I didn't get out of here, I'd be another burden for Ray to deal with. I felt my way along the counter. The door was closed. Had Ray shut it? Must have, to limit oxygen to the fire. I grabbed the handle, but the hot metal singed my skin. I jerked my hand back. What the hell? The flames were nowhere near it.

But fire was roaring in the other room. The form of the two men appeared as one silhouette, Ray pulling his grandfather along, wheezing and coughing.

"Marissa." He snapped my name like a reprimand. "Jesus, get the hell out."

"I'm trying. The handle..." I steeled myself and reached for the knob again, ready to twist it open as fast as I could. The knob burned my fingers. And wouldn't budge.

"It's locked." I yelled over my shoulder.

"What?" called Ray.

The men shuffled up behind me, the elder man limp in Ray's grasp.

"Take him." Ray transferred his grandfather's arm from around his neck to mine.

I braced against the old man's weight, made heavier by his inability to support himself.

Ray touched the handle and jerked back his arm. "Ah." A beat later, he fumbled with the locks, then waved his hand. "Son of a bitch!"

In the hiss of the flames was a breath of laughter. Fear pulled my gaze to the back of the house. Flames licked around the corner.

Ray twisted toward me, eyes wide. "Was that…"

I set my jaw. "Oh no, you don't, Old Man." I wouldn't let him trap us to burn like puppets.

Ray's grandfather grunted in question and swung his head toward me.

"Not you." I had no time to explain. "Kick it. Break it down." I shuffled backward with the old man.

Ray jammed his boot against the wood again and again. The air further thickened around us, and his breath sounded more labored. The door shook in the jamb with each kick, but otherwise didn't budge.

Eyes burning from the heat and smoke, I glanced back. The fire would reach us soon. If I didn't help Ray, we'd die here, and I wasn't about to give up. Not without a fight.

I guided Rusty to the table and shifted his weight to a chair. "Stay here and keep your head down." No problem there. His head thudded against the table.

Ray's kicking had grown more sporadic. He kept an arm across his mouth and breathed into his shirt sleeve, but he moved slower.

Tightening my scarf around my neck and raising it like a bandit, I touched his shoulder to signal I was beside him. I matched his every kick, desperate for clear night air. My scarf wasn't working as a filter, and the burn moved down my throat into my lungs.

Ray's occasional cough had become constant. Every movement appeared an effort, valiant but ineffective. The door might as well be made of steel.

I grabbed his sleeve. "This isn't working. What about the window?"

He doubled over in a harsh cough. "Can't. Rusty."

I sent his grandfather a desperate glance. He sprawled over the table, eyes closed. "We have to try. I'll go out first, you push him through." I tugged Ray toward the old man. "Let's get him over there."

The heat had grown fierce, another force to battle.

Outside, sirens wailed. Faint, so they were too far away. Every moment we waited our chances grew slimmer.

"Hurry, Ray." I reached for his grandfather, but Ray slumped to the floor.

"No—" I stumbled to him and slapped his cheek. "Get up. Hurry, Ray."

Coughing, he turned his head away.

In a crouch, I froze, panic scattering my thoughts. What options did we have? We were trapped.

Anger built inside me like steam. I lifted my head and glared into the fire. "You won't win, Old Man. I won't let you." Tears welling against the sting in my eyes, I grabbed my handbag and cradled it to my chest. A wave of smoke billowed into the kitchen and enveloped us. A fit of coughing overwhelmed Ray. I unfastened the scarf, dragged myself closer to the two men and laid it across their heads. As I stretched over them, my handbag toppled onto the floor, its contents tumbling out. A clang sounded, something metal falling out.

The star. I groped along the linoleum, sorting items in my mind's eye as I touched them. The moment my fingers found the metal, I snatched up the star and held it against me. In between coughs, words spilled from my mouth—wishes and prayers and curses and damnations.

Shouts came from the direction of the driveway. Flashing red lights through the panes resembled a leering smile, cartoonish yet terrifying, that loomed toward us in a pulse like a heartbeat.

A floodlight poured through the window, erasing the smile and illuminating the smog in a splash of gray. My head grew light again, my eyelids grew heavy, and my hand slipped along the floor. The star was impossibly cool against my skin.

Thudding footsteps pounded through my head. A crash. A shower of glass shards and wood splinters. Silhouettes moved inside the blinding light. Hands dragged me to my feet. Without consciously doing so, I tightened my grasp on the star.

"Ray? Rusty!" Coughs wracked me when I fought to reach back.

"We got them," a man said.

My head spun, or maybe my body, I couldn't tell. Only that I floated, weightless, out of the thick haze to where the sweet night kissed my face.

****

I gulped in the clear air and choked out the remnants of smoke.

The firefighter set me down near the outdoor fireplace. "Anyone else inside?"

Through my mind flashed the crude red features. The undeniable presence of some*thing*. Try explaining that to the crew. My nerves exploded in a chuckle, a completely inappropriate response.

Remnants of smoke lingered in my throat, and I coughed. "No. No, just the three of us."

Emergency workers hovered over Ray and his grandfather, who slumped in the loveseat in front of the fireplace. My rescuer gestured to a tall woman and asked her to attend to me.

I held up a hand. "I'm fine. Take care of those two."

"I should check you out to be sure."

I shook my head and waved them away.

A firefighter trudged past, and I recognized the smudged face beneath the rubber hat. "Javi!" My arms trembled as I threw them around his neck.

"Oh my God, Mar. What the hell happened?" He glanced at Ray and said no more.

"We're not sure." I held back the tears threatening to flow.

Someone called to him, and he released me. "Take care of her," he told the emergency worker.

"I'm fine." But he'd already jogged off toward the smoldering cottage.

"Sit down, at least." The woman turned me away and guided me toward the spinning red lights of the ambulance behind my SUV.

"Seriously, I'm all right. Take care of them." I nodded toward Ray and Rusty, but uniformed workers were already loading the grandfather onto a gurney and then wheeled him toward the ambulance.

Ray jogged alongside his grandfather. "I'll be over soon."

Ray waved away any attempt to guide him to the

emergency vehicle. "I'm staying." He glanced back at the cottage, where firefighters swarmed, then at me.

From his pained expression, I could tell he wanted to be in their midst. Doing something to help. Standing helplessly by and merely watching was torture for us both.

He strode over to me. "You should go to the hospital, get checked out."

"No, I'm staying, too." How could I leave him like this? He looked angry enough that he might do something foolish.

The emergency worker closed the back doors, then climbed inside the ambulance. Ray jammed his hands in his pockets as the headlights retreated down the driveway. The vehicle swung onto the road and sped out of sight.

Wordlessly, we turned to the cottage. Steam rose from the roof and escaped through the broken windows. From what I could see, the fire hadn't left much that was usable.

"Was your grandfather staying with you?" I finally asked.

He stared into the distance where the ambulance had gone. "He lived in the back cottage for the past four years."

I didn't know what else to say. A little late to apologize for ruining their lives.

Javi came up behind Ray and clasped his shoulder. "Rough night, man."

"The worst."

Another firefighter eyed Ray. "There's something suspicious about this fire."

Ray blanched. "Is that an accusation?"

Oh God, this was not the time to let Old Man Gloom's effects get the best of them.

"He was in his house," I said, pointing to the larger structure, "when the fire broke out in the cottage."

"How can you be sure?" the firefighter asked.

I squared my shoulders. "I was with him."

"For how long?"

Had this conversation turned into a formal investigation? "Long before the blaze started. Ray never left the kitchen, so he couldn't have set any fire."

Another guy muttered, "They were igniting their own fire."

I whirled and grimaced at the three men, and their grins faded. "Do you always turn on a colleague so quickly? Ray is your friend."

"Which is why we make certain to clear him of suspicion immediately."

I crossed my arms. "How thoughtful of you."

"I was the first inside," one said, "and I'm not convinced yet."

Anger restored my flagging energy. "What? That's ridiculous."

Ray laid a hand on my arm, and said to the man, "If you have something to say to me, say it now."

The man brushed past the other and stepped closer. "All right. The fire should have destroyed that little house by the time we arrived. But the three of you were on the floor. With this weird…bubble around you."

Ray looked at the firefighter like he'd lost his mind. "Bubble? What the hell are you talking about?"

My mind registered a weight in my hand. The star. I still held it. I slipped it into my pocket.

"I can't explain it. I've never seen anything like

that before. It hardly looked real. But I saw it, goddammit."

Ray winced. "I still don't get your point."

"All I know is, that bubble surrounded you three. In my experience, most people don't survive blazes as strong as that one."

There was no humor in Ray's laugh. "So you think I set the fire in the back, even though I was inside my own home, and then somehow created this bubble around us so the flames couldn't touch us." Each word he spoke was louder than the last, and Ray stepped closer until he was in the other man's face. "...rather than do what I was trained to do. Get people to safety and go back to fight the flames."

"I don't know," the man snarled. "I didn't say it made sense."

Ray's jaw hardened. "Yeah. You're right. It doesn't make sense. Not a lick. Why don't you get the real issue off your chest, once and for all, Tremont?"

"Real issue?" Tremont repeated slowly, like a taunt.

"You're upset that I'm up for a promotion. Not you." Ray jabbed a finger into Tremont's chest.

The man staggered backward but recovered quickly. "Don't be an ass."

Javi stepped between them. "Enough. Everyone's emotions are running high. We could have lost you tonight, Ray. One of our own. That hurts."

Another firefighter said, "And people talk. We can't have any rumors following our squad. Let's not share whatever optical illusion you thought you saw, Tremont. No mentions to your family or friends, or on social media."

"Or at the bar," Ray muttered, then shuffled his feet, shoulders hunched. "Are they done inside? I'd like to go assess the damage."

"Not a good idea, Ray. Not tonight. The bedroom floor gave way under Harvey."

Ray shrugged. "There's no basement, so it's not like I'd go far."

A shudder went through me, imagining him falling through the ground to nowhere, as I had.

Javi shook his head. "There's also no structural support. The roof could cave on your head. Wait till tomorrow, at least. Please."

Ray raked a hand through his hair. "Yeah. Yeah, you're right. I'll stay outside, but I need to see." He strode off and circled the ruined structure.

Javi nudged me. "Hey, you sure you're all right?"

I wanted to melt against him. "Since you guys came, yeah."

"Man, I feel so guilty."

"Why?"

"If I hadn't nagged you to come over, you wouldn't have been caught up in this mess."

"This has nothing to do with you. Who knows? If I hadn't visited, maybe Ray would have gone out somewhere, and his grandfather might have..." Tears surprised me, and I scowled at the ground so my cousin wouldn't see.

He pulled me against his bulky uniform. "Shh, don't think about it. Everyone's safe."

I nodded against the rubbery surface. "Yes, everyone's safe."

Within minutes, Ray returned, shoulders hunched low.

"How bad is it?" I wiped my face dry. If Ray saw me crying, he'd only be more upset.

But he couldn't seem to take his eyes off the smoldering structure, like the reality still hadn't sunk in. "It'll take me months to rebuild. Pop will have to move in with me."

"I'm sorry." My heart grew heavy as lead. "Will the hospital keep him overnight?"

"Probably. I should go check on him. I'm no use here." He glanced back at the main house, its frame intact.

I could practically hear his thoughts. What if that burned while he was gone? On its own, fire was an unpredictable force. Under these strange circumstances, there was no way to be certain another accident wouldn't happen, an outburst from a straying ember…

I focused on Ray to drive that thought from my mind. "Are you all right to drive to the hospital?"

"Fine. What about you?" He swung his head toward me. "Want me to drop you at your apartment?"

I hugged myself and forced a pleasant expression. He had enough to worry about. "No, my car's here, I'm good. You go look after your grandfather."

A nod, then he slid me a look I couldn't decipher. Serious. Full of doubt, like someone who'd just awakened and wasn't sure whether he was still dreaming. Then he turned to his colleagues and thanked them, grasping shoulders as he moved through their midst.

Javi clapped his arms around Ray and rocked him in a bear hug. "Thank God you're all right, man."

"Yeah," was all Ray said.

When Ray headed for the house, I remembered my

jacket, still on a chair in the dining room.

I jogged after him. "Don't lock up yet, my things are inside." Hopefully, I'd left the phone with my jacket.

"I have to change my shirt anyway." With the awkwardness of a sixth grader, he waited for me to enter first.

Everything inside was as we'd left it. I lifted the jacket, checked the pockets. No cell. "Damn."

"What's wrong?"

"My phone, I lost it somewhere." I hated to complain about something so insignificant. "It'll turn up. You sure you're all right to drive? You seem a bit dazed."

"I'm good. Thanks for your help."

I snorted. "Yeah, almost getting you both killed." I fussed with folding the jacket so I wouldn't have to see his expression damning me a second time.

"No, thanks for your help with Pop. I couldn't have gotten him out of there alone."

A deep ache filled my chest. He wasn't blaming me. My throat thickened, so I turned and slung the handbag straps over my shoulder. "I hope he's okay." A terse smile, and I aimed for the exit. "Night."

"Hey."

I froze, hardly able to breathe.

All he said was, "We should talk more."

I nodded. "We will."

He heaved a trembling breath. "Stay safe."

"You, too."

Behind the two fire trucks, a crowd had gathered, neighbors, I guessed, the usual gawkers. Among the faces was one that sent a chill to my soul. The familiar leer of the guy I'd glimpsed at the bar on the first night home. The man who was Old Man Gloom in the flesh. And who was stalking me.

I steeled myself. The only way to deal with a stalker was meet him head on.

I kept him in my sights and hurried to catch him. "Hey you."

He froze, but his gaze snapped to me. He shifted behind three men and was gone.

"Hey—" I rushed up, scanning their legs for an extra pair. "Sorry." I skirted around them, but none of the faces was his. No sign of him retreating in either direction. Opposite Ray's house, trees and brush crowded together, then dropped away along a slope, revealing a spectacular view of the mountains.

Shoulders slumped, I huffed. Had I imagined him? Was Ray right? Was my mind playing tricks on me?

"Marissa?" a woman called.

I turned and scanned the faces around me.

Ashley hurried toward me. "What are you doing here? Conrad sent me to cover this story."

"Sorry. You didn't have to come. I'm here." The words just fell out of my mouth, all nonsense.

Confusion contorted Ashley's perfect face. "Conrad said he couldn't get hold of you."

"Conrad," I repeated in a haughty huff. God, now I sounded like her, but hearing Ashley use Weller's first name pricked at my already agitated senses. I shook it off. "I lost my cell." Damn, and in my rush to leave Ray's house, I'd forgotten to search the yard for the phone. "But I've already spoken to everyone here. So you don't need to interview anyone." Not nonsense at all. The firefighters were exhausted. If Ashley asked too many times, someone might mention the weird bubble. Or their suspicions about the fire's origin.

Ashley tilted her head. "You didn't get pictures. You couldn't have, if you lost your cell. Unless you thought ahead and brought a thirty-five millimeter?"

The insinuation came through loud and clear. "No. No, I didn't bring a camera. I didn't 'think ahead'. It was all very confusing, and very frightening." I heard myself yelling and closed my mouth to stifle the outburst.

Ashley winked. "I'll just go snap some photos. You'd better...rest." With a pointed look of accusation, she whirled, and her heels clipped along the stony ground.

Was that woman ever not put together? Her outfit was perfectly color coordinated, not a hair out of place. By contrast, I must look a mess. Thank God Ashley hadn't pointed a camera at me. I might have decked her.

A chill came over me, and I rubbed my arms. Walking back to the house, I scanned the ground, then retraced my path to the cottage. Halfway between, I spied my cell. When I picked it up, the shattered face caught the light.

Damn. Of all times not to have a phone.

The fire trucks began to pull away. The crowd broke up, meandering to their homes. Soon, I stood in the driveway alone. The scent of wet charcoal tainted the air. Other than an occasional bark of a dog, or a vehicle passing at the intersection, all was quiet. No reason to stay there, yet I hated to leave. That meant giving up, giving in. Too many questions lingered, puzzle pieces that didn't fit.

Tonight wouldn't yield any more clues. I needed to

go home, though I doubted sleep would come. Or if it would help. So, I did what came naturally. I wrote.

Releasing my thoughts on paper, a professional hazard, but writing always helped me sort things through in my head. Within the next half hour, I'd wrapped up an article. At first, it had been a way to make sense of all that had happened, then it was a way to ensure my colleague wouldn't probe too deeply into the case. If Ashley disturbed Ray's grandfather at the hospital, Rusty might let something slip, something he'd seen or heard, or a fact that could provoke more questions, more anger, more threats of revenge.

I had to do whatever I could to prevent that. No matter how much Ashley would be insulted, stepping on a colleague's toes was a professional low, this was about bigger worries.

I didn't trust my emotions not to cloud my judgment, so I read the piece several times before submitting it to the editor. The accompanying email explained I'd been at the scene as the blaze broke out. That should trump anything Ashley had sent in.

Yeah, having to deal with her tomorrow would be fun. But hey, we were professionals. Ashley should understand I'd gotten the scoop first-hand, and she should have been the one to back off. Somehow, I couldn't quite envision that scenario occurring in real time.

Chapter Thirteen

In between bouts of fitful sleep, an endless procession of thoughts kept me awake. Second-guesses and what-ifs, topped with heavy doses of self-blame. I shouldn't have let Javi goad me into visiting Ray. If I hadn't, then his property wouldn't have burned. His grandfather wouldn't be in the hospital.

At five a.m., I gave up. No point staying in bed when I could go to work and do something useful, or at least find out whether anything else strange had happened last night.

A shower didn't rouse me as I'd hoped. Bleary-eyed, I went through my morning routine by rote...until I walked outside.

Another dust storm had blown in from the mountains and covered the city in red. Thicker than last time. As the wind carried the dust away, the streaks resembled scars, much like the indelible scar from that first festival. I'd carried it year upon year, inside me. An invisible mark, but now it burned.

For revenge. *Venganza.*

I'm ready, Old Man.

Fired up, I drove to work and went inside. "Morning," I called to the security guard. Too early yet for the receptionist, and the quiet of the newsroom was sheer bliss. I'd need to down a pot of coffee before I was ready to face my colleagues.

Please let it be a slow news day.

Once the coffee maker was chugging away, I checked the online edition of the *Chronicle.* The story about the fire at Ray's house appeared on the front page above the fold, with my byline beneath. A satisfied sigh escaped when I saw that Ashley was listed in the photo credits, and at the end of the article, she was named as a contributing correspondent. That should help her bruised ego.

I bet Weller had cursed me for the extra work of combining the two stories, though he must have appreciated my insider information.

Next, I opened my email. One from Weller stood out. *See me in my office first thing tomorrow.*

I glanced over at the darkened room. "Soon as you get here." Not likely for at least another hour and a half, maybe two. The editor was notorious for his long work days, but I doubted he'd arrive before seven.

Heavy footsteps at six forty proved me wrong.

They abruptly halted. "Tahy."

I sat straighter. "Mr. Weller. Good morning."

He strode toward his office. "You're early."

Without waiting for the order, I followed him in. "So are you."

"I couldn't sleep. Apparently, you had a busy night." He gestured to the chair in front of his desk. "You look like hell."

I plopped into it. "Unfortunately." On both counts.

"So you just happened to be at Mr. White's house when the fire broke out?"

My face flushed hot. "Yes. I know you sent Ashley to the scene—"

"I couldn't reach you."

"My cell was destroyed in the confusion." I shifted in the chair. "I'm going to the phone store for a replacement today."

"See that you do."

"Right. I'll follow up on the elder Mr. White, too."

"Yes." Weller sounded distracted. "Good idea."

After an awkward silence, I clasped my knees and pushed myself up. "Okay then. I'll get back to work."

He tapped a pencil against the top of the desk. "It's odd."

"What is?"

"Since May, the city has tumbled into one nightmare after the other." He narrowed his eyes at me. "That's when you came to Santa Fe, isn't it?"

"Yes," I admitted. "But I have no frame of reference to make that same comparison. The last time I was here, I was five. I don't remember much from then."

"I suppose not."

When he said nothing to follow up, I inched toward the doorway. "I made coffee. Want some?"

"No." His answer sounded hollow.

An empty sound that gave me the willies. "I'll be at my desk if you need me."

He grunted in acknowledgment.

The unspoken release energized me. I fled to the break room.

Thirty-five minutes later, the click of heels along the floor was like a time bomb ticking down. Three. Two…

Ashley slammed her purse on her desk. "Since when are you such an early bird?" She didn't wait for me to respond. "Oh, right. When you became a suck-up."

I rubbed my aching forehead. "I'm not a suck-up."

"Really." The deadpan delivery dripped of sarcasm.

"It's a simple case of me being in the right place, right time." Or the opposite.

"Funny how that keeps working out for you. Funny as in strange. Or suspicious."

That made two people in the space of an hour who hinted I was guilty of some crime. Or lots of them. "A professional journalist doesn't accuse a colleague of…whatever you're accusing me of."

Ashley poked her finger against the desk top hard enough her glossy red nail was in danger of breaking. "A professional journalist doesn't steal a story from said colleague."

"I'm sorry, Ashley. Really, I am. But I told you last night I had more facts than you."

"So you did."

"And by the time you arrived, the firemen were already leaving. It made sense for me to write the article."

A snort, then, "Keep telling yourself that."

Oh shit. I couldn't blame Ashley for being angry. If anyone had done the same to me, I would squawk, too. My newsroom credibility just self-destructed. No one would want to work with me.

"I'm sorry, Ashley. Last night was crazy. Awful. Crazy awful. And I wasn't thinking clearly."

"Exactly why you shouldn't have written that article. You were emotionally involved. In whatever way, you were part of the story."

The cardinal rule. I'd broken it, and Ashley was

sniffing out the cause. "You're absolutely right. I apologize." I heard the flatness in my own voice. Not especially convincing.

Suddenly shrewd, Ashley asked softly, "What are you hiding?"

"Pardon?" I sputtered.

Ashley ran a cold gaze across me. "You must have had a reason for butting in. There are certain facts that you wanted omitted. Is that it?"

Was I that transparent? "No, of course not. That's crazy." The accusation lacked conviction. A dead giveaway to my guilt.

Ashley's expression soured. "Did you hate me before you came here?"

How perfectly narcissistic of her. "I didn't remember you." I wished that I still didn't.

Ashley propped a hand on her bony, well-dressed hip. "Then why are you trying to undermine my career?"

Weariness loosened my self-control but somehow, I kept a straight face. "Which one, the writer, or the actress?" When Ashley's nose flared and her lips became a jagged, thin line, I stood. "Look, I've apologized twice about the story. I promise to be more respectful about professional boundaries in the future. Last night was a highly unusual set of circumstances. I hope you can find it in your heart to forgive me." And put this incident of poor timing behind us.

Ashley's turn was militarily precise and sharp, her back straight as if someone had shoved the proverbial stick up her rear. She slammed items around on her desk, then shot to her feet and marched to the break room.

Yeah, today was going to be a blast. I busied myself with looking up the address of the phone store. My relief at seeing other *Chronicle* employees arrive was short-lived. From the way they gave me a wide berth, they'd all read the morning edition. If they hadn't heard the background story, Ashley was sure to fill them in. She hadn't returned from the break room, and her shrill voice carried through the newsroom.

Do not engage. Do not protest. I picked up the phone and dialed the hospital. "Have you released Mr. White?" When the receptionist said no, I asked if he could have visitors.

"From ten this morning until eight o'clock tonight."

"Great." My press card would serve as an excuse, but the questions I wanted to ask Rusty White would be strictly off the record.

If I left the building now, I might avoid a lynching.

Before my hasty exit, I had enough semblance of mind to grab an extra star.

****

The hospital room was quiet. I crept inside, and my hopes sank when I saw Ray's grandfather. Asleep, deeply. Might be a long wait. If I could get away from work later, I'd check back. I tiptoed toward the door.

He called, "Leaving so soon? You just got here."

I sent a smile over my shoulder. "I didn't want to disturb you."

"Too late. I've been disturbed since the fire." Rusty squinted, then put on his glasses. "You're the girl who helped me and Ray the other night."

I walked to his bed side. My nod was awkward. "How are you? I thought the doctors would let you go home today."

He grumbled. "These damn doctors aren't happy until they prod and poke me full of holes."

I wrinkled my nose. "Ouch. Wish I could spring you from this prison, Mr. White."

"Call me Rusty. Please." His chuckle resembled a cackle, but his expression hardened. "Except, I've no home to go back to."

What a horrible feeling that must be. "Ray will rebuild the cottage. He said so." I wouldn't repeat that he'd feared it would take months.

Rusty appeared distracted, lost in his thoughts.

I hated to bring it up but had to find out. "What happened last night, Rusty?" I dragged the chair closer to the bed.

"You should know."

The words sent an icy shiver down my spine. "Not as much as I'd like. You're not a smoker, are you?"

"Gave it up years ago."

No chance a stray ash had sparked the blaze, then. "Did you see anything strange? Or anyone."

"No." He stared out the window.

I suddenly understood the literal meaning of sitting on the edge of my seat, but I did it for nothing. He'd clammed up. All I'd succeeded in doing was upsetting him. I was about to apologize.

"I didn't need to see," he said. "I heard."

I leaned forward, every nerve on edge. "What did you hear?"

"More like a 'who', but I can't be sure. Ach." He waved dismissively. "You'll think I'm a crazy old man."

Pretty much the same thing Ray had said. "I'd

never think that." What I did think was that these two didn't talk about anything beyond the weather or what to eat for dinner. What was up between them? I sensed they kept each other at arm's length.

"You're too nice." The way he said it, he didn't mean it as a compliment.

"You mean naïve? I'm actually neither." I grinned. "But when I first moved back to Santa Fe, I thought I might be losing it, too. Because I heard things in the night that I haven't heard since I was a little girl."

He squinted, searching my face. "You're a Tahy."

And he must know the implications of that. "You know about my brother."

"He died the night of Zozobra." Tilting his head, he held my gaze. "In a fire."

"Not just any fire. It was Old Man Gloom himself." I lowered my voice and spoke more distinctly. "And I think he's come back." When Mr. White's only response was a wary look, I went on. "I think he followed me to your house. And I'm…" A lump formed in my throat. Staring at my hands, I swallowed hard. "I'm so sorry."

"You can't blame yourself for what happened."

His disbelief might have been a comfort in another situation. "He knows I've moved home, and he doesn't want me here. Especially with Zozobra coming up fast." I tossed my hair back and tried to shake off the willies. "Now who sounds crazy, huh?"

At a noise from the doorway, we looked over. Brow furrowed, Ray stood there, glaring at us.

Despite my best effort, a chuckle burbled up. "Hey, Sunshine."

"What are you doing here?" So serious.

I mock-frowned. "Not a very nice welcome."

"I agree." Rusty pulled himself higher in the bed. "We taught you better manners than that."

We? Had Mr. White helped raise Ray? The two men locked gazes like bucks locking antlers.

Ray glanced away first. "Are you feeling all right today, Rusty?"

"Peachy. I'm ready to leave." Mr. White's gruffness softened.

Ray nodded. "I'd feel better if you were home, too."

Rusty huffed. "*You'd* feel better?" His shoulders jerked as he shook his head.

"You know what I mean." Ray's glance touched me for an instant, then he jammed his hands in his pockets.

"I suppose I do." The old man rested his head against the pillow. "But does it matter where I am?"

I gripped the bed rail. "Yes. You'd be better off at home where Ray can look after you."

Rusty's closed-mouth chuckle was all the response he gave.

I eased back. "I'd better get back to work." I rose and surprised myself, and Mr. White, by kissing his cheek. "Take care."

He caught my hand and squeezed. "And you, young lady."

The phrase made me laugh. No one had called me a young lady in a long time. "I'll see you." To Ray, I jerked my head toward the hallway. "Can I talk to you a sec?"

He looked uncertainly at his grandfather. "Yeah. For a second."

Great. No pressure. "I'll make it fast." I fished in my handbag as I walked. My fingers found the cold metal, and I pulled it out. "As soon as you get home, hang this on your house."

He winced and began to shake his head.

"Don't argue. My aunt gave me a bunch of these. She was adamant that everyone put them somewhere outside their homes. The more open the spot, the better. If I read her right, the stars provide some sort of protection." I pressed the ornament into his hand. "Please. You need as much protection as anyone." More, if my instincts proved right. I hoped to God I was wrong.

He blew a sharp breath. "Okay."

"Try to get him home soon."

"I will." He turned the black ornament in his hand. "Thanks."

"Would you mind if I visited him again?"

"Course not. He actually seems to like you."

This trip to the hospital wasn't a total loss, then. I surprised myself a second time by kissing Ray's cheek, too. "See you soon."

"Yeah." His smile didn't last long, but the warmth was enough that I was satisfied to walk away. He'd follow through with the promise to hang the star. But I'd still make sure next time I went to their house.

Outside the hospital, the sight of a man's figure arrested me. He kept to the side of the building where shadows gathered, but I saw him clearly enough to know he was watching me. Again.

It was the same guy from last night—from the bar. A younger version of Old Man Gloom. And wherever he showed up, disaster was never far behind.

I clenched my jaw, anger fuming through my flared nostrils. "Hey." I rushed toward him.

In a watery blur, he slipped around the corner.

"Wait." I couldn't let him get away. Not without knowing the truth.

I raced after him. The instant I cornered the building, darkness enveloped me. A thick, palpable darkness, that at once seemed to slam into me, and to stretch out forever in front of me. Unable to see, I lost my footing. The ground slipped away from beneath my feet, and I floated down. Panicked, I grasped for anything, but my hands found only air.

I willed myself to calm down. Think. If this wasn't a dream, I had to do something, fast. Aunt Zelda's words came back: *Keep this with you.*

I clutched at my shoulder, and my fingers closed around the straps of my handbag. Somehow, I hadn't lost it. I followed the strap to the bag and unzipped it. My mind sorted each item my fingers touched. When I found the pointed metal, I closed my hand around the black star I always carried with me.

The blackness shifted, a quick jerk like a hiccup. I squeezed the star, and the darkness thinned and ebbed away like the sea pulling back upon itself.

Not far back enough to release me. With my other hand, I grasped the silver flame pendant I wore. The metal warmed beneath my touch.

The darkness forcibly pushed me backward. A rush of wind filled my ears. Daylight dialed up, from weak to strong, and my feet found the ground again. With a yelp, I stumbled back, and then righted myself.

Gasping, I glanced around. The hospital stood to my right. Another building was beside it, the corridor between them dark but not impossibly so.

I stood there until my heart rate slowed enough that I might not fall on my face if I walked.

Chapter Fourteen

I didn't know which was worse, not being able to tell anyone what had happened or having to face my coworkers again. Not that I had a choice. I could only avoid the newsroom for so long before I'd land in deeper trouble. After the strange experience, I had to take a long walk to calm myself, but I found I'd developed a sudden aversion to shadows, and the bright sunlight created deep ones.

After a few blocks, I decided facing my angry colleagues would be easier than the shadows, so headed back to the car. The quick stop to the phone store stretched longer than I'd have liked, but at least I had another cell when I returned to the newsroom.

Aside from Ashley, no one showed outright irritation with me. Whatever had distracted Weller earlier still seemed to have a hold on him. Everyone else was either out on assignment or working on stories.

I kept my nose in my work, too.

My cell chimed. Zelda's name appeared in the display.

Just the person I needed to speak with. Probably calling to remind me about tonight's meeting, no doubt. "Hello, Aunt Zelda."

"Marissa, dear. Sorry to bother you at work."

"You're never a bother. Besides, we're committee associates. I have tonight's meeting on my calendar."

And I had Zelda in my sights. One way or the other, I'd wrangle the truth from my aunt.

"Wonderful. Don't forget we're not at the usual site."

"Right, we're taking a field trip to the warehouse." I nearly had forgotten, though. Maybe because I wasn't looking forward to going there. "Can you text me the address again? It's been a crazy day, and I don't think I'm going to have time to stop at my apartment beforehand."

"I was hoping you could come to dinner again." Disappointment dripped from every word.

"I wish I could, but I have some things to finish up at work. I may be a few minutes late for the meeting." I braced for an explosion through the phone.

"A few minutes is fine. Just don't miss the entire meeting." She said it pleasantly enough, but the underlying warning was clear.

Still, I had dodged one. "Never. The committee's an extension of work for me." Hopefully a one and done deal. Let some other schmuck have the pleasure next year. "See you later."

At hearing the blues riff, I checked the cell again. A text from Zelda with the address. I messaged a thank you and returned to the article I'd started, but my concentration was shot. Normally, I could pound out a piece within fifteen minutes and send it off to the editor. I shuffled through my notes, the handwritten ones and on the tablet, but kept losing the thread of information I needed.

I pushed away from the desk, grabbed my mug, and refilled it at the coffee maker. Tepid and awful-tasting, I tossed the contents of the mug down the sink and dumped out the pot. No one should have to suffer drinking that goop. Absently, I went through the motion of preparing a new batch. The gurgle and hiss of the machine was sweet music to make my blood dance, long enough to get through the committee meeting, I hoped.

****

The warehouse sat a few blocks away from Fort Marcy Park, where Old Man Gloom would burn on September 2. I angled my vehicle beside my aunt's car and crossed the wide gravel drive. The wide doors stood open, and bright light flooded out. No one noticed my approach. The too-bright overhead lights flooded the large indoor space, revealing activity everywhere. In the center of the room, some committee members grouped around the volunteers constructing the effigy.

The figure's wooden frame had taken shape, an all too familiar one. Simply stepping into the same room with it put my senses on high alert. Silly, nothing would happen. Old Man Gloom wasn't even fully formed.

My aunt appeared at my side. "Are you all right?"

"Fine." Zelda knew better, but I would pretend for the benefit of the others. Pretend the roar of the flames didn't suddenly echo in my head, didn't mingle with my brother's screams. Pretend that being near Old Man Gloom in any form didn't set my skin to prickling.

The festival was two and a half months away. Before then, I had to find a way to deal with the residual fear of that night. I couldn't shake the feeling that this year's Zozobra would bring more tragedy.

I turned to my aunt. "When are you going to let me in on whatever secret you're keeping?"

Zelda's surprise was awkward, and seemingly

practiced. "Secret?"

"I'm going to find out eventually. We need to talk." We thought too much alike for my aunt to hide the truth from me for too long.

Tomas Gomez strode up. "Ms. Furtado, may I have a word." Mr. Gomez drew away an apologetic Zelda to discuss a scheduling detail.

I skirted the assembly section in the center of the warehouse. Thinking of the effigy as a giant puppet helped. A marionette subject to the will of the puppeteer. If only that were true.

Focusing on my real job would help block my fears, so I sought out Mrs. Brock for an update on the fundraising. I took notes on the small note pad I kept in my bag. I gave Mrs. Brock a business card and asked her to email whatever records she could share.

Then I talked to the people who helped to construct the effigy. George Blake did most of the preparation himself.

"That's a lot for one guy." My earnest admiration came through in my voice.

"After all these years," Mr. Blake said, "I know every step by heart."

"So you've been building the Old Man for a long time?"

"Since 1967." Hard to miss the pride as he spoke.

"Impressive. Can you give me a step-by-step description of the procedure?"

I wrote fast to keep up with him as he talked. Within weeks of the festival's end, he began to put together next year's figure. He constructed the fifty-foot frame in four separate parts in his own garage. Each year, he colored the hair different from the previous year. He created the enormous head, replicating the terrible eyebrows, the large menacing eyes, and the wide smile that also passed for a grimace.

I jerked my head toward the effigy. "So, all his features are finished?" I hated to think of that face.

George chuckled. "Of course. This year's no different from any other."

I wished that were true. "Tell me more."

He cheerfully went on to describe how the committee members then helped move the parts to the warehouse, where they added two hundred yards of fabric. Sewing the effigy together with about a half million stitches took weeks of work.

"Then what?" I prompted.

George shrugged. "Then we stuff him with paper."

"Any particular sort of paper?" I asked.

He gave me a look suggesting I'd lost my marbles. "Absolutely. The festival is all about purging troubles, so we use bags of discarded records, anything from obsolete mortgages to old legal records, divorces and such. Anything that people want to put behind them and forget about. We usually get about ninety bags."

"Wow." I jutted my bottom lip as I wrote. "From where?"

"Residents and businesses donate them." He puffed out his chest and grinned. "Some save up all year just so they can see them go up in smoke."

About what I'd expected. None of this sounded out of the ordinary. I must be missing something. How did the spirit enter the wooden frame each year? "But you let anyone come to the warehouse and add their written troubles to the effigy, right?"

He nodded. "They take them there, or to your

newspaper."

"Yes, we've had dozens of contributors." Even from out-of-towners. Whether they lived in Santa Fe or out of state, I'd ensured that each donor received a black star, as my aunt had demanded.

"And when we are ready to stuff Old Man Gloom full of everyone's troubles, we invite those people to help. Otherwise it would take days to stuff those ninety bags into the frame."

"That's a few days before the festival, right?" At his nod, I said, "Great, I'll have a staff photographer capture the fun on film." Hopefully, he'd capture more than that in the photos. If people garnered evidence of ghosts with their cameras, I might just be able to document the spirit of Zozobra. I'd love nothing better than to have proof I could confront Zelda with, and demand her to explain it away.

"You'll be there, too?" he asked.

"I wouldn't miss it." Or I'd hear about it forever. "Could you describe what happens next? You haul the puppet to Fort Marcy Park and attach it to the scaffold," I prompted.

"Yes, that's pretty much it until Thursday evening."

"The night of the festival," I clarified. "When you burn him." I kept my gaze averted from the effigy, but from the corner of my eye, I could swear I saw the thing shudder.

"And everyone's troubles along with him. That's the whole point of Zozobra, isn't it?"

"Right." The pivotal point, it would seem. "Thanks for your time. If you think of anything to add, could you let me know?" I fished out a business card and handed it to him.

He tucked it into his shirt pocket. "Of course."

After he walked away, I couldn't bring myself to go any closer to the puppet. Constructed or not, the thing gave me the creeps. Taking photos gave me an excuse to keep my distance. Then I interviewed a few volunteers. Then I ran out of excuses.

My aunt stayed near the half-constructed effigy. Avoiding me, no doubt, but that could only work for so long. Sooner or later, Zelda would have to face me.

The committee members left, a few at a time. Meeting adjourned, I thought. Except that Zelda remained close to George, helping him work on the figure.

I might as well give up, for now. I steeled myself and approached my aunt. "I need to take off."

She glanced up long enough to say, "Take care, darling."

Odd, her letting me go so easily. Until she added, "See you at the next meeting."

I couldn't stay in the same room with Old Man Gloom another second. "Night."

The urge to run was a force pushing me forward. I barely subdued it. Behind me, the effigy was a palpable presence. When I had the sense of that ghostly presence rising up, floating above the effigy and everyone gathered around it, my neck hairs bristled. *Don't look back.*

My SUV sat at the end of the row of vehicles, damning me to walk into deeper darkness. Didn't the warehouse have an outdoor spotlight? "I'm going to mention it to Aunt Zelda," I muttered. "A potential accident waiting to happen…"

A tidal wave of breath billowed from the building and flowed toward me. Gaining, rather than losing strength.

I was being watched. I could feel a gaze crawling over my skin.

The parking lot was empty other than two committee members heading to their cars. I waved and hurried to mine. After jerking the door open, I scrambled inside and slammed the button to lock all the doors. Once I was on the road, the headlights gave everything an unnatural grey appearance. Objects that looked interesting in daylight took on ominous shapes.

"Quit freaking yourself out, Mar." I turned the radio up loud and sang along with Beck. *Baby, you're a lost cause.* The irony made me laugh.

For a moment after pulling up outside the apartment, trepidation held me in place. The sense of being watched had faded, but not entirely. As I stepped out of the SUV, a different sensation crept across my skin. Insect-like black forms flitted from tree to house, shadow to shadow. They didn't make a sound individually that I could discern. Their collective hum vibrated through me like an army of ants, tiny feet prickling into me.

Whatever they were, it was no coincidence they'd showed up now.

I hurried up the stone walkway. Once inside, I frantically scrubbed my arms but couldn't erase the tingling. Several deep breaths in and out helped calm me, but shadows lingered in the corners of the room. The adobe fireplace beckoned but would have overheated the small rooms. Instead, I lit the candles on the table in front of the sofa, and the thick one with four wicks atop the tall iron candelabra to the side of the fireplace. The flickering glow soothed me, and I curled into the corner of the leather sofa and pulled a pillow to my chest.

The flames reached higher, then collapsed, in a rhythmic dance that lulled my senses.

Chapter Fifteen

My eyes snapped wide open, but I found myself in darkness. At some point, the candles must have burned out.

I rose, crossed the room to the front door, and stepped outside. Pebbly ground registered beneath my bare feet as I walked in the night. Stars twinkled through the branches of the trees, more numerous than there should have been. No lights shone, though I should be on Griffin Street. Odder still, I could discern no outlines of buildings anywhere. The apartments, and my neighborhood, were gone. I stood on barren land I didn't recognize. No familiar landmarks were in sight other than the peaks I knew to belong to the Sangre de Cristo Mountains.

Somewhere in the distance, from the direction of where the city Plaza should be, rough voices rang out in what sounded like Spanish, and another language I didn't recognize. Gun shots echoed, and more shouts. The commotion drew me forward, and I swiftly glided over fields, the rows of plants guiding me ahead.

Tall structures just beyond the fields meant civilization. Finally. My heart lightened, unburdened from the worry of being lost. I crossed between two of the four large pueblos. Each stood three stories high, situated to form a crude square, vastly different from the parklike setting of the Plaza.

Uniformed men surrounded a group of Native Americans. To my mute astonishment, the soldiers wore old-fashioned Spanish military outfits, complete with the tall silver helmets I'd seen in museums. This might have been a scene from one of the exhibits, except the soldiers jabbed at the people with their long rifles, forcing them into a huddle. Some of the Native Americans wore what looked like colorful ceremonial costumes, others were dressed in plainer garb. Whatever they'd been doing, they weren't celebrating now. They were afraid for their lives.

More townspeople clustered in groups along the pueblos. Fearful cries of women mixed with angrier shouts of young men. Several girls tugged older women toward the ladders leading to the upper level of the pueblos, probably to their homes. Their gazes returned to the square as they climbed to escape the melee.

The Spaniards forced the huddled group toward the end of one pueblo structure. Unlike the windows in the homes on upper levels, the windows in this section had bars. Outside the jailhouse, the soldiers bound each Native American with rope.

A striking-looking soldier strode to the center of the square and halted beside a wooden pole. If I'd seen him elsewhere, I'd have thought him magnificent. His silver helmet gleamed brighter than the rest, and medals decorated his crisp red jacket. From the set of his jaw, and the glint in his narrowed eyes, he intended to inflict harm on these people.

His authoritative voice rose above the din. He spoke in a thick accent, probably in Spanish, but I understood each word too clearly.

He gestured to the prisoners. "Bring him to me."

Another Spaniard grabbed one of the indigenous men from the group and dragged him to the center of the square. The Native American glared at the commander as the second soldier tied him to the pole.

The commander paced around him in a slow, menacing circle. "You have been warned too many times. Have we not made our rules clear enough?"

The prisoner jutted out his chin.

"Spanish law forbids you to perform these pagan rituals." The commander stopped in front of the man. "Why do you persist?"

The prisoner's chest rose and fell with sharp breaths, but his face registered only anger.

"Your stubborn disregard of the rules has condemned you to punishment." The commander swept his hand toward the others. "All of you must pay the price for your sorcery and collusion with the Spirit of the Mountains."

Spirit of the Mountains? Only then did I notice the slaughtered deer hanging alongside one pueblo—venison the Spaniards had earmarked for themselves, but the Native Americans had offered to the spirit.

I searched the faces of the indigenous people looking on. Some were teary-eyed, most revealed horror or showed agony. Only one man stood slightly apart from the rest. His white robes flowed in the breeze. The glow of firelight across his features registered a mixture of anger and disgust as the soldiers carted away the lifeless buck.

The Spanish official signaled another soldier, who came forward carrying a cat o'nine tails.

Oh no. I strained to turn my head so I wouldn't have to watch, but my body had become stone-like. The soldier raised the whip and cracked it through the air, slicing the poor man's back. His body undulated with pain, but he restrained his cry. Red welts puckered on his skin. The next lash cut deeper into the welts, and darker red dripped from the cuts.

Shrieks rose above muted sobbing of the other townsfolk. Men watched silently, fists as clenched as their jaws, flinching as the soldier brought the whip down again and again.

Stop. Please. I wanted to cry out but had no voice. I wasn't truly there. This scene had taken place centuries and centuries ago, in the late 1600s. I was being shown this atrocity for a reason.

I searched for the man in white robes, but the place where he'd stood was empty.

The soldier meted out the same punishment to three other Native American men, an excruciating horror I was forced to witness.

The Spanish commander strode into the center of the square again, this time halting beside a taller wooden structure. "The law is clear. The one who organized the rebellion must pay the ultimate sacrifice."

At his signal, a soldier tossed a rope over a taller wooden structure, securing one end with knots. The end that dangled over ended in a loop. My blood chilled when I realized what they were about to do.

A soldier led a horse beneath the structure. Two others marched an older man to the animal's side. They tugged the prisoner to a stop, dropped the noose over his head and tightened the rope around his neck. They forced the man to mount the snorting beast, whose flared nostrils, wild eyes, and pinned ears indicated a primal understanding of the horror awaiting. No sooner was the old man situated on the horse's back than a soldier smacked the animal's rear.

In the suspended moment before the rope snapped tight, the old man called one word in the hushed silence: *venganza.*

Revenge.

The noose choked off his yell, but the screams of others sounded as his body shuddered, fighting off death. But death claimed him, and he went limp. Soldiers dragged away the men they'd flogged to prison cells. Wails of anguish filled the night, agonized cries, and tearful, angry echoes of *venganza.*

The wave of voices carried me backward, flowing swift as a leaf atop a river along the route I'd traveled. Like the echoes, the scene faded. But the bitterness remained embedded in the reddened dust.

****

The brutal violence startled me to consciousness, my heart still wildly fluttering in my chest, sweat dampening my skin. Cool leather was smooth against my cheek. I knew I was safe at home, that the murders were long past, but the horror remained a blood-soaked stain on my consciousness.

The candles had been snuffed out by their own melted wax. Muted sunlight, with a reddish tinge, splashed across the walls.

Not another dust storm. With a weary sigh, I sat up and rubbed the sleep from my eyes. Last night's vision still weighed heavily on me. I wasn't sure I was up to another day of insanity, but a full workday stretched ahead of me.

By the time I'd physically readied myself, I was more mentally prepared as well. Or thought I was.

From the time I arrived, the *Chronicle* phones rang nonstop, people calling with complaints, crime, accident tips, and demanding answers.

Like the vision I'd had earlier, the newsroom seemed to spin around me, the other reporters spurred to action. Rooted to my seat, I could only watch. Something niggled at the back of my mind. Writing articles about everyone's troubles was tossing gasoline onto the wildfire. I had to do more.

And I had questions of my own. Where was Luis Valdez? How could I find him? How could I stop these assaults by an intangible being?

The old saying popped into my head—fight fire with fire.

It might be just the answer I needed. All I had to do was figure out how.

Grabbing my purse, I called out, "I have to follow a lead." Where, I had no idea. My body moved on sheer intuition, and with an urgency I didn't understand. All I knew was that I had to go. Now. The rest would reveal itself to me.

As I drove, some inner magnet pulled me. And it was leading me to my aunt's house.

Her silver car sat outside, so she must be inside. I leapt out of my SUV and didn't bother to close the door before running to her door. My left hand pounded the wood while my right jabbed the doorbell. "Let me in, Aunt Zelda. You can't ignore me any longer."

The door whooshed open, and I nearly toppled onto her.

Wide-eyed, she surveyed me. "Are you insane?"

I gritted my teeth. "I'm getting there."

She peered past me. "Come in before someone

calls the police." She clamped a hand around my wrist and pulled me inside. "What is all this about?"

I wrung my fingers. "Why is all this happening? Because I moved back? Or because of the Zozobra centennial?"

For once, she didn't ask what I was talking about. Her pursed lips and arched brow told me she understood. "Come and sit."

"I don't want to sit. My nerves are about to jump out of my skin." Once I began to speak, the flow of words became an unstoppable torrent. "These visions steal my sleep, and they're so upsetting, I can barely focus on my job, and that's getting to be a real problem, and the fact that Old Man Gloom has returned as a young guy doesn't help my peace of mind, nor does the fact that the boy I interviewed disappeared, and his family blames me—"

Zelda briefly squeezed my shoulder. "Take a breath, dear. What visions?"

Her touch had a clarifying effect. I suddenly saw everything as if it were laid out before me. "Of lightning and *Ptesan-Wi*." I flailed a hand as I recounted them. "Of Fire Eagle and the other men who first named Old Man Gloom. Of Ashley Stirling burning from the inside out. Of the Spaniards torturing and killing the Pueblo people who lived here God knows how long ago." I pinned her with a look. "Why? You know, don't you?"

"I suspected, but I wasn't sure." She strolled to the kitchen. "Do you want some coffee?"

Coffee? I wanted to scream, but I followed her. "Fine. But what do you mean, you weren't sure? About which?"

177

"You."

Her beatific smile deflated my blustering. "Me?" I sank to the bar stool at the kitchen island.

Zelda puttered back and forth, pouring water into the coffee maker and spooning coffee grounds. "Yes. Your mother was right. I suppose I didn't want to admit that I needed your help. But I do."

I braced my elbows against the counter. What had my mother known about Santa Fe that I didn't? "Why am I having visions?"

She pulled two mugs from the cabinet. "Because you are a descendant of the Chin family."

Chin was my aunt's maiden name, and my mother's. A vague memory teased my mind, but all I knew about my mother's family was that she didn't associate with them. "Why does this family have so many secrets?"

"Because we must." In a roundabout way, my aunt was responding to my questions, technically, but volunteering nothing.

"Why? Can you just explain?" I wanted to take hold of her, make her stop moving long enough to give me a straight answer.

She turned and crossed her arms over her chest. "Someone as protected as you can't possibly understand what my parents went through. They were Korean in a time when it was dangerous to appear Asian in America."

My thoughts raced. "Because of the Korean War?"

"My parents were deeply spiritual and had moved to Santa Fe, the city whose name translated to Holy Faith. Because of the racial mix of people here, they thought they could fit in, that no one would question their loyalty to America. The Korean War sent them into a panic. Since World War II, anyone who looked Asian was considered dangerous, a threat to national security. Many Japanese were forced into a prison camp in this very city."

"In Santa Fe?" How could I not have known? Or had I buried it in my subconscious?

"Oh yes, in Santa Fe. Complete with barbed wire, armed guards atop towers with search lights, and tear gas." Zelda's bitterness was evident, until she added, like a disaffected tour guide, "In the Casa Solana neighborhood."

"I had no idea." How frightening for my family, to live under such a terrible shadow. "So that's why we abandoned everything Korean." Such a loss of heritage.

My aunt bowed her head. "A necessary pretense." The coffee machine gurgled, and she busied herself again. "The prison camps left a permanent impression on my parents. They never got over the fear."

A fear they had deeply ingrained in their daughters, apparently. My mother married a Navajo, Buck Tahy. My parents raised me as Native American, never speaking of the Korean culture.

After the fire that took my brother from us, my family's fear changed. The threat changed. My parents hadn't wanted to leave Santa Fe and what was left of our family, but they couldn't risk losing me, too.

Zelda set the steaming cup in front of me, and I studied her. Was that why my aunt married a Latino man? She could pretend to be Latin American and raise Javi that way?

"I can tell by the look on your face that you're piecing things together. Maybe not in the correct order," she warned, watching me as she sipped.

Had she loved her husband? My right to know ended where her marriage began. I had no right to ask about such personal matters.

The festival was another matter entirely. "Tell me about the star ornaments."

She chose her words carefully. "They are unique to the centennial event."

"Because you're worried what Old Man Gloom might do?" When she didn't deny it, I pressed further. "How could small, black decorations possibly protect people?"

The look in her eyes told me I was a foolish child, but she explained, "They've been blessed three times over. By medicine men. By priests with holy water. By shamans."

"Shamans?" That was a twist I hadn't seen coming.

Zelda shrugged. "I know a few."

Sure, what could it hurt? Better overkill than inadequate protection. Something told me my aunt was holding back. "What else?"

She pursed her lips.

A shiver went through me. "What else?"

"Do you remember the day you first arrived home? We stopped at your old address?"

Why bring that up? "Yes."

"At the time, I avoided your question about the land."

"I'm not following. What question?" Then it hit me. Someone had disturbed the dirt. "You dug there? Why?"

"We needed to add sacred ingredients to the ceramic mix."

"Michael's ashes," I whispered.

"The key to protecting people. I should have asked your permission."

I shook my head. If she had, I would have thought her crazy. Now I knew better. "The process must have worked. Those nasty little demons, or whatever they are, avoid the houses where the stars hang."

Cradling her mug between both hands, she leaned forward on the counter. "What nasty little demons?"

I went still, feeling like my sparring partner had just dropped out of our little verbal match. "You haven't seen them? I thought you heard the clicking noises, too." I'd felt so certain that she had.

Zelda searched my face. "Tell me about them."

I did. At least, what little I knew. About hearing them from afar, then sensing them swarm through the streets. "And each time it happens, they seem to be stronger than the last."

"But what are they? Can you see them?"

"Not really. From what I can tell, they're not tangible. They might be some kind of energy. When they move in a swarm, they remind me of black ashes."

"What else?"

"I can hear them. They make my skin crawl." I shrugged, as much to indicate that was all I could think of, and to shake off the shiver that hit me.

"He's gaining strength," she whispered. She appeared to stare into the distance, but her roving gaze indicated she was searching inside her head.

Her sudden flurry of upset gave me a bad feeling. "But you have other protections against him, right? Some extra voodoo for this year's festival?" I regretted using any words she might find demeaning. I just had no frame of reference for any of this.

From the sunroom came a shudder of wings and a squawk. "*Mudang eomeoni*," Phoebe called.

"What's that supposed to mean?" Had my aunt been tutoring the parrot in a foreign language? Eccentric, even for Zelda. And whatever Phoebe said, hadn't been Spanish. "Did she just speak in Korean?" When Zelda flicked her gaze to mine, then away, I knew my guess hit home. "Who taught her? You?"

"It doesn't matter." My aunt set down her cup and walked to the door. "I have an appointment I can't miss."

My hands clenched the mug tight. "I have to know what I should do about Luis Valdez. If you can't help me, then who can? Will you at least point me in the right direction?"

"Meditate on the matter." She opened the door and waited.

A laugh of disbelief escaped. I pushed to my feet. "Fine."

As if I had patience for sitting around, doing nothing. The last thing I wanted to do was spend more time inside my head. It had become a strange and dangerous place, and I was woefully inadequate to solve its mysteries.

Conjuring a vision was a skill I had yet to learn. I tried each night to summon *Ptesan-Wi*, but the efforts only gave me a headache and robbed me of more sleep. Harrowing days turned into torturous weeks, and I worried sick for Luis' welfare. I'd checked with the police so often they'd grown annoyed and basically told me to stop calling, that they'd inform me if they turned up any information.

I wasn't holding my breath.

Nor had I bothered Zelda again, so was surprised one Wednesday when she texted me:

—See you tonight at 7—

The committee shindig. Now that it was mid-July, they'd ramp up the planning part and get together more often. Good thing I had no social life.

—I'll be there.—

I wouldn't admit that I actually looked forward to the meeting in the cathedral, the one place immune to the gloom infesting the rest of the city.

By evening, my weary soul cried out for the peace. Mrs. Brock and George Blake had arrived before me, and I greeted them, then hesitated.

There was my aunt's chair, still empty. How tempting to claim a seat at the table. But out of deference to the rest, I sat in my usual place, slightly behind my aunt's chair.

Zelda rushed in but came to an abrupt stop when she saw me. "Marissa. You're here."

"I told you I would be."

She unwound the scarf from her head and sat. "Yes. Good." Her professional demeanor took over when Tomas Gomez and Peter River entered. "Let's get started, shall we?"

What a relief to have others in the spotlight of Zelda's ire for a change. My aunt conducted the meeting like a maestro, mostly reviewing agenda items that had been planned in detail long ago, and before I knew it, she announced the meeting's conclusion.

"See you soon." She wound the scarf around her head.

My cue that I could leave, too, so I shouldered my

messenger bag strap and headed for the hallway. Had my aunt's many-tentacled reach failed to ensnare me? "You mean, at the fundraiser this weekend." I half-held my breath in hopes Zelda would laugh and tell me the committee didn't require me to attend.

She walked beside me. "Absolutely. Will you be bringing a date?"

I toyed with my pen. "I thought of asking Javi to go." Springing it on him at the last minute wasn't my best idea, but I had no others.

"I believe he has plans. He mentioned a girl, I forget her name." Zelda ducked her head coyly. "Surely you've met a few nice young men by now."

Sure, I'd been here all of what, a month and a half? I wasn't exactly out hunting husbands.

I pushed open the heavy wooden door. "I'll bribe someone if I have to." In the wan yellow of the streetlight, I met my aunt's fake smile with one of my own. "All for a good cause, right?"

"Any man would be proud to go with you."

Funny, my aunt almost sounded sincere. Of all people, Zelda knew the kind of emotional baggage I schlepped around. I'd been ready to purge myself of it, but sometimes the weight seemed double.

On the drive home, I weighed my options. Bill Larsen would be there as official *Chronicle* photographer, and I could time our arrival to coincide, but that wouldn't fill the dinner seat beside me. Another staffer? I imagined Bernard from HR fidgeting next to me. No. Mike Fisher? The good night might turn awkward, and so would our working relationship. No, no, no.

Maybe Javi knew someone?

But I already knew who my cousin would suggest.

I skipped the family drama and just called Ray. His deep voice acted like a balm to my senses.

"Hey. How's Rusty?" Real nice, ignoring Ray's well-being. I mentally smacked my forehead.

"Grumpy as ever. But he's home, safe and sound." If I'd offended him, he hid it well.

Avoiding the window, I couldn't shake the memory of those things outside. "So you hung the star?" I closed my eyes, praying he'd say yes. And praying the ornaments actually did shield people. I still wasn't convinced about any bubble protecting us during the fire.

"Surprisingly, I did."

Tension released like a dam break. "Good. Hey, I have a favor to ask. Feel free to say no."

"Okay, shoot."

"The festival planning committee's holding a fundraising dinner on Saturday. Any chance you'd go with me?"

A beat of silence. "Are you asking me because Javi's busy that night?"

Should I lie? "Well…" Well, damn. I'd hedged.

He grunted. "What you're saying is *yes*. Then I'm saying no."

I didn't expect the pinprick of hurt. "Not fair," I tried to joke, but even sounded pathetic to my own ears. "You owe me a dinner."

"I thought it was the other way around?" No teasing in his tone.

I'd blown my chance with him. "Never mind. I get it." And now I was pouting. Shit.

"I was only joking, Marissa." He sounded so

serious.

If he wanted honesty, I'd give it to him. "That's mean."

"Guess I'm not such a nice guy after all."

Yes, he was. Better than I'd given him credit for. "A little mean streak is good for the soul sometimes."

"I'll remember that." Another beat. "I'm also a pushover. So what time are you picking me up?"

That was a twist. One I kind of liked. "Five thirty. Wear something nice. It's semi-formal."

"A suit?" He whistled. "That's a tall order."

I should warn him. "One more thing. Because the *Chronicle* assigned me to cover the festival and all its illustrious proceedings, I have to corner some people for interviews, snap a few photos. But it shouldn't take long."

His *hmm* became a growl. "Then this doesn't count."

"What do you mean?"

"You still owe me a night out. And not some business function. Just the two of us, alone."

A bubble of happiness floated up from deep inside me. I held it in, let it dissolve throughout my body, like warm sea foam spreading beneath my skin. "You drive a hard bargain."

Chapter Sixteen

On the one night I didn't try to conjure a vision, I fell into one as soon as my head hit the pillow.

People streamed out of the cathedral. From the long skirts and stylish hats, I guessed I was back in the 1920s. A marching band struck up a tune. The drum strapped to one musician's back bore the black letters "The Conquistadores." The band led a procession down the street and circled behind City Hall. I was caught up in the marchers, and when everyone stopped at the paved lot, a chill hit me when I saw why.

There hung a shorter version of Old Man Gloom than I was accustomed to, but no less terrifying. The effigy stood only twenty feet tall, and his features were more crudely drawn. In a semicircle in front of him, several small fires had been lit but glowed an eerie green.

The band segued to a more somber funeral march, and people in black robes filed in, hoods pulled low to hide their faces. One of them turned his head toward me, and I glimpsed Fire Eagle's face within.

A man stepped to one side of the effigy and introduced himself as city attorney Jack Kennedy. He waved toward the effigy. "I hereby proclaim a death sentence upon Zozobra."

By the theatrical way he announced it, this was the newly christened Zozobra, so this must be the first festival conducted in public rather than in Shuster's back yard. In naming the effigy, the men had unintentionally summoned the spirit. Zozobra swayed. The leering smile gave no indication of the aggravation of the spirit within.

Kennedy pointed a revolver over his head, then drew it down slowly. He took aim at the puppet and pulled the trigger. At the shot, the green fires sputtered into red and blazed higher in front of the effigy. The robed man who'd revealed himself to me as Fire Eagle stepped out of line, chanting as he touched a torch to the hem of Zozobra's long garment. Flames leapt into a tall column, shifting colors as they climbed higher.

At another bang, I startled. Fireworks whistled and exploded in all directions around Zozobra, who twisted in agony at the flames consuming him. No one but me heard his screams.

The crowd sent up a rousing cheer. The band launched into La Cucaracha as a group of people in bright costumes danced into their midst, waving torches. The men in black suddenly stripped away their black robes, and people clapped at seeing the robes beneath were harlequin style. They dispersed through the spectators, leading the rest to the street where bonfires glowed. All of them but one.

Fire Eagle remained behind. He shuffled his feet in a ceremonial dance, back and forth in front of the effigy. The colors of Fire Eagle's costumes blended with the flames engulfing Zozobra. As the sound of merrymaking retreated, Fire Eagle's voice rang clear in a sad lament.

Maybe Fire Eagle had heard Old Man Gloom's screams, too. The lines of his face deepened as if sharing the spirit's pain. Waving its flaming arms, the effigy flailed uselessly, trapped in the wood and cloth prison, doomed to burn along with the papers housed within.

No one but Fire Eagle remained to witness the burning, and he chanted as fire ate away the fabric, unveiling the sparse frame beneath. The wooden skeleton writhed as flames forced it to collapse—head sinking between the shoulders, torso into legs—all finally dropping into a charred heap of embers.

Only when the embers died into black bits did Fire Eagle's chanting fall away as well. We stood shoulder to shoulder in somber silence.

"The people thank you for your honorable sacrifice." He bowed to the charred remains, then faced me as he straightened. "This is but the beginning. The greater the sacrifice, the greater the struggle." Beneath heavy lids, his eyes shone bright. "The sacred one will guide you, daughter of lightning."

I dipped my head in acknowledgment. When I looked up again, the abandoned lot faded as it receded from view. The bonfires along the streets shrank to pinpoints, then mingled with the stars above the city.

****

Bargains were made to be broken.

The thought kept running through my head as I showered, and it stayed with me as I padded into the bedroom and reached into the back of the closet for the little black dress I kept for special occasions. I slipped into the sheath, a blend of silk and spandex that clung in all the right places, then I angled left and right in front of the full-length mirror and wondered if I should have bought something less sexy for the occasion. Too late now. So I put on silver earrings and bangles. With black heels, the dress practically qualified as a dangerous weapon. A weapon that had the potential to backfire. If I weren't careful, I might be the one injured.

With that in mind, I drove to Ray's house and pulled the SUV into the gravel driveway. Climbing in and out presented a challenge, but I managed to maneuver in a ladylike manner. He opened the back door before I reached it.

I set a hand on my hip as I assessed him. "Wow. You cut a sharp figure in that suit, Mr. White." The charcoal color set his blue eyes ablaze and contrasted nicely with the violet shirt.

His smile was halfway between shy and sly as he swept his gaze up my length. "No one will notice. All eyes will be on you. You look…" He whistled.

"The kind words of a gentleman." I dipped slightly, an awkward curtsy. "Thank you."

He craned his neck and adjusted his tie. "If I stay a gentleman all night, it'll be a miracle."

I could only imagine how ridiculous I looked when heat rose in my face. "I believe in miracles, don't you?"

"Not tonight." He stepped toward me. "Tonight is for more earthly matters."

Fluttering swirled in my belly. The night hadn't even begun yet, and it was way too early to react like some silly schoolgirl going to her first prom. That's what it felt like when he escorted me to my SUV and opened the door for me.

"So gallant," I teased, and climbed in. The movement hiked the fabric high on my legs, and I tugged it lower.

Like a gentleman, he averted his gaze. "I shouldn't

have asked you to drive."

"Why not?"

"What if your dress…" He flailed a hand helplessly. "…uh, wrinkles?"

No chance of that. There wasn't enough spare fabric.

"You're sweet." I couldn't remember the last time a man was so thoughtful. When Ray looked at me, he didn't look through me. The last few guys I'd dated made me feel invisible. Or interchangeable, like a place marker easily swapped out for another.

Ray saw the real me. The best part about the way he studied me was there was nothing judgmental about it. All he projected was acceptance. It freed me from awkward inhibitions, although that freedom didn't come easily to me. To act myself was to let down my guard and allow Ray in. I wasn't sure I was ready for that. Until he sat in the passenger seat and aimed that shy-sly smile at me again.

Even when we both stared ahead through the windshield, I was all too aware of his every movement. We talked like an old married couple…about the venue, the guests, the festival, and the success of the committee's fundraising efforts. But underneath the conversation, an electric tension filled the air until I worried my old vehicle might burst from the strain.

By the time we reached East San Francisco Street and walked toward the hotel, I was as high-strung as a racehorse at the gate. Less than a block away, the twin towers of the Cathedral Basilica of St. Francis of Assisi that rose at the end of the street had a calming effect on me. When Ray slipped his hand into mine, the initial electric spark gave way to a steady warmth as we entered.

We stood at the entrance to the La Terracita room where the elite of Santa Fe had gathered. Three walls of glass with teal panes reflected the white tablecloths and the strings of white lights criss-crossing the vaulted glass ceiling. The concentrated candlelight flickering caught my eye. Nestled in the center of the hors d'ouvre table, rows of candles surrounded a tabletop version of Old Man Gloom. The small model replicated the effigy too well, especially the exaggerated facial features. My skin pebbled into goose flesh.

"There's your aunt." Ray inclined his head toward her.

Zelda might have been a movie star. Her beauty was matched only by her tightly contained energy. Beside her, everyone else appeared a faded image. With her hair swept up, the slant of her black eyebrows accentuated the sparkle in her dark eyes.

"Do you need to check in?" he asked.

"No need. Here she comes." I beamed in Zelda's direction as she whisked across the room, her beaded midnight blue dress catching the muted light.

"Marissa. You're finally here."

I made sure my smile didn't falter. "We're right on time."

"Committee members were due earlier." She turned to Ray. "Nice to see you again."

"And you, Mrs. Furtado. You look beautiful."

She brushed her hand through the air. "Aren't you a darling? Please, call me Zelda. You two are at table three." Zelda gestured but rested a staying hand on my arm. "There's a chair for a *Chronicle* photographer at your table, too. You did ask for a photographer to attend tonight?"

"Mr. Weller promised one would be here." I strained to search the faces of the other attendees, but no photographer.

Zelda only said, "Mm."

"I could always take some shots on my cell." Thank God I'd made certain to charge my phone.

"Your cell?" Hand pressed delicately to her chest, my aunt made no effort to hide her horror.

"The photo quality is almost as good as a thirty-five millimeter. But only as a last resort. I'm sure the photographer will arrive soon." I sent a worried glance to Ray.

He pressed lightly at the small of my back. "Shall we go find our table?"

"And the bar," I murmured after we walked out of my aunt's earshot.

"Oh yes."

I spotted a few committee members and pulled my cell from my clutch purse. "I'd better grab some photos until the real photographer shows up. Would you get me a glass of wine?"

"Sure you wouldn't prefer tequila?" he teased.

I answered in all seriousness. "Maybe later."

"Go ahead. I'll have your drink waiting."

"You're an angel." I cursed my newly uninhibited tongue and fanned the heat from my face as I walked away.

Tomas Gomez greeted me. "You look beautiful tonight, Marissa."

Mrs. Brock squeezed my hand and held me at arm's length. "You're positively glowing."

"You both look wonderful. I love that dress, Mrs.

Brock. Do you mind if I take some photos?" When her smile faded as I raised my cell, I explained, "The staff photographer's running late. I hope you don't mind posing more than once."

"Not at all." Mr. Gomez tugged his lapel and drew himself tall.

The images weren't half bad when I flipped through them, so I thanked Tomas and Trisha, and moved on to my next victims. When I cornered Zelda and Peter, beneath her smile was an undeniable glare, a how-dare-you-cheapen-my-event expression that I was certain to hear all about later.

Ray rescued me. "Here you go."

I took the wine he offered. "Just in time." I raised my glass in cheers and sipped. At the appearance of the photographer at the entrance, I choked with excitement. "Bill's here."

Zelda arched one brow as if aiming me in her sights.

I waved in his direction. "The photographer."

"How nice he could fit us into his schedule." She swept up her glass in passing and launched herself toward him.

I frowned at Ray. "Sorry, I'd better go mediate."

"Sure," Ray said with an easy air.

I hurried to catch up to my aunt, but she'd already cornered Bill and was halfway through instructing him.

"Hey, Bill. Thanks for giving up your Saturday evening." I sent a pointed glance to Zelda.

He pursed his mouth, a sour curl of distaste. "No problem. I'll get started." He swung the digital camera in front of him and fidgeted with the settings.

"Fantastic." I oozed appreciation enough for both

of us. His appearance wiped one task off my To Do list, though Zelda was certain to have other duties for me. Once Bill set to work, I waited for the avalanche.

Zelda merely said, "Remember…you represent the committee tonight." Then her face lit up, and she greeted a donor as if he were long-lost family.

I slipped away and found Ray chatting to George, who excused himself when I approached. "Sorry," I told Ray. "This isn't much fun for you."

"I'm fine. Like I said before, you still owe me a date."

"This absolutely does not count as a date."

"I wouldn't go that far." He caught me around the waist and drew me close.

A thrill rolled up my spine and coiled my breath in my chest. "You're pretty devious, aren't you?"

"Just tired of waiting."

The coil tightened, but I felt light enough to float. The only thing keeping me grounded was the intensity in his expression. That same feeling came back to me as when I'd looked at photos of him that my cousin had posted online. Looking at him, I could fall into the sea foam depths of his eyes. Rather than my old fear that I'd drown, I wanted to swim deeper.

My aunt's amplified voice through the speakers couldn't break us apart. She asked everyone to take their seats, indicating the servers entering through the kitchen doors with carts loaded with food.

"Guess we can't skip the meal." Ray arched a brow.

"I'd never hear the end of it." The flutters in my belly left no room for an appetite.

Ray took my hand, and we headed to our table.

After dinner, we sat through the obligatory speech. I took notes as Zelda implored the attendees and general public to fill the coffers, detailing the good the money would do. My cold statistics didn't compare to her descriptions of the students whose lives would be enriched and the city programs that would flourish rather than fail. Zelda was born for this role, and I couldn't wait for the final tally of contributions.

As my aunt spoke, my view of the world shifted. Almost as if I'd fallen into a vision, the world telescoped away from me. Ray sat close enough for his leg to brush mine, and I smelled the ocean scent of his aftershave. His baritone voice resonated along my skin, but I observed him as if from a great distance, as if with a stranger's eyes. The square set of his shoulders commanded attention, the stance of a man who was sure of himself and his purpose. Where I'd once glossed over his qualities, I viewed them as deeper aspects of his personality. Far from a weakness, his niceness was integrity. His handsomeness was an outward personification of his goodness. He was caring and gentle, yes, but I'd also glimpsed his steely determination, his strength. Not merely physical strength, but his strength of character. I'd never underestimate him again.

So when Zelda introduced the band and encouraged everyone to dance, I didn't hesitate as Ray turned to me and took my hand. He led me to the center of the floor and into his arms.

He murmured into my ear, "I'm glad you moved away when you were little."

"Oh, really?" I sputtered, uncertain whether to be insulted or not.

"I'm glad you're back now, of course. But this way, you never had to see my awkward teenage phase."

"Don't tell me you weren't a football star? Track star? Some kind of sports star."

"I played a few sports. I was never a star."

Add humility to his qualities. "I can't imagine you suffering through an awkward stage. Not like me, I'm sure."

"Ha, impossible. You had grace and poise when you were five."

"I did not." Dammit, I was blushing again.

"You were always beautiful."

His compliments flowed so naturally, I almost believed them. I hid pleasure behind a smirk. "God, I bet you were a lady killer even as a teenager, weren't you?"

"No." There was that seriousness again. "I don't play the field."

"Ever? In Javi's online photos, you were always surrounded by females."

"Maybe he only posted party pictures? Javi's the ladies' man, not me." He drew me closer against him. "I thought you didn't remember me before moving back to Santa Fe?"

"Only from Javi's pictures," I lied, then the need struck to change the subject. "So, you're a one-woman kind of guy?" I teased.

"Yes." Dead serious now.

"Good to know." I was surprised at just how delectable I found that tidbit. "But you never married?"

"Not yet. How about you?"

As we danced, the room seemed to spin around us instead of us moving across the floor. An odd sensation, but I wanted to stay in that center of calm with Ray. Nothing else could touch us.

I hated to admit I'd never considered marriage. "Not even close." It seemed an indicator of weakness.

"Haven't you ever been in love?"

Teasingly, I echoed his earlier reply. "Not yet. How about you?"

He held my gaze, and the blur of the world fell away. "I'm not sure, yet."

He pulled me close, and our bodies moved to the music in perfect time. For those precious moments, I had no worries. Nothing else existed except him and me, wrapped in a sublime bubble.

I tried not to think about how easily bubbles could burst.

****

The evening wore on without incident. By ten o'clock, the first guests began to leave. The perfect time to make our getaway. Ray stood close as I said goodnight to Zelda, and I blushed at hearing my own voice, breathy with anticipation.

My aunt gave Ray the once-over, as if she hadn't known him for years, or maybe she was seeing him in a new light. "Good night."

"I really enjoyed the meal," he said and took my hand.

I gave a light squeeze, a warning not to overdo it. He took the cue, and we walked outside to my SUV. He held the door open, but as I climbed inside, he was chivalrous enough to look away.

We drove in a comfortable silence to Ray's house. In his driveway, the moment might have been awkward with anyone else, but the anticipation of what might come next held me in its grips. I wasn't sure whether to cut the engine or not.

Ray took the decision into his own hands and reached over and twisted the key off. "Tonight was great. Thanks."

"Thanks for giving up your night at the bar to go with me."

"Anytime." He leaned in slowly.

I wanted to give in to the magic of the moment, but I cupped a hand against his cheek to block him. "I have a confession to make."

He slumped back against the seat. "You couldn't wait until after I kissed you?"

God, I should have. "You might not want to, after you hear."

He loosened his tie and sprawled his legs. "Hit me."

I'd already ruined the mood, but this might have long-term effects. Still, it had to be said. "I already told you I've seen Old Man Gloom. But he also spoke to me. Twice. The first time when I was five and again after I moved home."

Lips pursed, he gave me a single nod. "Well? What did he say?"

"One word. *Venganza.*" When he squinted at me, I translated. "Revenge."

A few long seconds later, he said, "You think this has something to do with the festival."

"This year marks the hundredth anniversary of Zozobra," I clarified, then shrugged. "None of this sounds logical or makes sense on paper." As a writer, it pained me to say so. "All I know is, I feel the truth of it inside."

199

"Rusty would probably agree," he said softly, as if to himself.

"He would?" At Ray's reluctant nod, I unlatched the door. "Then let's go talk to him." I was already rounding the front of the SUV when Ray lowered one foot to the ground.

"We might have to bribe him."

"Whatever it takes, Sunshine." I extended my hand.

His eyes narrowed, but he chuckled and let me pull him out. "You'd better be more diplomatic with Rusty than you are with me."

"I'll be the epitome of charm and delightfulness." I slammed the door and tugged him toward the house.

He looked at me askance. "Sure you have it in you?" The repressed laughter changed his voice.

I climbed the front step and whirled to catch him in my arms. "Positive." I pressed my lips to his, intending on a short kiss.

He wrapped his arms around me and held me there. Not that I needed convincing.

****

If slightly more disgruntled in his new surroundings, for the most part Rusty appeared his usual self. He'd nestled deep in the pinto-print chair. He grunted at Ray but interrupted his television viewing for a longer look at me. "You clean up nice."

"Not often." I hated to admit it. "But my aunt insisted I dress up for the fundraising dinner."

Rusty grated out a deep chuckle. "She's still bossing the festival planning committee around, eh?"

"Among other people," I admitted.

"She's quite a woman." He shook his head,

reminiscent of the shake a dog might give to clear its ears.

The leather cushions sighed as I sat on the sofa adjacent to his chair. "Were you two friends?"

"Eh. Friend-ly, I guess. Hard not to notice such a striking woman. Especially when she's extra bossy."

"Uh oh, I hope you didn't serve as one of her underlings." I said it as a joke, but in truth, wanted to learn his role in Zozobra, the festival, and especially what he knew about Zozobra, the spirit.

"When I was younger, I volunteered plenty. Not in any official capacity, but I got to see your aunt in action."

I was about to apologize when he added, "She's really something. You know, she was only seventeen when she took over as chair of that committee."

"Right, in 1964. I read about that, but I don't understand how a minor could take on such an important role in the community."

A shrug, and Rusty grew thoughtful. "They needed her. Her safety protocols secured the burning ritual, so it didn't get out of control again." He rested his head against the back of the chair and went back to watching the television show.

At first, I had thought my aunt eccentric, but her rules served a purpose—at least, Zelda believed they did. She knew better than me the dangers Old Man Gloom posed.

I glanced at Ray, who hesitated before taking a seat beside me.

Having him close gave me the courage to brave the harder questions. "Zelda's in danger, isn't she?"

Absently, Rusty nodded. "Every year."

"This year's different," I said. "It's worse."

His mouth twitched. "I believe it may be. A hundred years of anything," Rusty said, "and a man's soul cries out."

Ray fisted a hand against his knee. "It has no soul. It's a hunk of wood dressed in fabric."

His grandfather grunted. "You'll never understand if you close your mind."

I slipped my hand into Ray's. "He's right. My aunt believes the same thing, though she's understandably tight-lipped about it."

"Most people won't admit that they think Old Man Gloom is real." Rusty narrowed his eyes. "But they know. On some level."

"Not Old Man Gloom," I said. "The spirit inside the effigy."

Rusty let out a sound, half groan, half sigh. "Fire Eagle knew. He told us a long time ago. My father didn't believe him then."

"He knew my great grandfather?" I asked.

"Fire Eagle was part of that first circle of five. The ones who created Zozobra. So was my father."

Now I understood. "That's why one of the men resembled you."

Ray's hand tensed in mine. "You saw my great grandfather?"

"In the photo," I stammered. "Hanging in the hallway at the *Chronicle*."

"Oh, man." Mouth in a grim line, he slid his hand free from mine.

"What's wrong?" I'd done something I shouldn't have, but what?

He flailed a hand. "There's no getting past it, I

guess."

"I'm not following, sorry."

"I had to hear about this superstitious nonsense all my life." The glare Ray shot at his grandfather lasted only seconds but carried the weight of a lifetime.

Of what, I couldn't be sure, but his reaction had me stumped. "Ray, it's not nonsense."

Unfazed, Rusty remained silent.

"It's time to get real. Isn't it?" He pushed to a stand and said to me, "Sorry, I can't listen to any more. I just…" He pressed his hands down as if putting on virtual brakes, then strode out the back door.

I caught the inside of my lip between my teeth. "I apologize if I brought up a sore subject." Odd that Ray had listened to me spout off in the car, but when his grandfather joined the conversation, Ray shut him down.

"He's not fond of the subject," said Rusty.

"But he knows the threat is real."

"Oh, yes."

"What can I do, Rusty?" I wasn't sure if I referred to Ray, or the spirit.

"Give him time."

I nodded. "Guess I've done enough damage for one evening." And just when it had taken an interesting turn.

Rusty shifted in his chair. "My father spoke very highly of Fire Eagle. Everyone else said that Fire Eagle went a little bonkers."

Something about the way Rusty glanced at me spurred me on. "Do you know the real story?"

"A little of it." He looked up at me. "But Zelda knows all of it."

All I needed to hear. I leapt up and planted a kiss on his cheek. "Thanks, Rusty."

As I made my way toward the back door, he called, "You can find him at the fireplace. He stares into those flames like he's at church."

Halfway out the door, that caught me up. Rusty's face gave nothing else away, so I slipped outside. Loud crackles and pops echoed across the back yard. Ray leaned forward, elbows propped on his knees, focused on the blaze dancing within the white stucco's portal like it contained the oracle and he was seeking the secrets of the universe.

Hard to interrupt someone so enraptured, so I stood to the side of the bench. Only for a second, then he turned.

"Hey. Sorry about that."

I sat beside him. "I didn't mean to dredge up anything between you two." Obviously, their family had dealt with Old Man Gloom for too long, and the spirit had wedged between them.

"You have nothing to apologize for. I over-reacted. Rusty…" His breath strangled the remaining words into silence.

I clasped my hand in his. "Corny as it might sound, everything will be all right." Even between the two of them.

A slow smile erased his intense frown, and as he searched my face, Ray visibly emerged from the gloom encasing him. "Not corny at all."

The glow of firelight played across him, and I wished I could melt into that warmth. "I have some things to finish before then."

"Now?"

"Putting them off will only make things worse." I leaned in to kiss him.

"Did I ever tell you you're beautiful and strange?"

"You forgot amazing. Wonderful. Mystic—" Another kiss cut off the word. I surrendered to the moment, into the blissful world where only Ray and I existed. A temporary escape, but enough to give me strength to face what came next.

Chapter Seventeen

The women in my family had great power against spirits and people. Against one another, the odds were more evenly balanced. My aunt may not have wanted to reveal much about my great grandfather, but my stubbornness matched hers.

I called her the moment I climbed into my SUV at Ray's house and wouldn't take no for an answer. I had to speak with her. Tonight.

"Fine," my aunt snapped. "But hurry up."

I arrived at her house in record time. Zelda let me in and gestured me to the sofa, then sat in the chair and curled her legs under her, wine glass in hand.

"I need to know everything. Starting with Fire Eagle." More than what I'd learned in the visions. He had to be the key.

After a long exhale, Zelda began. "For as long as I can remember, Fire Eagle lived in a shack in the Sangre de Cristo Mountains. We tried many times to move him into town, but he refused. He told us he had to stay close to where the spirits ran free. Where they danced. Where they needed to remain. Away from Santa Fe. He said it was his duty to guard them." She seemed to gather herself. "He died the summer before you moved."

In 1992. The summer before my first festival. When my brother died. "Why didn't anyone say anything? There was no funeral…" I hadn't known my great grandfather well, but no one even mentioned his passing.

Sadness filled her eyes. "We didn't find out until the day after Zozobra. When he didn't show up for the festival, I sent someone to look for him. He had passed about a week before." Surprise crept into her voice, even now.

"Of natural causes?" I asked, not really wanting to know.

Zelda's hard glance was answer enough.

"Do you think that's why Old Man Gloom killed Michael? Because Fire Eagle wasn't there to stop him?"

"Perhaps." She sounded as hollow as her gaze.

Trauma had touched every one of us. But I still needed to piece it all together. "And that's why my parents moved to California."

Absently, she ran her thumb across the rim of her glass. "They feared for your safety. You know that."

I did. But, knowing didn't ease the pain. Even at five years old, I knew running away wasn't the answer. So much about our family was still so screwed up.

I rubbed my head. "I found an old photo of the committee. From 1964. The year you became chair."

She cut her gaze to me. "Yes, I was seventeen."

"Seventeen," I repeated in disbelief, though she'd confirmed what I already knew. "Not even of legal age. Why would a teenage girl want to join a festival planning committee?"

"For the same reason you did, dear. Duty."

Tired of this little dance, I sighed. "Zelda, seriously." Time for her to come clean.

"I am serious. It is my duty to perform the rituals.

Fire Eagle taught them to me when I turned sixteen. For years, my mother helped, as well. Our family has an obligation to protect the people of Santa Fe, who don't understand the real significance of Zozobra."

"Fire Eagle knew about the danger of naming the effigy." I understood that much.

"Yes. That same year they named Old Man Gloom, Fire Eagle built the cabin in the mountains, I'm told."

I was still trying to connect the dots into something that made sense.

Worry tinged Zelda's solemn expression. "It's late. You should go home."

My back curled, sure as if she'd knocked the air from me. Tossing me to the curb? Now? "Aunt Zelda…"

"We'll talk more about this. Enough for tonight. My head is killing me." She used her authoritative tone and shooed at me.

Arguing would do no good. Much as I hated to put my heels on again, I stepped into my shoes and sucked air between my teeth. My poor feet would pay for this night.

When I stood, I felt fifty pounds heavier. Until I processed everything, I had nothing else to offer my aunt. No ideas to save the day, no grand superhero finale to eliminate the threat.

My feet throbbed as I followed her to the entrance.

She smiled over her shoulder at me. "Great job tonight, Marissa."

It took me a moment to realize she meant the dinner. Already, it seemed like weeks ago. "Thank you."

She held the door open. "Good night."

That was it, then. I was dismissed. "Night."

When I stepped out into the night, the wind rushed around me, tangling my hair around my face. I brushed away the strands, but each time, they plastered across my cheek, my eyes, as fast as I could push them away. My vision blocked, I slowed to avoid tripping.

"Dammit." I swiped, but the breeze pushed them back. I stumbled off the path. "Sonofa—"

Abruptly, I stilled myself and closed my eyes. The tension in the air blew around me like the wind. Old Man Gloom wanted to aggravate me. He was laughing at my angry response, and he wanted more.

I wouldn't play into his hands. "No way, Old Man." With a deep breath, I finger-combed my hair and knotted it to one side. A simple motion, but I'd reclaimed control of my hair, at least. Gusts puffed at my face, but the strands remained bound. I hummed a lilting tune. The wind screeched past me like a wounded animal.

The air stilled until the night turned peaceful.

With a smile of satisfaction, I walked to my vehicle, radiating electric positivity.

****

Maybe I'd finally discovered my superpower.

With a blues riff, my cell announced a text message. My grin stretched ear to ear after I swiped the phone screen. The positivity I sent out into the universe was returning good things to me. Like Ray. His message read:

—Still think MMA isn't your thing?—

I typed my reply:

—I'm reconsidering.—

I was a far cry from some sort of a super hero, but

an upbeat outlook would help me overcome a sparring defeat, at least.

Ray:

—*How about tomorrow morning? Loser buys dinner.*—

My smile quirked as my fingers moved.

—*I thought the winner was supposed to buy?*—

His answer came seconds later.

—*Twisted my arm. See you in the morning?*—

I didn't hesitate, either.

—*I'll be there. And that's not all I intend to twist.*—

I re-read the last part, and then deleted the sentence before hitting send. After the fundraising dinner, I'd fled his house so fast that I may have left his boxers in a twist. I'd treated him terribly, practically as an afterthought. Only because the weird, urgent circumstances had demanded it.

I just hoped the semi-calm of the week carried over into the weekend. Despite my sarcasm in nicknaming him Sunshine, Ray truly did create warmth and a good feeling, and it was time I had more of that in my life. And time I gave back more of that, too.

By the time morning arrived and I was entering the fitness studio, I was reminded of how woefully out of shape I'd grown. I hadn't kept up with running or yoga or spinning. Somehow, biking after work had lost its appeal. The possibility of running into Señor Zozobra, or the swarm of black things chasing me, stole the fun.

Watching the others warm up erased any possibility of fun as well. I was about to be slaughtered.

I lifted my chin and squared my shoulders as I followed Ray to the mats, but my positive mind control sputtered. Time after time, he proved me right by laying me flat. My reactions were slow, and I took a pounding. I was glad when the two hours were up.

"Guess you can't use me as a success story." I winced as I stretched.

"Success requires practice. You have to come to class more often."

"You're not embarrassed by me?" I half joked.

"On the contrary. I see great potential."

For what? I wanted to ask but pressed my lips together.

He lightly clasped his arms. "So. We still on for tonight?"

"You're not getting out of it again." My insides did a salsa dance. We'd be alone again. This was going to get very real, very fast.

He leaned close. "Neither are you."

The salsa became a flock of swallows swirling through the sky. I hugged myself to stay steady against the whirl of thoughts. Like, he might be sorry afterward or maybe, disappointed. I might not be ready to jump into another relationship.

But this was just dinner. Who said anything about making it long-term?

"Hey." His hand warmed my arm in a gentle touch. "You all right?"

He'd noticed me silently freaking out? "Great. Absolutely fantastic." How smooth of me. "So, what time?"

"Six sound good?"

"Yes. But this time, let's go casual. Since we already did the semi-formal thing."

"But you clean up so nicely," he teased.

"Don't worry." I shrugged a shoulder. "I'll make myself…presentable."

His grin broke into a smile. "Casual sounds perfect."

"Yeah." It did. A little too perfect. The flutters were kicking up in my belly again. I had to get out of there before I made a complete fool of myself. "See you tonight."

I practically floated out of the fitness studio, and my SUV might have been a flying carpet on the drive home. I spent the rest of the morning cleaning the apartment, a chore I tended to eschew in favor of more interesting activities. Like sleeping. Tidying up kept me in motion, at least, and I worked off some nervous energy before getting ready for dinner.

Slightly superstitious, I decided against the black top I'd purchased for our initial disaster date. Silver jewelry was a staple, and the flame necklace had become a daily necessity. If I didn't wear it, the pendant's absence felt like a phantom limb.

I slipped on a silky cobalt blue blouse and jeans, and my worn leather boots. At least some part of me would be comfy tonight.

On my doorstep at six sharp, Ray was Mr. Punctuality. I opened the door, and he scanned me open-mouthed.

"Hey. You look amazing." He oozed sincerity.

I couldn't help but grin. "So do you." He'd smoothed some product in his hair, and the tousled look suited him. So did the black t-shirt, the old jeans with just the right fit, and his scuffed black boots.

"Stop teasing. You said casual." Sounding apologetic, he scanned himself.

I grabbed my handbag. "You do casual very well." The mix of angel and bad boy was irresistible. Best of all, he had no clue about the effect he had on women. He was certainly having an effect on me.

He extended an elbow. "Ready?"

Wow. Now that was formal. But I slipped my arm through his. "As I'll ever be."

We were halfway to his truck when I realized, with a gasp, how rude I'd been.

"Did you forget something?"

"My manners. I'm sorry. I never asked if you wanted to come in."

His grin went lopsided. "You can make it up to me, later."

The swallows in my stomach went Cirque du Soleil. My throat went dry, and I couldn't speak, so I climbed into the truck when he opened the door.

He sent me another grin, more uncertain, as he started the truck. We drove mostly in silence, the small talk awkward stuff about the radio station, what type of music we liked, where to eat.

"Not la Fonda," I blurted. I didn't want any visions interrupting my night out. "I heard it's haunted." True enough. Legend had it that the ghost of a salesman who'd lost his company's fortune leapt to his death down a deep well. When the restaurant was built, the La Plaza dining room sat directly above the well, and diners have reported seeing an apparition walk to the center of the room and disappear into the floor exactly as he'd disappeared into the well so long ago. With my luck, that would be the middle of our table.

"How about the Dancin' Cowgirl?" he asked.

"I've heard good things about it." Such as, it

tended to be a rowdy crowd, which would fill in stretches of silence. "I'd be fine with the El Malena fajita truck, really."

"He's gone for the day. Plus, no margaritas."

"Well then, that settles it. Lunch only at the fajita truck." Margaritas were sounding better by the minute. They might help me come up with less lame jokes as the evening progressed.

We headed for the Dancin' Cowgirl and stood fidgeting while we waited for the hostess. "Dining room or patio?"

"Patio?" Ray asked me.

"Yes." The rumors had proved true. Inside, the Dancin' Cowgirl crowd was loud, maybe a bit too, though I loved the cowgirl flair of the place. As we trailed the hostess, I admired the Old West memorabilia featuring trick riders, sharp shooters, and all manner of cowgirl.

The outside crowd was more subdued, but not by much. A guitarist played at the far end of the patio. Small lanterns, strung above the metal and wooden bistro tables, provided a romantic atmosphere, though the sun hadn't yet set.

The hostess led us to a corner table close to the building. A server in tight jeans and bandana around her neck appeared almost immediately. The brim of her hat was almost as wide as her smile. I didn't hesitate to order a margarita. Ray asked for a beer.

We exchanged nervous smiles before looking over the menu. Once we had our drink, Ray raised his glass. "Cheers."

A wave of guilt halted me. "First, let me apologize."

"For what?" His sunny expression wavered.

"I had such a good time with you at the fundraising dinner. Then I ruined it."

"No, you didn't. I did." He set down his glass and reached for my hand. "I'm sorry I ran out on you that night."

I'd give him some leeway. "Technically, you were already home, so I ran out on you."

"I shouldn't have waited so long to get in touch with you."

The lonely girl in me wanted to agree, but his sudden seriousness gave me pause. "Rusty said I should give you time, so I did."

"Rusty," he muttered, but chuckled.

"Ray…" God, I really hated to ruin another date. I pleaded with my eyes for him to open up and just tell me whatever. If he told me to shut up about Old Man Gloom, I would. I'd never mention it again to him. Or try not to.

He braced an arm against his seat and leaned toward me. "I guess my grandfather clued you in on our family connection."

"No. I'm still clueless."

"Hardly." He blew out a breath. "This is a long story."

"I have all night." Realizing what I'd implied, my face went hot. Thank goodness for low lighting.

But he was too lost in his thoughts to tease me. "I'm going to lay it all out, then. You already know that both our great grandfathers were part of the group that founded Zozobra."

"And helped give the festival its name."

"Even before they took the festival public, things

began to go wrong."

"Like what?"

"People claimed their problems came back on them double. There was more trouble in the city."

"Just like there is this year."

"Yeah." He sounded reluctant. "I didn't want to believe it. Whenever Rusty tried to talk to me about it, I'd shut him down."

"But you knew, didn't you? Isn't that really why you became a firefighter? Because you felt that same need to protect people?"

"I was there the night your house burned down. I saw your brother in the window. He was yelling to me."

To Ray? My throat tightened. "What did he say?"

"He told me to watch over you. I swore that I would. Then you and your family disappeared." He glanced around, then went on. "I heard something else in the fire that night. Did you?"

"Michael," I whispered, trying desperately to recall something, anything besides his frantic cries. "I don't know. At the time, I thought he was yelling...to me. But I was screaming, too, and so was my mother. Everything's jumbled in my head."

When I looked up at Ray, his eyes had become a bottomless sea, illuminated in their depths by a powerful light. The impression I'd gotten of him in Javi's photos had been completely wrong. Ray radiated a force that I didn't understand, except that it was the opposite of the gloominess embodied in the spirit.

"Don't go chasing after him anymore," Ray said.

He looked so sincere. So worried. I hated to disappoint him. "I have to."

He grasped my hand, stroked his thumb across the

top, seemingly lost in thought. "Then I will, too. I'll be right by your side."

"I'm not sure you can."

"I'll be by your side, anyway."

The power of what he said encased me in a sort of haze. It wrapped around us both and blocked out the rest of the world. The server came and went like a shadow figure in a dream. Time slipped off track and was irrelevant. We ordered our meals, finished them, and shared a few glasses of wine.

Then Ray was driving me home and then opening my door outside my apartment. I climbed out and into his embrace. "Stay awhile." I didn't want to let him go.

The stars hung crisp in the summer sky. Like two halves of a whole, we leaned on each other and walked to the door.

Once I snapped on the lights, the haze dissipated. He shuffled his feet, awkwardly boyish.

A case of shyness hit me, too. "Come in."

He took a few steps, glanced at the sofa and the small coffee table, the only furniture in the room. "Are you sure you actually live here?"

I set my purse on the kitchen table, hoping he wouldn't notice how the tile top angled up to a backsplash and connected it to the wall. I suddenly felt like a fraud, an imposter living in someone else's house. "I kept things sparse because I wasn't sure how long I planned to stay."

He leaned a shoulder against the arched entryway to the other room. "In the apartment? Or Santa Fe?"

I sent him a wry smile. "The apartment."

"Any verdict, yet?"

"The place is nice enough. We'll see." Not a

217

subject I wanted to explore at the moment. "Want a beer?"

"Sure."

A jab of pain shot through my inner thigh when I bent at the fridge. His boots thudded up behind me.

"You okay?" he asked.

"Just sore from this morning. That's the last time I fall for the I-promise-I'll-go-easy-on-you routine." Grinning, I handed him the beer.

He set it atop the table, then dug his fingers into my shoulders and moved them in a circular rotation. "Better?"

"Sublime." I wouldn't tell him the injury was in my groin. He'd already rotated his hands down my back.

"You're so tight," he noted. "Your muscles are screaming for a massage."

"They're moaning in ecstasy at the moment." Head drooping, I lazily looped my arms around his waist. His breaths had grown deeper, faster. His warm scent filled my senses.

"Mar," he said in a look-over-here hush.

Intrigued, I looked up, and his face flushed with pleasure. He stopped massaging and closed his arms around me. Our lips met in a kiss, sweet and intoxicating at first, then ravishingly hungry. My body was electrified, and I stood on tiptoe to press deeper into him. Our hands were everywhere, dragging across hips and waists, neck and cheek, grasping hair, locking us together. We were two butterflies fluttering against one another in mid-air.

An insistent noise intruded, and he eased away. "Dammit."

My brain function returned enough for me to identify the noise as his phone. "Work?" *Don't answer.*

Checking the cell display, he winced. "Yes. Sorry." He answered, sighed, said, "No one else available?" Another sigh. "Okay. Yeah." He slid the cell into his back pocket. "One of the girls scheduled for tonight called in sick."

"And you have to substitute."

He pressed his forehead against mine. "Sorry."

"Me, too." I rubbed his back beneath his shirt. "We can go out some other night."

"Huh, and I don't have to pin you to the floor to get you to agree?"

My smile felt drunken, but not from alcohol. "All pinning will be optional."

Hips against mine, he pressed me against the wall. Blue blazed in his eyes, and I wanted to fall into that fire, let it consume me, and afterward, I'd rise again from the ashes, renewed. Ready to burn again.

He stroked the hair from my face, then lightly touched his lips to mine. "I could come back after the shift's ended."

"You'll be exhausted by then."

He barely shook his head, as if he couldn't tear his gaze from me. "Not for a long time."

"Tomorrow's Sunday." I said it to myself, to mark our place in time because it had become a hazy stream again.

He gave a nod.

"You don't have anything planned?" I asked.

He shook his head once.

"Neither do I."

The blue in his eyes ignited into flame. "I'll be here

at ten after six."

My "Okay," came out in a whisper, nothing like the rush of need washing over me like a waterfall. When he kissed me goodbye, then pulled away, I spun like a leaf adrift, then floated. The roar of his truck's engine, the headlights swinging through the windows like search lights, the crunch of tires on gravel. Only after silence settled was I released from the magnet hold of the wall.

Cool, wet metal registered on my hands as I put the unopened beer back in the fridge. Still abuzz, I floated to the bedroom, my senses vibrating with Ray's warmth. Each memory of his touch sent a new wave through me. The memory of the intensity in his eyes jolted me anew. The vibrancy washed over me in a steady hum, one that a small voice in my head told me I should recognize. I lay on my bed, barely touching the mattress. The hum carried me through the hours one by one.

At six o'clock, I drifted out of my bedroom and through the living room, drawn by the pull of his energy. It pulsed near the entryway, and I opened the door. Headlights approached, the truck jerked to a stop. Ray flew out, a blur as he rushed to my open arms.

I breathed in his warm scent. "You came back."

"Yes." He kissed my forehead. "Yes." My nose. "Yes." My mouth.

His *yes* reverberated through me. The hum burst to life.

I should have recognized it earlier, but it had been so long. Now I knew what it was.

Happiness.

Chapter Eighteen

The Monday morning staff meeting at the *Chronicle* had become a freak show these past few weeks, with new little horrors popping up every day, and Weller dishing out assignments for us reporters to cover them. I'd come to expect the worst.

This morning, I braced for disaster, but there was none.

Weller scowled as he shuffled through his notes. "Pretty quiet today."

"Even at City Hall," joked Fisher.

Leaning an elbow against the table, Ashley muttered, "Don't jinx us."

The absence of trouble made me uneasy. It was too quiet. As if Old Man Gloom were gathering up his minions, saving the worst for last. The proverbial calm before the shitstorm of gloom. With less than two weeks before he was scheduled to burn, I had to wonder what Señor Zozobra was up to.

The sound Weller made when he cleared his throat rivaled an earthquake. "We have many events to cover in the coming weeks. Close on the heels of la Fiesta is the Ren Faire, with the Wind and Chile Fiesta the following week, immediately followed by the Concorso."

"Concorso?" I wondered aloud.

Ashley affected a sickly expression. "A fancy term

for car show." The way she dragged out the last two words, she considered it tantamount to torture.

"Your obvious love for the sport just bought you a press pass to the Concorso, Stirling." Weller grinned like a toad and went on. "This week, world-class riders and their mounts arrive for the Equestrian Event. Tahy, why don't you and Larson take a run over there on Friday and try to come up with some new, interesting angle?"

Fisher chuckled. "No beating a dead horse, in other words."

"Right." From their sarcasm, I gathered that task would be nearly impossible to put a fresh face on a longstanding event. I had a feeling I'd share Ashley's pain.

Weller grunted. "I hope your sources can dredge up some news worth reading. Pound the pavement, if you have to. Man in the street head shots to accompany some issue-related question. Or something mundane. But get *some* content." He waved a finger in my general direction. "Oh, and Tahy, write an update on committee goings-on. Spice it up, if necessary."

"You mean, lie?" My smile pulled into a smirk. He knew as well as I did that the committee itself was about as lively as the life-sized sculptures of the dinosaurs just south off Cerrillos Road. And about as immovable.

Others snickered, but then scrambled away the moment Weller dismissed us. He was less quick, and I held back, too.

"Mr. Weller? I've been meaning to ask…why was no other *Chronicle* staff assigned to be this year's committee liaison before me?"

"Who told you that?" he practically spat.

"No one. I gathered—"

"In fact, there were two. Freddy Ortiz served for a few months before he resigned his position at the paper." He spoke as if reciting a practiced spiel, and without looking at me.

Right, Ortiz. He was the reporter whose leaving had allowed me to return. "What happened to the first one? Did the committee scare him away?" I joked, though I could easily imagine Zelda's glare inspiring a permanent cower in anyone.

Still not meeting my gaze, he said, "She...left for personal reasons."

"Oh." Sounded like too much of a coincidence. I wondered who she was and made a mental note to ask around. Jill, at the front desk, had proved a good source for such news.

He rose and finally leveled his gaze at me. "If you don't have enough assignments, I can dredge up a few more."

Obvious hint taken. "I'll let you know after I finish."

I skirted around him and out the door. As I headed to my desk, Ashley's stood vacant. I envied her, being out in the sunshine, but for now, my work was here. After refilling my coffee mug, I wrote the committee update piece faster than I anticipated and emailed it to the editor with a satisfied sigh.

My desk phone rang, and the display showed FRONT DESK. Perfect timing. "Hey, Jill. Did you read my mind?"

"What? No. I was calling to ask if you took the star decorations?"

My pleasant mood fled. "No, why?"

"I can't find them anywhere. People have been coming in all morning, and I ran low, and was going to let you know I needed more. But I took a quick rest room break, and when I came back, the box was gone."

"The container and all?"

"Yes. I'd shoved it under my desk, close enough to reach but out of sight, you know? There were maybe twenty left."

"And now they're gone?" Box and all. My logical brain said any thief would grab the container for convenience sake, but another small voice argued that would allow him or her to steal them without having to touch them. Which would be a bad sign.

Jill heaved a sigh. "I guess that answers my question about whether you took it."

"No, not me." I pinched the bridge of my nose. "But I'll bring you another one today. All right?" As I spoke, I typed an email to the web content manager, requesting her to post a notice on the *Chronicle* site so anyone who didn't receive a star today would be able to retrieve one. Soon.

While asking Jill to let walk-in donors know, I pulled out my cell and dialed my aunt. I switched phone calls like a trapeze artist switching swings.

"Marissa?" Zelda sounded confused. "Aren't you at work?"

"At the moment, yes." In fact, I was already heading out the back to the parking lot. "But I need a refill of the stars. We ran out, suddenly."

"Suddenly?" Doubt came through in the sharp downturn of her voice.

I climbed in the SUV. "Do you have more at your

house? I'd like to come pick them up now, if possible."

"No, we moved them last night," Zelda said. "To the warehouse."

"The warehouse?" Dread stole my voice, and the words came out as a whisper. "Is someone there to let me in?" I didn't want to be alone with the effigy for even a few minutes.

"Of course not." A loud breath, and then rustling, as if she shifted the cell in her hands. "Give me twenty minutes. I'll meet you there."

"Thanks." I ended the call, then wondered aloud, "How does she do that?" Make me feel so incompetent, and then I always thanked her for it?

I drove as slowly as I could across town, even stopping for a chai latte along the way, but still arrived at the warehouse before my aunt. The midday sun heated my auto interior, and the SUV's air conditioner left much to be desired, so I reluctantly climbed out and waited in the shade of the building.

Hurry, Zelda. Before the spirit of Old Man Gloom pays me a visit. The effigy within usually gave off a palpable presence. A malevolence. Today, all I could sense was a void. The emptiness was even stranger than the ill will.

All remained quiet until my aunt's vehicle crunched along the gravel driveway. Rather than relief that nothing weird had happened, I was again struck with the notion that the spirit was elsewhere. And up to no good.

No sooner had my aunt stepped out of her car than her tirade began. "You should have let me know long before now that you were running low."

I stood my ground, literally. "We weren't. The box

somehow went missing."

She halted beside me. "Missing?"

"Or was stolen." Her scrutiny was worse than being subjected to the rack, every moment tightening like a turn of the screws. "It's just gone."

Her eyes narrowed. "I don't like that."

The lack of finger pointing came as a relief. "Neither do I. That's why I called you right away."

Her *hm* held a tincture of doubt and bewilderment, then she unlocked the side door and flipped on the light switch. With no one else around, the buzz of the fluorescent lights overhead sounded louder than usual. Old Man Gloom sprawled in the center of the space in disconnected parts. His head turned toward the back wall, I was glad to note. No eerie stare from the puppet, but I'd bet his eyes would be empty anyway.

"He's not here," I whispered, and rubbed my arms.

"Who?" my aunt absently asked as she headed toward a metal cabinet.

"Old Man Gloom."

While unlocking the storage unit, she inclined her head toward the giant puppet. "He's right there. And he's staying there until the day before Zozobra." She sounded defiant.

She was pointedly ignoring my real meaning, but I wouldn't argue. "Don't you normally move the frame a few days ahead of the festival?"

She pinned me with an admonishing look. "There's nothing normal about the centennial event." She dragged a heavy box off the shelf and opened the top. "Ah, here we go. Grab the dolly over there, please."

The metal contraption handled three boxes easily, but even with wheels, the load was a bear to move. The wheels squeaked as I steered the dolly. My poor SUV groaned as I dropped each box into the back.

"Lock up," Zelda said, "after you return that to its proper place."

"I will." I wheeled the empty cart alongside her as she walked to her car.

A wave, and she climbed in. "Talk to you soon."

Without hesitation, I pushed the dolly inside. The effigy lay as cold and dead as before.

I stared at it but discerned no aura of evil. "Where are you? And what are you up to?" Only silence answered me.

With no other excuse to linger, I locked up and drove to the *Chronicle* to make my delivery. Jill spotted me entering and rushed over from her desk.

"Let me help. Those things weigh a ton." She took hold of one corner, and together, we hauled the box and set it beside her chair.

Straightening, I rubbed the tension from my lower back. "Thanks. Let me know if you start to run out." I'd keep the other two boxes handy, just in case.

"Believe me, I will. Everyone wants one of these commemorative stars." The chair cushion sighed under her weight. "I'm glad we don't have to hand them out every year."

Speaking of previous festivals… "Hey, I have a weird question. Do you remember the last *Chronicle* liaison person? And why she left?"

"Yeah, weird is right." Eyes wide, Jill shook her head. "She claimed to be sensitive to ghosts. Lord, she had a story for every house she lived in, who haunted it and why, sometimes grisly details about their deaths. I went to lunch with her a few times but stopped going when she acted more spooked every week. Nervous and jittery like you wouldn't believe. Then one day, she didn't show up for work and never came back. We found out later she'd moved to Seattle."

I made a mental note never to confide in Jill. "She never gave an explanation?"

"Not officially, but…" Jill swept her gaze left and right, and whispered, "A few staffers said she kept talking about a ghost. Every time she worked for the committee, the spirit did something nasty, though she'd never say what, exactly. Which was unusual, given how she loved to talk about the paranormal. HR wrote the incident off as a mental breakdown and recommended treatment. Guess she came up with her own remedy."

"Interesting." For most people, the spirit came through as an irritation or sadness, a magnification of their own troubles. Bad luck for my predecessor to take a job that put her in direct contact with a hostile spirit.

Now that bad luck was mine.

****

The uneventful day left too much of a lull and played havoc on my imagination. My curiosity built to near bursting. At least if I had a hint about what Old Man Gloom was up to, I could prepare. I didn't like being left in the dark like this. Not one little bit.

When Fisher called out, "Happy hour," I couldn't follow fast enough. I welcomed the bustle of a crowded bar.

Ashley, however, didn't budge from her seat except to shake her head. "Not tonight."

A chill snuck over me and prickled up the back of my neck. "You're not coming?"

Her fingernails clacked over the keyboard, and she

took sudden interest in whatever appeared on the screen. "I have plans."

"A date?" *Please, not with Señor Zozobra.* Then added, "He *called* you?" Shock lifted my tone up an octave or so, and I managed to stop myself before adding, *on the phone?*

"No." Turning toward me, she drew out the word in wary suspicion, and went still, like a rabbit who found itself facing down a wolf. "I ran into him today."

How convenient. Or it might explain why I hadn't seen the corporeal spirit recently. He was stalking Ashley. My mind was racing, but my body seemed to move in slow motion. Untold horror might await her, but I couldn't warn her. And if I didn't lighten up, she'd bolt.

"Come on," I teased. "Happy hour won't be the same without you." Yeah, that was over the top.

She sent me a look of disgust mixed with confusion, then pretended to weigh her two options. "Let's see…hot guy? Or coworkers I see all day long? Not much of a decision."

My muscles tightened, the strain of holding back the "*Stop her…*" screaming in my head. "Why not bring him to the bar?"

After a cold glare, she asked, "Why would I want to do that?"

Because at least I could keep an eye on her there? Get an up-close and personal look at the man who'd swept her off her feet? Hope piled against hope that I was wrong, and that he was an ordinary guy.

But all I said was, "Why not?" A shaky delivery, at best.

"I think I covered it under the 'Coworkers I See All

229

Day Long' clause. Plus, nothing kills the romance faster than everyone talking about politics and work."

Cold fear twisted in my stomach. "Ashley, seriously. I wish you'd reconsider. How well do you know this man?"

A laugh bubbled from her perfect red lips. "Honey, you need to get out more often. That is the whole point of dating. To get to know him."

"But he might not be what you think he is." She would be alone with him, and he could take full advantage of her vulnerable emotions.

With a toss of her head, she gave a sultry, open-mouthed laugh. "Guess I'll find out. I'm hoping to get to know him very well."

I bit the inside of my cheek. Should I warn her? I could imagine how that scenario would play out:

Me: You can't go out with him tonight. Or ever. He's the corporeal version of Old Man Gloom. An evil spirit in the form of a man.

Her: You are more bonkers than I thought. Adios.

And then I'd be quietly fired. I'd have to find another way. "Please be careful."

She hooted a laugh. "You are too much, Marissa. Were you house bunny of your college dorm? I don't need anyone watching over me. Thanks anyway."

Yet if anything happened to her, I'd never forgive myself. I was the only one who knew the truth. I needed more information. "So, where are you going?"

"Not," she came down hard on the "t", "to la Fonda."

I tried to sound casual, though my heart pumped hard. "Out to dinner? A movie?" The young Zozobra sitting in a movie theater eating popcorn and watching a romcom? That was too much to wrap my head around.

She paused to assess me, in wonder rather than hostility this time. "You just don't give up, do you?"

I mimicked her cool with a fluttering wave and turned away. "I was just making conversation. Forget it."

She exaggerated a sigh. "I told him I needed a kickass margarita, so I'm meeting him at Raphael's. They make the absolute best margaritas, with fresh-squeezed limes and gold tequila."

"Raphael's. That's a few miles outside Santa Fe, right? Almost to Taos?" Which would make it more difficult to spy on her. She'd easily play into his hands.

She slung her laptop bag over her shoulder. "It's an easy enough drive. And afterward, maybe I'll let him take me to the Ojo Caliente hot springs." She arched her brow suggestively.

Oh God, no. I was sure I must seem like a lunatic to her, so I forced a grin. "Much more romantic than happy hour." And much more dangerous. The hot springs might become boiling hot.

She *tsk*'d. "Aw, don't look so sad. You'll find a man of your own."

If talking about guys would keep her here, I'd bury my discomfort beneath a casual pleasantness. "Already covered." Feigning a coy smile, I shrugged. "Maybe."

"Really?" She set her bags on the desktop again. "Anyone I know?"

Bingo. Now to reel her in, if only for a few minutes. Until I figured out what to do. "He's a firefighter. Ray White."

"You little vixen." She rested her elbows atop her briefcase and relaxed over it.

All I had to do was keep talking. "We've only gone out a few times. Well, technically, once," I realized with a shock. Since our second date, we'd spent some spare time together, but officially hadn't dated.

None of that mattered. The hum of happiness lived inside me.

Rustling noises snapped me out of my head. Ashley lifted her bags. "You'll have to tell me more. Tomorrow."

While I'd become lost in my thoughts, I'd lost Ashley. She was already heading toward the rear entry, her step so light she might be walking on air.

By the time I thought to call after her, she was outside.

"You'll have to tell me all about your night, too." My murmur faded. Except tomorrow might be too late.

Only a few people remained in the newsroom, too engrossed in their phones or computers to notice me. The outlines of desks, walls, split into two, phantom images overlaid the original and shifted apart in a slow carousel ride around me. The phantom figures gathered their belongings and departed. My stomach churned as the spin continued while the place quieted, then spirit images of my coworkers entered, worked at their desks, got coffee, worked, and left again. There was Weller, and Mike Fisher, and Larsen the photographer, Juanita from IT, Bernard from HR. I even saw myself, in transparent form, moving around the room, doing my job.

The scene kept revolving as the workday played out to its end. Repeatedly, my spirit-self glanced over at Ashley's desk. Her chair had remained empty throughout this bizarre theme park ride. As *Chronicle* staff began to leave, the phantom images began to settle over the solid parts of the newsroom. The floor no longer spun. The walls, offices, and desks slid to a halt and stayed static. The same people who'd stayed late were still in their chairs, concentrating on finishing their work.

My head still spun, though. I pressed my hands to my desktop until I steadied. Nothing could calm my thoughts. My pulse pounded in my ears. Sleepwalking dreams were one thing, but visions while I was awake completely rattled me.

And I wasn't sure what to make of what I'd seen. Was this a sign that Ashley wouldn't show up for work tomorrow?

Thousands of tiny pins prickled at my skin. *Not if I can help it.*

I fumbled my cell into my hands and tapped through the screens. My fingers flew as if they knew who to search for before I did. I pressed the contact name, and on the second ring, he answered.

"Javi," I said breathlessly.

"Hey, Mar. What's up?"

Bless his endlessly cheery self. I hoped it would see him through a favor. "Are you busy?"

"Right now? Well…"

I squeezed my eyes shut. "Can I take you for a drink? It's really important."

"Are you all right?"

Not really. My breaths were becoming shallower, my heartbeat erratic. "I'll pick you up, okay? Are you at home?"

"At the station. But—"

"Please, Javi. I really need you to do this." Without

asking any more questions, I hoped. I probably should have called Ray instead. Then I could have pretended to Ashley that he'd asked me to dinner at Raphael's, a more plausible excuse to crash Ashley's romantic dinner with the vengeful Zozobra. Or at least keep an eye on them.

"Yeah, sure," he said. "Happy to." Though he sounded anything but happy.

After ending the call, I acted as if by rote, instinct urging me on. I was in my SUV. I was driving. I saw nothing except the road ahead of me and the nightmarish images in my head. Ashley's body engulfed in flames, from the inside out. Then somehow I found myself outside Javi's place and blasted the horn.

He jogged outside and leaned his elbows against the passenger window frame. "Mar, you're worrying me."

How could I explain so he'd want to help? Without lying? "Sorry. I need to rescue a friend from a creep." The simple truth. Hopefully it would work.

"Why didn't you say so?" He slid onto the passenger seat and tapped the dashboard. "Let's go."

"Thanks." I slammed it into gear and took off. "I owe you."

"Don't kill me before you can repay me." His teasing rang hollow as he glanced over with obvious nervousness.

I knew I was driving like a maniac, but an urge was driving me. Undeniable, but blind. I acted on intuition, without question. If I didn't find Ashley, she'd be lost. And I'd be to blame as much as the spirit.

"So how's work? Was your day as quiet as mine?"

I chattered just to fill the silence and take my cousin's mind off the crazy drive north up Highway 285.

As he kept up the flow of conversation, he slouched a bit, legs sprawled. He might have been relaxing…or bracing for impact. Either way was fine with me. I couldn't have slowed down if I'd tried.

A few minutes later, he interrupted the small talk. "Raphael's should be coming up soon."

"There it is." At seeing the lighted restaurant sign nestled among shrubbery, I jammed on the brakes and veered into the parking lot.

Javi let out an audible breath. "Yeah. We made it." He made a quick sign of the cross.

"I hope we're not too late." I jumped out, and Javi caught up to me on the walkway.

"What do you think's going to happen in a public restaurant?" He opened the brass-framed glass door with *Raphael's* stenciled in gold.

I swept inside ahead of him. "I don't know. This guy's a predator. And Ashley's vulnerable." I scanned the faces of those waiting for a table, then searched the candle-lit room for any sign of her.

"Ashley," he repeated thoughtfully. "Do I know her?"

"Maybe. Her maiden name's Martin. Married some guy named Stirling, but he broke her heart."

"Oh yeah. The same girl who lived a few blocks from you when we were kids?"

"Yes." Oddly enough. Fate had a funny sense of humor.

"You're friends with her?" He didn't bother to hide the surprise.

"Sort of. She's a reporter at the *Chronicle,* too." At

his look of disbelief, I shrugged. "I don't want to see her get hurt again."

"I'm proud of you, Mar." Javi clamped a hand on my shoulder and squeezed. "But she may not be happy about this little intervention."

"In the long run, she'll understand." I checked the time on my cell. "Maybe she took her time getting dressed?" To my relief, Javi didn't mention my Mario Andretti impression again.

The hostess speared us with a look. "Two for dinner?"

"We're going to the bar," he told her.

The dining room was to the right, and the bar to the left, but it had a direct line of sight to the entrance. "Okay."

I made my way to the opposite side so I wouldn't miss her.

Or him. A shudder hit me at the thought. How could the young Zozobra appear in public without arousing suspicion or notice? Did a corporeal spirit have money to pay the bill? Too many ridiculous questions of logistics filled my head, and I pushed them away to avoid the distraction. All I needed to learn was what sort of hold he had over Ashley. And how to break it.

A flash of blonde glinted in the entryway. *Ashley.* Alone, for now. With bright eyes and flushed face, she strained on tiptoe to look across the people seated in the dining room. Her glow dimmed, not finding the one she'd come to meet.

The upward curve of her mouth froze, then fell as she spied us.

I waved her over. Another glance around, and she

gave in.

Javi perked up. "Mm mm mm," he said through his grin.

I jabbed my elbow into his side. "Behave." Although, a devious little voice in my head whispered, Javi might be just the shiny object to dangle in front of her starry eyes. Hadn't she expressed an appreciation of His Hotness earlier?

"Hey Ashley," I said as if I had no clue she'd be there. "You remember my cousin Javi?"

A brief glow washed over her. "Who could forget? Hi, I'm Ashley Stirling." She shook his hand a beat longer than necessary.

"I certainly couldn't forget you." His smile turned sly.

So did hers. "You were in a few of my classes in high school, if I recall."

Just like that, they began talking like old friends. I was invisible to them. Which gave me the perfect chance to maintain a watchful guard.

A blur beyond the wide windows caught my eye, and a chill wrapped around me tight as a mummy's shroud. I couldn't move. My muscles mummified, locked in the black gaze of the young señor standing outside.

I fought to crack through the hold and shook it off. Rather than shrinking beneath his glare, I dredged up an energy inside me, and willed the thought in his direction. *You lost. Go away.*

His eyes narrowed and broke down whatever force I'd mustered. A vise squeezed my heart. Pain sliced my chest. Cold crept into the opening.

As if from a distance, I heard Javi's laughter. Then

he spoke, clear and close. "Right, Mar?"

His voice flooded me with such warmth, Javi cut through the ice choking me. I turned toward him and opened myself to the full effect of that warmth. "Yes." To whatever he'd said.

"See, I told you she needed one. Two margaritas for the ladies, please. Ginger ale for me. I'm on call," he confided to Ashley.

On call for desperate relatives? I wouldn't argue. The less I said, the better.

Ashley had made herself comfortable on the other side of Javi, and they talked like old friends.

Another glance out the window revealed only a couple huddling together as they walked away. The stranger was gone. It occurred to me he might have slipped inside, come to claim Ashley, but I couldn't see him indoors, either. Nor could I sense him. I was struck with the same void that had hit me at the warehouse. Señor Zozobra had fled. But to where?

The bartender slid the two margaritas toward Ashley and me with a flourish, and I fussed over how delicious it was. For the next few hours, I nursed the one drink while Ashley downed a second. Javi talked her into a third.

She held up a hand. "I can't afford a DUI."

"I'll drive you." He turned to me, and pointedly glanced at my half-empty glass. "You're legal, right, Mar?"

Probably not, but I nodded. "Absolutely. Yes, you should do the chivalrous thing. I can follow you to Ashley's and take you home from there." Which meant I'd just volunteered to tag along. "It's the least we can do."

Ashley blinked. "What do you mean?"

"Well…" I shifted in my bar stool. "I feel bad you were stood up."

Her jaw hardened. "Yes, I guess I was."

Javi looped an arm around the back of her tall chair. "Everything turns out for the best."

She beamed a smile at him that could guide ships in through stormy seas. "You might be right."

I hoped he was.

At least my impulse to invite Javi hadn't steered me wrong. I'd have to pay closer attention to those instincts from now on.

****

I tossed my handbag inside the SUV and waited while Javi escorted Ashley to her car, parked in the next row back, and closer to the roadway. A single screech pierced the air then shot like a missile past me. Darkness veiled whatever the thing was, but I knew exactly where it had originated: Old Man Gloom. Normally, I had the sense the swarm of troubles sought out people who were beaten down by life and too weary to fight off new layers of anguish.

Tonight was different. The spirit unleashed this shrieking wraith. And as I suspected, it wasn't alone for long. The swarm came at me in whistling shrieks, a fleet of tiny black kamikazes dive-bombing my head. I batted them away with one hand, tugging the door wider with the other. Stupid to let go of my purse. The star inside would have warded them off. I ducked my head and got one leg in. Ahead of me, Javi was just rounding the front of Ashley's car. Clinging to the door, I flailed an arm overhead. Javi waved and climbed in.

I dove inside the SUV and groped through my bag.

The black ornament lay at the bottom. No sooner did my fingers touch its smooth, cool edges, than my breathing eased. I dug the star out and set it in my lap before pulling the SUV behind them as Javi steered onto the highway. The black swarm hovered above the roof of Ashley's car like a cloud, but apparently neither she nor Javi noticed. The vehicle handled smoothly, hugging the turns like a race car.

The cloud dipped low behind the back end. The next instant, my windshield was masked, every inch an impenetrable shield of black.

Panic jolted me into a rigid state. "No!" My heart filled my throat, choking off air. I jammed my foot on the brake, fumble-jabbed the wiper control, and released the spray until I thought it would empty. As if fluid could erase the invisible tarp. Stupid thought, but I wasn't about to give up and pull over. I kept driving, glancing out the side window every other second to gauge whether I'd strayed beyond the painted lines. The tires hit bumpy ground, and I jerked the steering wheel to the left. Too far. A horn blared, and a pickup heading the opposite direction missed me by what seemed like inches.

I yanked the steering wheel to the right, and the SUV bounced over rocky terrain. My pulse raced, my blood heated beneath cold skin, and then I jammed on the brakes.

"Get off." I opened the window and thrust the star outside. The nearest corner of the windshield cleared, like someone had peeled away an opaque vinyl cling. I set the black ornament on the glass. The thick swarm rolled away from the rest of the windshield. My full view of the road ahead was restored.

I gulped a huge breath. "Oh God." The trouble-things were bolder, more aggressive. I'd be lucky to make it home if this kept up. I had to improvise, quick.

Up ahead, the white car sat on the side of the road, flashers blinking. The backup lights shone, and the car reversed.

Javi jogged over, the headlights illuminating his deep scowl. Watching for any sign of an attack, I rolled down the window.

He leaned an elbow against the door. "You okay?" His irritation signaled the swarm of troubles must be infecting him.

"Uhh…" My voice shook with that small effort. "Yes. Give me a second, okay?" I rummaged in my bag and pulled out a couple of hair ties. "I need to do something. Oh, and I need you to do something too." I grabbed his wrist and tugged him to the back, pulled up the rear panel and drew a star from the box I kept there. "Keep this on you?"

"What? Why?"

"Just humor me?" I used my best pleading voice. "Plus, one more favor? Leave the star outside Ashley's house. But don't let her see you. She'd get royally ticked off." Better that Her Highness get angry than get attacked.

With an exasperated *tsk*, he shoved the ornament into his shirt pocket. "Fine. I should know better than to ask." He walked away, his grumbling out of earshot.

I hurried to fasten the ornament to the wiper blade in front of my driver's seat.

A wave, and I got in again and put on my blinker. Javi pulled the sports car onto the road, and with shaky hands glued to the wheel, I followed.

Sudden swarms of screaming black insects still appeared in waves, but each attack burst in front of me like squid ink, then split around the vehicle at the last moment. Repelled by the star I'd fastened to the front? It was worth the extra weight of lugging the ornament around.

The attacks continued until we stopped at Ashley's place. Javi walked her to the door and handed over the keys. Once she was safely inside, he peacock-strutted to the SUV.

"She is one amazing woman. Do you know how many journalism awards she has?"

I pretended to glance around for oncoming traffic, then headed toward Javi's. He didn't appear to notice that my knuckles turned white as I steered, my shallow breath hardly allowed for speech, or my eyes might bug out of my head.

Apparently, my cousin had been riding on a high. That worked in his favor, the buzz of happiness shielding him while he drove. I wondered how Ashley had fared but didn't know how to ask without arousing more suspicion. Javi probably thought I was looney tunes. Or he hadn't noticed.

"That car." He whistled. "What a sweet machine. Drives smooth as a dream. You know, I always thought Ashley was cute, you know, attractive in that high-maintenance way, but man, up close she is beautiful. Any man would be an ass to stand her up."

I only half heard. Partly because I'd blocked out the gushing, glowing praise for my coworker. Partly because I sensed Señor Zozobra's anger had bloomed into rage, like electricity waiting to zap me with razor spikes. All I wanted was to get home and lock my doors.

"Whoa, slow down, Mar." Knee braced against the door, Javi burbled out the words mixed with a nervous chuckle. "Are you sure you're all right to drive?"

"Fine." But I realized I'd arched over the steering wheel like a gargoyle, and so eased back. "Thanks again for coming along tonight, Javi."

"No problem. Not that I needed to since the creep never showed."

"Yes, he did. He was outside, but he didn't come in when he saw us with Ashley."

"Seriously? How weird is that?"

My cousin didn't know the half of it. "Told you the guy was off the rails." And now I'd fueled his need for revenge by thwarting whatever plan he'd devised for Ashley.

I pulled to a stop outside Javi's. "Thanks again."

"No problem. Night."

"Take care." I wanted to warn him further, but he'd have laughed it off as a joke.

The shrieking swarm flew in and clung to the adobe walls.

"No, no, no." What were they doing? Javi wasn't safe in his home. I scanned the exterior for any sign of a star, but the single light beside his door cast too many shadows.

I climbed out, unfastened the one from my wiper blade, and walked to the rear of the SUV for another of the extras. Holding a star in each hand, I snuck up to the entrance and looked for somewhere to set it. The light fixture had just enough space to tuck the ornament between the wall and the light.

The screaming storm cloud lifted up and vanished

into the night. But I knew it was far from over. Old Man Gloom would unleash whatever minions he could summon against me to retaliate for my action tonight.

I grasped tighter to the remaining star. "Game on, Old Man."

Chapter Nineteen

The vision began before my eyes had fully closed. I flew above the streets, their beauty marred by the ugliness of the people inhabiting them. From snarling mouths to fisted hands, the residents of Santa Fe showed their miserable attitudes. The scenes changed fast, so I knew I was viewing events that had occurred over several weeks.

A powerful presence appeared beside me. *Ptesan-Wi.* She must have wanted to show me these events. Without speaking, she said, *Look.*

I gazed into the distance. A dark grey cloud swirled around the highest mountain peak. White Buffalo Woman's voice spoke in my mind: *The spirit grows angrier, more restless.* Soon, I sensed, he'd lash out more aggressively.

She lightly touched my wrist, and we dipped lower, then slowed as we came upon a crowd. A photographer's camera flashed. I peered past the people to see why they had gathered. Three young men stood with a teenager, a girl so strikingly beautiful I couldn't look away. Thick black hair flowed to her shoulders, her almond-shaped eyes dark as ebony.

Zelda.

Wordlessly, I questioned *Ptesan-Wi,* but she made no motion to answer. She wanted me to pay attention.

The onlookers were a mix of young and old,

shaggy haircuts on the boys, the girls with long locks or beehived bouffants. We'd somehow traveled to the Sixties.

In the front row, off to the side, a middle-aged Asian woman held her head high. As the man closest to Zelda announced that my young aunt was the new planning committee chair, the Asian woman gave a resolute nod.

I knew her…or sensed that I should have. Fire Eagle stood nearby, but not beside her.

Once she began to speak, there was no mistaking the young woman was my aunt. No one else had such a deep, sultry voice. It must be 1964, when seventeen-year-old Zelda was crowned queen of the planning committee, a dubious honor.

Then the scene shifted. The sun-splashed blue sky darkened into star-filled night as the city spun around *Ptesan-Wi* and me. Another crowd sprang up around us, and then we were gliding through them. Up ahead, a spotlight shone on Old Man Gloom, who towered over our heads. As we neared, the effigy swayed over everyone, his terrible smile swinging left and right. The music of a marching band mixed with loud conversation and laughter. When the torch bearers filed in procession toward him, his groans turned to roars. I feared for the people.

Graceful as leaping gazelles, two women danced into sight, vivid red costumes flowing behind them. Their procession ended at the base of the effigy, though they continued to dance and chant. As they whirled, I recognized Zelda. The other was the older Asian woman. They moved in near-perfect tandem—their gestures as identical as their brightly colored outfits.

A memory from childhood teased me. The older woman sat in my aunt's house, her sharp voice calling out to Javi and me. *My grandmother.*

That day was possibly the last time I'd seen her. Why was she performing at Zozobra?

Zelda's unmistakable smoke-over-gravel voice flowed beneath the birdlike tones of my grandmother. Their chants whipped deeper into the spirit. The monster Zozobra writhed in agony. His awful shrieks drowned out the trumpet, his stomping was more thunderous than the marching band's drum. The spirit's pain showed on the effigy's face, and he strained against the bonds holding him prisoner.

Placid as ever, *Ptesan-Wi* watched beside me. As questions formed in my head, she answered in kind.

Fire Eagle's ritual had slipped its control over the spirit, which had grown stronger each year since 1926, when Shuster and the others christened the effigy. Zelda and her mother performed a second ceremony to reinforce the first. Together, they controlled the spirit, this year and in succeeding ones.

There was still so much I didn't understand. *For how long?*

White Buffalo Woman went silent, and the vision faded.

Chapter Twenty

Under Zelda's strict command, the planning committee scheduled each event leading up to Zozobra at least a year in advance. The date when they placed their own written troubles inside the effigy was practically set in stone. Zelda repeatedly reminded me to bring a photographer from the *Chronicle* to capture the stuffing ritual. Not necessarily wanting to appear on film, I would have simply shot some photos, but then realized having documented proof of my involvement wasn't a bad idea.

When my cell rang on the drive to the warehouse, I knew without looking who was calling. "I swear, Aunt Zelda, a staff photographer will be there."

Hopefully, Bill Larson would arrive before me. I'd promised Bill a six-pack of beer and said the committee wanted to start at 6:50 p.m., though technically they'd set the time at 7:00. I'd declined his offer to ride with him, offering the excuse that I needed to stay later on committee business and didn't want to hold him up. I still had nightmarish flashbacks of the first time I had to ride in the Death Seat of his car.

Bill had parked to the side of the open warehouse doors like a getaway car. The vehicle sported a few more dents and dings than when I'd ridden in it, so I was doubly glad I'd followed my instinct. And he wasn't the only one who wanted to make a hasty exit. I couldn't wait for this night to be over. But like the rest of the committee, I was expected to do my part for the ceremony. Unlike them, I'd folded a blank sheet to contribute. I didn't want to add any more fuel to Old Man Gloom's feeding frenzy.

My aunt surveyed me with a keen eye. "Marissa. Good, you're here. What's wrong?"

How did she do that? "Nothing." The single word came out in a long burble.

Her brow arched. I was busted.

She held out her hand. "Give it."

I feigned ignorance. "Give what?"

"I want to see what you're adding to the effigy."

Protest would only prolong the affront. A sigh, and I slapped the sheet onto her palm. "I don't see what difference it makes." I sounded like a petulant teenager.

She unfolded it, drew her mouth into a tight grimace, then handed it back. "Fix this. And hurry."

"Fine." I went through the motions of writing down my fears, but the details of that night came pouring out. I soon found myself even sketching the house on fire.

I folded it quickly so no one would see any of it. If no one else saw the image, I'd never have to explain Michael's outline in the window, my reaching out for him but falling down an endless spiral. Or the ominous figure whose silhouette blacked out the stars as it hovered over our house.

My grip tightened around the folded wad. If only burning this paper and all that it carried, turning them into blackened wisps, could ever rid me of the horror of that night. Funny, but all of my problems related to Zozobra and Old Man Gloom himself. Yet I was supposed to pose near the effigy and smile as I inserted my written contribution into the figure.

Bitterness twisted my mouth as I watched the committee members paste smiles on their faces and pose with the figure. Old Man Gloom was the cause of my troubles. Witnessing flames destroy the effigy holding all my sorrows—and everyone else's—would be the answer to my prayers. If it actually worked.

Zelda gestured to me. "Go ahead. They're waiting."

I screwed up the courage and carried it to the effigy. A few members still milled around, adjusting parts. As I reached to insert the paper into the figure, the workers lifted the torso.

Old Man Gloom turned its big ugly head toward me. And through leering lips, the whisper rushed out, as it did that fateful night, *"Venganza."*

Revenge.

His hushed laugh unleashed another invisible swarm. Chittering like a million venomous insects that circled around me, so fast that my vision swam. The cyclone began to drag me down. The same sensation of falling overwhelmed me. I shut my eyes against it, against the helpless tunnel imprisoning me, against losing touch with all that was real. All that I knew was slipping away through my grasp. I had no idea where reality ended and fantasy began. I'd thought that I'd known. Thought that I'd made that delineation when I was five. I'd drawn a clear line, like a magical circle, and enclosed myself within it to banish all that I couldn't explain, all that mystery and mysticism encompassed.

But that line had blurred. Worse, it had evaporated. And allowed fantasy to leach into my adult life. I was losing my hold on all that I believed to be true. All that I believed to be real.

I won't. I refuse.

I pried open my eyes. The swirling kaleidoscope trapping me at its center crackled and splintered. Then it shattered, each piece dividing upon itself. The process repeated and repeated. Fists clenched, I stood fast, determined to hold my grip on the world.

Not this time, Old Man. Through sheer force of will, I summoned strength from my deepest center. It radiated up like the first rays of morning sun, brilliant in bursting to life at the horizon. It spread to the farthest corners of the room, pushing back the darkness. The void separating me from all else grew shorter.

Determination rooted my feet to the floor, grounding me where I stood, firm and sure.

Zelda crossed the shortening void and patted my cheek. "Marissa. Answer me. Please."

The buzz faded from my head, and the fog cleared from my vision. I was in the warehouse.

Zelda aimed her movie-star smile at her colleagues. "My niece is fine. She grew a bit lightheaded, but now it's passed." She held her practiced smile as the other committee members dispersed. When the last had left, my aunt's sudden seriousness acted like a bucket of cold water on me.

Zelda's dark eyes skewered me where I stood. "Are you," she whispered, "all right?"

"Yes." Now I was. "But you were right. He's getting stronger." I spoke too loudly.

"Marissa." Zelda's nervous laugh gave her away.

"You know it's true. Where is my grandmother? Why did she abandon us?"

For once, Zelda was struck dumb.

"Time to continue our talk." And agree on some actual solution. If she knew some voodoo tricks, I needed to learn them. To help her subdue the spirit. This year, he was too strong, too volatile for any one person to control.

"Not here." She glanced around. "Come to my house."

****

Knuckles white against the steering wheel, I had tailgated my aunt's car the entire drive over. My nerves wound tighter when Zelda poured two glasses of wine and handed me one.

The glass trembled in my grasp. "You must be able to feel it, too. The power of whatever negative energy this spirit stirs up."

She gulped her wine. "Yes. At first, I thought I should discourage you from returning to Santa Fe. This year, of all times."

I paced, my thoughts in a whirl. "Tell me more about the history. I feel as if we're missing some obvious clue that can help us."

Zelda puttered around the kitchen. "I hardly know where to begin. Both families have protected the city since the festival's inception."

I swept the hair back from my face. "I know, I know. Fire Eagle was one of the five who started the ritual. But how did your parents become involved?"

"It's impossible to live in Santa Fe and not know about the festival. People of different faiths practice different rituals, but their commonality brings them together, especially in the face of danger."

Under the weight of what else my aunt might be

about to say, I sank to the bar stool and braced against the island.

Our family history was closely interwoven with the festival and with Old Man Gloom. Zelda's mother, Bong-Cha, was a *mudang*, a female shaman, as was my mother. My grandmother performed sacred protection rites at the festival and taught my mother to become a shaman as well.

My mother married Buck Tahy, a Sioux. I looked more Native American than Korean, but I always felt like an outsider, like my family was of low caste. Some children wouldn't play with me, Michael, and Javi. Other parents didn't socialize with our parents. Though no one questioned us outright, they knew there was something different about our family.

I didn't remember my Korean grandparents and never knew about my mother's spiritual side.

"My mother was a shaman." I repeated it aloud to convince myself, but it still seemed surreal. Except that the night of the fire, the words she'd chanted...I'd always known there was something strange about them. "Did Old Man Gloom threaten our family?"

"I'm not entirely sure," my aunt admitted. "I only know that when she moved you away, she feared for you."

Of course, that was why we'd moved away so quickly. "Why did you stay here? Weren't you afraid?"

"Familial ties to a shaman posed no threat to Old Man Gloom. But your mother did."

"How? I don't remember her performing at the festival."

"She practiced her rituals in secret. She kept Santa Fe safe from evil spirits until..." She knit her brows.

So I finished for her. "Until the night Michael was killed."

"I wish I knew more about what happened that night. She wouldn't speak of it. Nor would your father." Zelda held my gaze.

"Does Javi know about any of this?"

"No. I had to keep him safe. And that's why your parents never told you."

"We deserved to know the truth."

"Even if it put your lives in danger? No. Not until you'd grown."

Except now that I was older, ignorance had rendered me helpless. "What can I do, Zelda? I'm not exactly a shaman. I'd have no clue how to expel a demon or spirit or whatever Old Man Gloom is. But as you said, of all times to come back to Santa Fe, now was the worst. But…I think I was meant to."

She studied me. "Potential is power. A little training, and you could learn the rituals."

An incredulous laugh burst out. "Are you suggesting I become a shaman?"

"Before you returned, I didn't believe the abilities passed to you. I was wrong. If you wish to protect yourself, and those you love, yes. I'm encouraging you to become a shaman."

"I have no idea where to start." And couldn't believe I said that.

Zelda avoided my gaze, brushing invisible lint from her blouse. "My mother can teach you."

There was my escape hatch. "But they live overseas. I doubt she has Skype."

She shook her head. "My parents are in Austin."

"Texas?" Hours away, rather than half a world.

"When's the last time you visited? How do you know they're still there?"

"I speak to my mother a few times a year. Except for this year. I've called her more often as the festival grows nearer." My aunt was the essence of cool control, the counter-balance to my panic.

"Because you're worried that this year will be worse, too." I didn't need to frame it as a question. I could see the concern in Zelda's face. In the way she glanced into the night, a warrior at the ready.

"Yes," Zelda said on a sigh. "I think Old Man Gloom wants this festival to be memorable for the wrong reasons."

"This changes everything. Don't you see? Your mother's the only one who knows how to stop him. She has to come to Santa Fe." And she was the clue we were missing. That had to be it. "I can't believe you didn't tell me all this before. How could you have kept this from me?" With only days until the festival, how could I possibly prepare?

A nerve pulsed in her jaw. "I've already asked my mother to help. Many times. She's refused. Every time."

"Why? Doesn't she understand we're in danger? Everyone here is in danger."

"She fears the backlash. That if she performs the ritual, people will blame her for whatever goes wrong. Or worse, ostracize her."

To my mind, not a viable excuse. Grandmother had moved away long ago. "If she won't help, you and I will have to work together. What does the ritual entail?"

"I haven't witnessed her performing one for decades. From what I remember, the *mudang* dresses in

255

ceremonial garb, chants and sings."

"That sounds perfect. We'll bill it as part of the festival. No one needs to know it's real." Among all the other performances, no one would even notice.

"There may be an altar involved. Some burned offerings."

Dread churned my stomach. "Not animal sacrifice, or anything weird like that?"

"Herbs and plants, I believe. Nothing horrific, but some people may find it odd. We would have to tread very carefully."

"Have Tomas construct a curtain in front of the altar, and position it to hide whoever was behind it. We could call the ceremony a pre-burning, so the people holding the torches can't argue with that. Your mother could do it and no one would see her." I was babbling, but I was desperate.

Zelda *tsk*'d. "You're getting ahead of yourself. *Eomeoni* has refused to come."

She'd refused Zelda, but we might still have a chance. "What if I ask her?"

My aunt considered me for a moment. "I suppose if we don't try, we'll never know."

"Exactly. Call her." A thought hit me. "Wait. What name should I call her?" That part of my memory had gone dark. Had I ever known her as anything but Grandmother?

"The respectful way to address her is *Halmeoni* Bong-Cha. *Halmeoni* is the Korean word for grandmother."

"And Bong-Cha is her first name. It's beautiful." Repeating it brought back the embarrassment of my five-year-old self, the girl who pretended to forget the name when anyone asked. "What does it mean?"

"The literal translation is *ultimate girl* but can also refer to a mythical phoenix."

A phoenix. How fitting, though Ultimate Girl would make a great super hero name. I wished I had time to learn more of the language before Zozobra. I might be in for a crash course in Korean.

Zelda tapped through the screens on her cell, then handed it to me. "It's ringing."

I held the phone as if it were a bomb. "Aren't you going to explain first? Does she speak English?"

A click, and a woman's sharp voice streamed through the phone. She threw in a recognizable word here and there, but mostly spoke in Korean.

I tried to hand the phone back to my aunt. "I have no idea—"

Zelda rolled her eyes. "Tell her it's you."

Glaring, I slumped my shoulders in an exaggerated sigh. "*Halmeoni* Bong-Cha. I'm sorry to disturb you. It's Marissa. Your granddaughter." Not the best way to begin my first conversation with the grandmother I hadn't seen in decades.

"Marissa?" The shrillness had softened.

"Yes. Hello. I had no idea you were in Texas. I would have visited you." All those years wasted, wishing I had more family, and they were there all the time.

"Where are you?" she demanded.

"In Santa Fe. I moved back a few months ago."

"You are there for Zozobra?" The end of the sentence rose an octave.

"The *Santa Fe Chronicle* offered me a job. But I've wanted to come home for years."

Muttering in Korean. "A foolish mistake. Your timing is very bad."

"Yes." I glanced at Zelda, who pretended to flip through her day planner, but I could tell was listening intently. "That's starting to become clear to me."

"You should leave Santa Fe. You should all leave." My grandmother sounded adamant.

"I can't, *Halmeoni* Bong-Cha. People here don't know what's going to happen."

"And you think you do, foolish girl?"

Apparently, Zelda had learned her intimidation tactics from her own mother. But my *halmeoni* didn't know what I'd been going through. "If it's anything like my dreams, then yes. And I'm afraid for them. I can't leave when they're in danger, but I don't know how to protect them. Won't you help us?"

More muttering in Korean. "Zelda has already asked. I've already told her no."

Was my grandmother hinting she might reconsider? "Are you saying no to me, too?"

"Marissa." *Halmeoni* spoke my name like a caress. "I am old."

That wasn't a refusal. It gave me hope to keep trying. "I'm young. But I don't know the ritual."

A cackling laugh. "You are a smart one, eh? But my memory is bad. I might forget the important parts."

Forget, my ass. I bet my grandmother remembered every detail.

I made one final appeal. "He's following me, *Halmeoni*. Old Man Gloom has taken shape as a man about my age. I chased him once, and almost fell into this chasm of darkness."

Her sharp gasp sounded like the precursor to a

heart attack. "Never chase him into his realm." More Korean muttering. "You could have disappeared from this world."

Ominous sounding, like my grandmother knew exactly where I had gone. Maybe my grandmother had visited there.

That was beside the point. "He's sending everyone's troubles back over them. And he burned down my friend's house, and Rusty White could have been killed. I can't let him get away with this."

"Rusty." My grandmother said it with an unmistakable familiarity. "Is he all right?"

"For now. What if Old Man Gloom burns down all of Santa Fe? Could you live with yourself if that happens?"

"All right, all right," my grandmother snapped. "I will come."

I didn't congratulate myself yet. "Soon?"

"Book me a flight." She spoke in a no-nonsense tone. "Text me the link to print out the ticket."

"Okay." Not what I was expecting. "Will tomorrow work for you?"

"Let me check with my knitting club... Of course, it's fine. I will see you tomorrow night." The cell went dark. Grandmother had hung up.

I handed the phone to Zelda. "Her knitting club? Really?"

"No. If she joined such a club, she'd end up stabbing someone with a knitting needle."

I could only imagine. "How old is she, anyway?"

"She turned eighty-seven on March 21."

No matter how shrewd my grandmother was, was she too old to take on Old Man Gloom? "I'll make a note of her birthday. And start researching flights."

An hour later, I'd booked my *halmeoni* on a nine-thirty, and emailed Weller asking if I could possibly take a personal day the following day, explaining that my grandmother—whom I hadn't seen in nearly two decades—was visiting unexpectedly. I phrased the request in a formal and apologetic way, and the wait for a response was prickly. Weller said fine, so long as I'd turned in any articles on deadline. I had.

Zelda texted my mother the link to print the e-tickets, and she confirmed its receipt.

Who knew my *halmeoni* was a techno-savvy shaman? "This night is definitely one to remember." A game changer, probably in more ways than I could imagine.

Chapter Twenty-One

Halmeoni Bong-Cha was thin, but otherwise was nothing like the frail grandmother I'd imagined. Age had not diminished her height, and my grandmother stood nearly eye-to-eye with me. Her dark eyes were clear and bright, full of intelligence and mischief. Leading the crowd of those debarking the plane, she walked with a sure step and aimed directly for me.

"Marissa. I would know you anywhere." She wrapped her long arms around me and murmured in Korean.

It was like hugging a skeleton. "*Halmeoni* Bong-Cha. It's so good to see you."

"It has been much too long. But such things happen in families." She sent a pointed look toward Zelda.

Zelda extended her arms. "No hug for me?"

Bong-Cha embraced Zelda. "Let's get my bags. I hate airports. And everything about airplanes."

We retrieved three suitcases.

"I'm glad you plan to stay awhile." I was also glad the oversized luggage had wheels.

"Don't be silly. I must return to Austin after the festival. I brought enough ceremonial outfits for us all."

"Do we need more than one each?" I joked.

Halmeoni Bong-Cha glared. "Perhaps."

"Oh." Humbled, I carried the bag with my head bowed.

After we loaded the bags into Zelda's trunk and headed back to Santa Fe, *Halmeoni* appeared lost in thought as she stared out the window of the back seat.

"Did you have a good flight?" I hated to resort to small talk after so many years apart. I had so many more questions.

"Fine."

I threw up my hands. So much for conversation. My family wasn't exactly one for sharing feelings of any sort.

Without glancing in the rearview mirror, Zelda asked, "Are you hungry, Mother? I planned to make soy sauce crab."

"Not tacos?" The words sliced from between grandmother's thinned lips.

The next second stretched into infinity. I processed the implication—a mother's disapproval of her daughter's shame regarding her heritage. I struggled to keep my attention on the road ahead so as not to embarrass my aunt. From the corner of my eye, I saw Zelda's grip tighten on the steering wheel. The tension radiating from her could have made my hair stand on end.

But my aunt ignored the jab. "I bought a few bottles of soju as well."

"That will be fine." Grandmother gripped the seat and edged closer. "Marissa, on the phone you said Old Man Gloom was sending people's troubles back over them. How do you know this?"

I angled toward my grandmother. "I don't know for certain. It's a feeling that strikes me after the dust storms."

Halmeoni didn't appear surprised, only thoughtful.

"How many dust storms?"

"Since I moved back in May, there have been three. Which is way more than usual, according to residents." I sounded like one of my articles, factual and boring.

Grandmother studied me. "What's unusual about them?"

"Not so much the storms, except that they've all occurred at night. It's what happens the day after. Everyone seems to be in a terrible mood. There have been more car accidents, fist fights, and domestic disturbance calls this month alone than in all of last year."

Halmeoni's look of introspection grew intense. "Hm. What else?"

"I hear noises at night. They seem to echo from the mountain."

"What sort of noises?"

"It's hard to describe. Rustling, like leaves, or the sound of wings. Once, I felt the rush of wind, like a swarm flying past me, but I couldn't see anything much. Some small black…things. Like shadows. Like cast-off troubles that grew wings."

My grandmother's eyes narrowed.

"And I heard him laughing. Old Man Gloom. The night I put my paper into the effigy, he whispered to me."

Zelda glanced over, mouth agape. I should have mentioned it to my aunt, but I didn't want Zelda to think I'd lost my mind.

"What did he say?" Grandmother asked, as if we were discussing an actual person.

"Revenge." I locked gazes with my grandmother.

"Revenge for what? He has it backward if you ask me. I'm the one who wants revenge for what he did to our family."

Grandmother rested her hand on my shoulder. "You must set aside your anger."

"I've been trying. For twenty-four years."

"You must. Now. Or you will not be pure of spirit. If you are to perform the rituals, it is required."

A pretty tall order. I dropped my gaze to my hands. "Okay. I'll try."

"Truly, for your own welfare, you must."

"Do you really think I can?" I wasn't so sure. The pain of all that had happened had deeply ingrained itself in me, and I carried it in my bones.

A pat, and grandmother withdrew her hand. "Not alone, not this time."

I didn't like the implications of that, but I didn't want to hear anymore right now. I had enough to absorb, so fell quiet. The rest of the way home, the three of us rode in somber silence.

****

Zelda had barely turned off the engine when my grandmother climbed from the car and tapped impatiently on the trunk. "Open it."

Popping the inside latch, Zelda sighed. "It's going to be a long week."

Halmeoni glared through the back window. "No smart talk."

"Yes, *Eomeoni*." Zelda hurried to the back, keys jangling.

I wasted no time, either. I helped my aunt carry the luggage inside the house. From the sunroom, a squawk greeted us.

"Mudang Eomma," Phoebe called. "Welcome home."

My grandmother set the bag on the floor and walked to the parrot's stand. The two babbled and cooed to each other.

I stopped to listen. "Is *eomma* a variation of mother?"

"Yes," Zelda said, pursing her lips. "Mommy."

"Oh." I regretted my surprise had slipped out, but not even my aunt called Bong-Cha that. "They have a history, I take it."

Zelda kept walking, lugging the big suitcase down the hall. "Mother communes with animals."

"Sure." Why not? I was on the verge of believing anything.

"She gave Phoebe to me when you were a baby. I didn't particularly want a bird that might outlive me, especially one so moody as that parrot, but..." Zelda shrugged. "She's been a comfort to me, especially after the divorce. Having another living being to care for helps take your mind off things. Of course, I had Javi, but he had his own full life. Phoebe and I will grow old together."

Funny that my aunt mentioned the divorce. Zelda never spoke of it, had always changed the subject when anyone else brought it up. Her response was always the same. It was necessary, and she was fine. End of discussion.

"But you've dated, right?" I tried to sound casual, as if I were chatting with a girlfriend. "There must have been men who've caught your eye. You're so stunning, you turn every man's head."

Zelda came to an abrupt halt.

Now I'd gone too far. I braced for the rapid-fire lecture.

"I have had relationships. Discreetly. None have caused me to lose my heart. Or my head." She wheeled the bag. "And thank you for the compliment."

A grin crept over my face. "Huh." Imagine that. I had a conversation with Zelda, woman-to-woman. A first.

So intrigued by the breakthrough, I didn't pay attention to the approaching footsteps.

"Why are we loitering in the hallway?" *Halmeoni* shoo'd us along.

Zelda and I continued to Javi's old room. *Halmeoni* Bong-Cha opened a bag on the floor and meticulously laid out three colorful outfits across the bed. The vivid blues and reds invited my touch, but my grandmother slapped away my hand.

"They're beautiful," I argued.

Grandmother smoothed the fabric. "Let's hope the spirits share your admiration."

Right. We weren't going to play dress-up. These outfits served a purpose. "Is the ritual difficult to learn?"

"Not for my smart granddaughter." Grandmother patted my cheek.

Not exactly the answer I'd sought. I turned to Zelda. "You haven't been performing them since *Halmeoni* moved away?"

"I have, in my own way." My aunt sounded defensive and kept her gaze averted from us.

"The wrong way," *Halmeoni* said.

"What was I supposed to do?" Zelda folded her arms over her chest. "The committee voted against the rituals."

"The committee." *Halmeoni* practically spat the word. "Does the committee understand what is necessary to keep the spirits placated?"

Fingers tapping her arms, Zelda merely arched her brows. I knew better than to speak. I didn't want to ignite that powder keg.

"Exactly." Grandmother shuffled between the bed and the suitcases. "Your mother knew the importance of each step. She put all of herself into performing the ritual."

"I never knew that." I searched my memory, but so much of my past was lost to me. Only the pain stood out.

"I'm surprised you don't remember. You showed great promise, even when you were a few years old."

"Me?" Like my other memories, I must have buried that one, too.

"It will come back to you." My grandmother sighed. "If my daughter hadn't moved away, she would have become a legendary shaman."

Zelda's silence spoke volumes. My grandmother was insulting her, belittling her abilities, yet she offered no argument.

Always moving, Grandmother kept unpacking. "When your family left, the rift began. And now it's been twenty-four years of Zozobra, all the bad juju flowing in one direction. Old Man Gloom is tired of people putting their troubles on him. He is demanding his due."

I didn't want to ask what his "due" might be. "After all these years, do you think one ceremony will be enough?"

"I never said we would hold only one. You must undergo an initiation. Become a *mudang*."

A shaman. The strangeness just kept getting stranger.

"To answer your question, yes. Between the three of us, the ritual we perform while Old Man Gloom burns during Zozobra should hold him for this year. After I go home, the burden will be on you."

"I'll have to repeat the ritual every year?" I gaped at her.

"Unless you are powerful enough to sever the spirit from the effigy." Bong-Cha gave a shrug. "I tried and failed many times. Even that is no guarantee it will remain gone. The people of Santa Fe have forgotten the power they invoke when they ask the spirits to intervene in the goings-on of this world. So as long as Santa Fe holds the Zozobra festival, someone will have to basically dance with the devil."

And that someone, apparently, was me.

"You must remember that the first Zozobra was a small ritual held by only a few men, some friends who burned their troubles inside a handmade figure. They didn't understand that they were calling up the spirit. Asking him to carry away their troubles. They only knew that afterward, they shared a real sense of relief. But to them, it was a game. Until the early 1960s, when the spirit finally grew weary of bearing everyone's burdens, and no one offering him anything in return."

"Was that why the founder turned the festival rights over to the planning committee? Because Old Man Gloom became a threat?"

My grandmother winked at me. "I knew you were smart."

"What did Ray's grandfather have to do with any of this?"

"Rusty's father was one of the original circle, friends with Will Shuster. Those men were the first to summon the spirit. His son was a firefighter and understood about the spirit. He did what he could to protect Santa Fe, but he was killed in a fire."

Hungry flames had destroyed the cottage where Rusty lived, and nearly the three of us. "Oh, God. Ray and Rusty are still in danger, aren't they?"

"Not necessarily. Rusty had a good mystical force. Stronger than ordinary people, but not enough to fend off danger by himself. But there may be more to Ray than we know." She seemed lost in her thoughts, then went on. "But everyone else? Yes, they require protection. Which is why we aren't going to waste any more time. We must placate the spirit."

"What does the spirit want?"

"The same thing all of us want. Praise, encouragement, acknowledgement. Manners when asked for something. And finally, peace."

"If he'll leave us alone, it will be worth it." I hoped.

My grandmother faced me. "He may demand a sacrifice."

"You said we wouldn't need to sacrifice small animals."

"I am not speaking of animals. He may ask us each for an offering."

"Like what?"

"Deep prayer. An offering from our souls."

"I'm not giving up my soul to any spirit."

"Don't be silly. Not your actual soul. But in return

for removing everyone else's burdens, he may require us to share some of his burden. His pain and anguish."

Share the pain of fifty thousand festival attendees? No human could endure such a crushing weight.

"You're making me worry, *Halmeoni*." The first festival I'd attended had left an indelible scar, one I carried for year upon year. I didn't know how many more I could bear.

Halmeoni mimed whining. "If you cannot handle a little wailing and gnashing of teeth, I should not have bothered to come."

My grandmother made it sound so easy. Too easy. "There's nothing else? It doesn't involve any physical pain?"

"Is pain of your soul not physical? When your heart aches, is the pain any less real?"

"What about Michael? His pain was more than a little anguish." I bit back the sudden rush of emotion that thickened my throat.

My grandmother cast her gaze down. "His sacrifice has kept the spirit at bay for many years. Now we must pay retribution once again."

"With another life? And how many years will that last?"

Grandmother stepped in front of me and held my gaze. "No life will be lost while I am here. And if you do the ritual as I teach you, the spirit will accept others' troubles without demanding any more payment. If I didn't believe that, I would not have come." With a small smile, she gave a nod.

"I'm sorry. You're right." I had to keep my emotions in check.

Grandmother released me. "Of course, I am. If you

learn nothing else, learn not to argue with your *halmeoni*, especially when she is a *mudang*."

"What about when I become a *mudang,* too?" Those were words I never envisioned myself saying, but they didn't sound as strange as they should have.

"You will never match my knowledge or experience." Grandmother huffed, turned to Zelda, and jerked her thumb at me. "This one may not catch on so quickly as I hoped. She thinks she is already smarter than me."

"I don't, honestly. I was kidding." At my grandmother's skeptical glance, I shrugged. "If we can't laugh…" I might cry. But I'd never admit that to *Halmeoni* Bong-Cha.

"Laugh yourself into this outfit." My grandmother pointed to the costume at the end of the bed.

"Right now?"

"No, at midnight. Under the full moon. Yes, right now."

I gathered up the costume and headed for the bathroom. After changing, I returned to the bedroom, where my aunt and grandmother wore matching outfits.

When I stood with them, I felt the strong presence of another—my mother.

When *Halmeoni* assessed me, her eyes glittered. "Yes. Very pleasing."

I gulped. Pleasing to my grandmother? Or to Old Man Gloom? What could possibly do to please such a vindictive spirit?

What the hell had I gotten myself into?

****

At Grandmother Bong-Cha's command, Zelda drove the three of us to the base of the Sangre de Cristo

271

Mountains. Dressed in the ceremonial garb, I kept my face turned from the car window. "I hope no one sees us like this."

Grandmother tightened her mouth. "If you feel shame about what we are about to do—about what we are—then you should not come."

Great, I'd insulted her. "I'm not ashamed, but no one would understand."

"Simply tell them the truth. We are practicing for the festival."

"Right." The truth. Why hadn't I thought of that? Because it still sounded outlandish. My Korean half embraced this, but my Navajo-self urged me to do more. That our singing and dancing would not be enough to subdue the spirit.

To my relief, no one I knew stopped to peer in the windows, no police cars hid behind landmarks or billboards and raced after our vehicle with lights blazing. Nothing at all happened other than the sun inched higher in the brilliant blue sky.

I couldn't get my mother out of my head. Had she worn this same costume? Maybe the very one I was wearing? Why had she never mentioned this part of her life? Since Michael's death, my mother wore her grief like a veil of sadness. That gauzy barrier filtered her every smile, every glance. It softened her speech. She often gazed out as if the world around her was unclear to her, a far-off place she missed but couldn't reach. The veil imprisoned my mother, an impenetrable cocoon. Until the day she died, it never left her.

And nothing I did could change that. The sense of failure haunted me, not being able to fill that void left by my brother's death. It pained me, too, but rather than bringing my mother and me together, grief was a barrier between us.

By the time Zelda parked along an access road near the Sangre de Cristo Mountains, a fog enveloped me, as if my mother pulled me inside her cocoon to embrace me. The warmth of my mother's love wrapped around me. Her spirit rose from the car alongside me and walked with me to where Zelda and my grandmother waited.

If anyone had asked me to explain later all that my grandmother had taught me, I wouldn't have been able to find the words. When *Halmeoni* Bong-Cha spoke, my heart heard with greater clarity than my ears. Grandmother's teachings were inscribed in my bones, so I'd carry them always. The motions came as a natural accompaniment to the chanting. The exact words didn't matter as much as the heartfelt proffering, the outpouring of my soul. The flow of emotion, this outpouring from the heavens reached out and formed a bridge between the two worlds from where my mother, father, and brother were to where the spirit who was resurrected each year as Old Man Gloom resided. My singing lifted me up, up, up, where in the vast darkness, all else faded away.

All except the man with the wide, sad smile. His white robes spread around him, he sat quietly, an audience of one, listening to my song. My voice tore at my throat, clawed my insides, punctured my flesh and organs deeper than arrows. My heart bled in a flood of sorrow until I thought I might melt and float in the rush of current.

Far off, a flash caught my eye. Veins of brilliance split the void, then vanished. Thunder cracked as two pulses of light outlined a black cloud. The storm drew nearer, and unless it veered to another direction, we were in its direct path.

Electricity crackled through the air, then grew more dense as the storm came upon us. I kept singing. If I stopped, I would never become a *mudang*. I would fail my family. I would fail everyone.

Pouring my soul into my song, I walked toward the lightning. Running would have done no good anyway. There was nowhere to run. Ever closer, the jagged strikes seared the darkness. The air around me hummed with the energy, so I knew I was dangerously close. The heart of the storm beat all around me. I raised my arms and sang louder.

A bolt pierced my fingertips, skewered me, and nailed me in place. Pain electrified my bones, radiated through my flesh, and out my skin. My voice expanded across the skies, an arc of silk and steel. The white-hot light seared me in a baptism of purest fire. I was one with the lightning, my spirit ecstatic, whirling in its light.

Just as suddenly, the bolt of electricity receded. I collapsed. My superheated marrow was unable to hold me upright. The physical weakness, I understood to be temporary. Electricity sang in every cell and danced through my veins. I no longer had reason to fear. The lightning had imparted its power to me.

Yet I couldn't control my trembling limbs, so lay there shaking.

Then my mother's hands grasped mine and pulled me up. I held tightly, my voice reduced to whimpers.

"Marissa." She called from somewhere far off.

I wanted to beg her to wait, not to leave me. A

force pulled me toward my mother. A thin slice of light penetrated the darkness. My mother stepped into what seemed like a doorway. I kept my mother in sight, kept reaching for her.

"Come back, Marissa."

Soft hands patted my cheek, wet with tears. "Mother."

"Marissa." The voice sounded clear and strong. And close.

The doorway of light narrowed, became a bright line. Then it was gone. So was my mother.

I opened my eyes. Grandmother bent over me, with Zelda over her shoulder.

"Come out of it." *Halmeoni* lifted my head. "You went deeper than I expected. Are you back again?"

I pushed myself to sit up. "Yes. I'm fine." Grandmother hadn't exaggerated. I had been in deep. Returning to my world invigorated me, restored the energy that the ritual had sapped from me.

Grandmother squeezed my hand and held tight. "Take a moment before you stand. Let your head clear."

And allow my soul to fully return to my body. I still felt fuzzy around the edges, as if my outline blurred with every movement, and my spirit seeped beyond my skin.

"Mom was there." Surprisingly, speaking aloud helped center me.

Grandmother went still, her attention solely on me.

"Ever since I put on this costume, I could feel her with me. When we crossed into, wherever we went, and she guided me out again."

Grandmother blinked back tears. "I hoped she

would."

I gently squeezed her hand. "All clear. I feel good."

"Are you sure?" she pressed but began to tug me upward.

I stood without wobbling. "Positive. Except that I'm starving."

Pride and strength came through in *Halmeoni*'s smile. "So am I. Let's go eat." She linked arms with Zelda and headed for the car. "I hope you have plenty of soy sauce crab left."

"Absolutely." Zelda lit up in a rare grin. "Or I could make *bossam*."

"Yes, make *bossam*," my grandmother said. "Marissa must experience as much Korean food as possible."

I couldn't wait to dig into my heritage, especially if it was as tasty as my grandmother suggested. "I hope you'll share your recipes."

When we were riding home, the silence was no longer awkward. The rift Grandmother had mentioned earlier didn't only apply to Santa Fe, I realized. When we'd lost Michael, it had created a rift in our family. My parents and I had fled to California, and my grandparents had moved to Texas. The family had fractured and remained that way.

My mom had shown me the way back.

As soon as my aunt parked in the driveway, I scrambled out, cursing the voluminous skirts. "Zelda."

"Yes?" My aunt turned.

I caught her in a hug. "Thank you. For all you've done."

Stiff in my embrace, she stuttered, "Me? I haven't—"

"Yes, you have." I drew away but linked our hands between us. "You showed such courage in staying here. You are the center who drew us all together again."

Gratitude shone in her smile. "You made the decision to move home."

"I probably wouldn't have if you weren't here. You and Javi. My family." I pulled my grandmother into another hug. "We can't lose this."

Zelda tightened her embrace. "We won't."

"We won't," Grandmother echoed. "Where is Javi? Why is he not here?"

Zelda broke the circle. "He promised to come after work. He can't wait to visit with you." She ushered us into the house, chattering about Javi's commendation the year before and dinner while we changed.

We were in the kitchen, the delicious scent of steamed pork and vegetables teasing my palate, when Javi arrived. If he'd beamed when he first saw me, he was over the moon to see our grandmother. He caught her up in a typical Javi bear hug.

"You've grown half a foot!" *Halmeoni* exclaimed.

"You're still too skinny." He held her away to look at her. "You haven't changed at all. What's your secret?"

Laughing, she said something in Korean, then motioned him to the island. "Help us make dinner."

"Sure I won't mess it up?" he teased.

"It's easy, but much work." She picked up the knife and arranged the ingredients in front of her.

Javi frowned at her, then me. "I don't get it."

"Come, and I'll show you. Both of you." She waved us closer.

I took my place beside Javi, waiting for

instructions.

Our grandmother's long, nimble fingers worked fast—first chopping the pork, then wrapping a piece in lettuce. She held it out to him. "You will love it."

Taking the tiny portion, Javi examined it with a disbelieving frown. "Maybe, but I'll also starve."

She waved her knife in the air. "Not if you repeat the process, again and again."

"Ah." Javi nodded. "Easy to do, but you have to do it many times."

Grandmother set him in her sights. "You're here to visit with me, aren't you? Not to say hello and rush off?"

"You're absolutely right, as always. There's no rush whatsoever."

"Good. Then we'll eat a delicious meal in the leisurely way it's meant to be enjoyed."

A grin at me, and I knew my cousin had surrendered. Good for him. He knew better than to argue. We prepared our own portions, trying the two dipping sauces.

Javi hooted and waved at his mouth when he sampled the second. "What is that?"

"*Saeujeot*," said Zelda. "Salted, pickled shrimp."

"Extremely salted." Mouth puckered, he squinted as he shook his head.

Grandmother grunted. "Of course, you'd prefer the *ssamjang* with chili paste."

"And soybean paste," added Zelda.

"Your palate needs a Korean education." Grandmother grilled him about his job, his love life, what he'd been up to in the few years since they'd visited her in Texas.

My parents and I had been the outsiders, out of touch with the rest. A pang of hurt sliced through me, then regret. I was no longer a child. I should have made an effort to contact them.

Javi nudged me. "You full already? I thought you ladies worked up an appetite today. What were you doing again?"

Zelda didn't miss a beat. "Practicing the ritual that we will perform at the festival. I told you, already."

"Right." Javi furrowed his brows, studying each of us in turn. "All three of you are involved this year? How come?"

Waving at him, grandmother said something in Korean. "You don't need to worry. We women can handle everything."

He held up his hands. "Believe me, I am the last person to argue with that. Women have all the power. Way more than any man."

Halmeoni turned to Zelda and jutted out her chin. "You raised your son well. I'm proud of you both."

"Me, too. When did you get so smart?" I said it teasingly, but I meant every word.

Nonplussed, he shrugged. "I was lucky enough to be born to a family of highly intelligent and capable women. Sometimes I feel kind of left out."

I threw my arm around his shoulder. "Not a chance." And from now on, I'd never make the mistake of thinking I'd been left out, either.

Chapter Twenty-Two

The sound that echoed from the Sangre de Cristo Mountains as I readied for bed that night sent a chill through my marrow. It was the wind moaning, the low call of a mournful coyote, the echo of the ancients crying out against the wrongs done to them.

I rubbed my arms and listened at my bedroom window, afraid to look outside but more fearful not to see what was approaching. The dark sky above the mountains turned dense and blocked out the stars. If those were storm clouds, the disturbance was isolated to the mountain.

I had a feeling it wouldn't stay there long. With Zozobra taking place tomorrow, this was no coincidence. This was a warning.

Since my grandmother's arrival, I'd spent every spare moment with her and my aunt preparing for our main event at the festival—the showdown with Old Man Gloom. When I wasn't physically with them, I sensed their psyches alongside mine. I visualized the three of us encircling the corporeal spirit, and with each chant, he grew smaller and smaller until he disappeared entirely. Every triumph in these visions strengthened my own spirit. I stood taller after every battle. My confidence in our victory was as solid as my bones. And the flesh around my bones vibrated with lightning, waiting to be concentrated for a strike.

We'd practiced the ritual so many times, the songs and dance steps repeated in my dreams. So many times, surely the spirit had taken notice. Maybe this was his answer.

A shadowy veil swept across the sky, too fast to be a mere storm cloud. It brought a storm of a different kind, and when it began to rain down, the patter sounded like manic laughter. It battered rooftops and windows, and it pounded the ground.

Anyone else would hear wind and rain. For a moment, I telescoped away from myself and had a different perspective. I saw myself as if from a distance, scheming with the women in my family, performing secret rituals with them, and preparing for a battle that no one else knew about.

Was I crazy? Even a few months ago, if I'd glimpsed a future version of myself, I'd have answered yes. Who acted like that? Who believed in shamans having power over supernatural beings? Not me, not until I'd moved here. Everything about my present life had a surreal quality to it. If I tried to explain any part of what my family and I had been up to, what we believed, we'd be locked in the looney bin.

Had the stress of the past year somehow twisted my mind? Had I listened to too many legends and fairy tales as a girl and imagined everything I'd encountered?

A movement in the sky sent a shudder through me that gathered in my heart, resonating deeper, until it threatened to explode. The black cloud-swarm whooshed directly overhead. Tentacles reached down into the streets, black fingers that felt along the neighborhoods in a frantic search for an opening. Any house not bearing a black star was vulnerable, and the flow of the cloud splintered and veered toward it.

With the exception of my family, no one else was able to see them. I couldn't even warn anyone, but I knew what would follow. People would become irritated and fight with one another as their troubles doubled back on them. Frustration would drive them to do things they'd never think to do otherwise.

The collective shrieks and patters from the swarm assaulted my senses. This was no figment of my imagination. The force might be invisible, but the evil intent was palpable.

Forcing a deep breath to calm myself, I did what came naturally—I envisioned my aunt, grandmother, and I confronting the spirit. The vision of our ritual replaced the view through the window.

Black flickers outlined the pane. I kept chanting, but my focus skewed to the intrusion. They gathered at my window in a show of power. To mock me. To prove me wrong.

It was working. I began to sputter the words, and my voice weakened, from steel to putty. The window blackened, tiny bits of black consolidating into a thick mass. Laughter sounded, distant but closing in fast. The spirit boomed every laugh at me, and each one hit me like a cannonball. I rounded with each assault. Zelda and *Halmeoni* vanished from my vision.

I was alone. And Old Man Gloom was coming for me. Every laugh pounded into me until I was doubled over.

Doubt blackened my mind, blotted my memory. Gasping, I could barely chant, puffing the words like smoke signals. My legs threatened to give out beneath me. If that happened, utter failure would follow.

My breath constricted. I couldn't tell if the flickering black bits swimming in my sight were from the swarm, or if I was about to pass out.

"Help me, *Ptesan-Wi.*" I made a point to speak aloud, but the words came out in a rasp.

A brilliant point of light appeared in my vision. *Ptesan-Wi's* presence was strong, though I couldn't make her out within the blinding light.

"You are the daughter of lightning."

My palm lay across my stomach. Electricity tingled beneath my skin, faint but unmistakable.

I would not give up. Not without a fight.

My body trembled with the effort of standing straight. With the last strength I could find within me, I gathered that electricity. Another cannonball struck me. The globe of energy wavered but didn't break apart.

Planting my feet wide and steady against the wooden floor, I willed the force into my hand. "I am the daughter of lightning," I announced, clear and loud and strong.

I hurled the bolt of electricity into the midst of the swarm. Through sheer force of will, I sent it beyond, to the approaching spirit.

He didn't laugh then. An agonized cry filled the air. The lightning burned him. For a moment, he floated, stunned and enraged.

I was dredging up what energy I had left, readying for another strike. It might not be enough to stop him again, but I would never stop trying.

He seemed to consider his next move. A low groan built up cyclone-fast into a tsunami of a scream, then he whipped around and shot back toward the mountain.

As he receded, the undertow tugged me into its

wake. I stumbled forward but caught myself.

The black bits peeled back from my window and swam away into the night. The last wisps of the cloud trailed from view.

Trembling, I eased backward until the bed came up against the back of my legs. I closed my eyes and smoothed the stinging prongs from the concentrated energy, allowed it to spread through me again and settle into my body. Only then did I let myself sit, but I was still wired. The surprise confrontation unsettled me.

My world seemed so fragile. Everything I'd worked for, trying to build a life here, was suddenly at risk. Despite my family's good intentions, a few days of preparation for what we'd face tomorrow seemed too little, too late. And I wasn't at all convinced I had the mojo necessary to face whatever awaited us tomorrow night. Exorcise an evil spirit? Not exactly my area of expertise.

Every part of my reality was at odds with what my aunt and grandmother expected of me. They'd have a better chance of success if they performed the ritual without me. I had nothing to offer them. I'd only get in their way. I was the Joker card, the anomaly that would throw off their chances.

I paced from my spot at the window, taking in my apartment. The place didn't look much different from when I'd moved in. It would be so easy to gather my few belongings. Bolt from this town. Disappear.

But to where? And if I did leave, I'd lose everything: my family, my career, Ray.

Pain stabbed my heart. Only a coward would consider leaving them unprotected. I'd never forgive myself if any harm came to them.

That's what Old Man Gloom was counting on, for me to surrender before the fight. Surrender was out of the question.

Maybe I'd been wrong when I assumed that my aunt's ferocity was part of her DNA alone. The spark of anger was rising within me, a fierceness new but undeniable. Tomorrow, I'd stand with my aunt and grandmother, a trinity of power.

I had run away once in my life. I wouldn't run away again.

****

Shakespeare had it right when he wrote: *That way lies madness.* But there was no other way for me, so I followed the path set out before me. Waiting at the end of that path was one hell of a roadblock: Old Man Gloom. I guessed tonight would either prove to be the end of the road for me or somehow a new path would open.

On the drive through the city, I took in every detail. The shadows that had descended in the night lingered, nestled into corners and deepening the shadows created by the rising sun. From the ashes scattered across the desert over the past one hundred years, the spirit had conjured up the burned bits of people's troubles and cast them back onto the city. Whatever troubles that people had before were nothing compared to this. For some, the burden might be too great to bear. People argued in the streets, slammed their car doors after they climbed out, and every face registered sadness or anger.

Old Man Gloom had promised revenge, and it had already begun.

I rushed into the *Chronicle*, intending to stay as short a time as possible before heading to Fort Marcy

Park where the committee members would assemble the effigy for tonight. Zelda would have my head if I didn't participate in every aspect of the events, and I'd promised to photograph the spectators, usually local kids.

Besides, everyone in the newsroom had fallen victim to the mass *ennui* as well. They were preoccupied with envy, bitterness, or worry, their gazes distant and cold.

Ashley was no exception. "Guess you're hot shit today." Her glance was a cold blade knifing through me.

Reminding myself that she wasn't to blame, I shrugged. "Shit, yes. Hot, doubtful."

"After today, we won't have to listen to Weller gushing about your festival articles."

"He gushed?" How had I missed that?

She snatched up her mug and arched over her desk, narrowed eyes glittering. "You'll be an ordinary cog like the rest of us." Her lip curled, she turned and walked away.

I'd give anything to be ordinary. If I said so, she'd go ballistic, interpreting the statement as bragging, rather than begging.

I studied her, the unusual curve of her shoulders, like the world weighed on her more than anyone else. I grabbed my cup and caught up to her at the coffee maker. "Ashley, did you hang that star on your house?"

"What? No." She sounded incredulous. "I'm supposed to drive a nail into a rental? I can't afford to give up my deposit money. Until the divorce is final, my finances are under strict control. I'm going to make that asshole pay." She slammed the pot onto the burner, and coffee sloshed over the rim. "And anyway, even if the landlord didn't complain, a black star would have looked awful."

Oh, God. The man who was Zozobra must have gotten to her. "I'm sorry for your troubles."

Ashley stared as if I'd said I was running off with the circus.

"If you need to talk," I said, avoiding her gaze as I filled my cup so as not to scare her off, "we can go out for a drink some night, and you can vent all you need to."

"Why are you being so nice?" She sounded suspicious.

I kept my voice firm but pleasant. "Talking about your troubles helps. It can't take away all of the burden, but even if it relieves a small bit of stress, I'm happy to help."

"Yeah. Sure."

"I mean it." My cell chimed with an incoming call. "Sorry, I have to take this. Hello?" I headed for my desk.

Zelda launched into her tirade. "When are you going to get here?"

"I have to finish a few things. Do you need me there now?" Anticipating her answer, I was already logging off my computer.

"Yes. Or no, if the committee caves to pressure."

"What do you mean?"

"Some members want to call off the festival." She choked out the words, as if strangled by frustration.

"They can't." That would ruin everything. Old Man Gloom would certainly win.

"Everything's in chaos."

Including my aunt, apparently. I'd never heard her so unsettled. "I'll come over now." A click, and the cell went dark. "I have to go."

Ashley had settled in her chair, back stiff as she clicked the mouse. "See you there tonight."

I hated to say this, but I did anyway. "Please, don't go to Zozobra. Stay home." I stopped myself from advising her to lock her doors. It might not help anyway.

"Why?" Her lip curled as if she were nauseated.

"It's going to be a madhouse. Worse than any other year." I waited for her to call me out, as I hadn't exactly been a regular attendee at the event.

She jabbed a glossy, blood-red finger through the air. "No way. My troubles are going up in smoke, and I intend to be there to watch."

So I would have to watch out for her. "Just...be careful."

"Aw," she sneered, "I didn't know you cared."

"I'm serious, Ashley. If anything seems off, get out of there. Please. I'd feel terrible if something happened to you." I stared at her, willing the words to get through whatever daze she was in.

Her eyes cleared, and she visibly sobered. "Okay. I'll be careful."

The tension that had gathered in my body flowed out in a breath. I hated to leave her. By tonight, she'd probably fall under Old Man Gloom's influence again. I'd just have to make sure she didn't fall victim to him.

I hurried toward the exit, wondering how the hell I was supposed to save the city. I couldn't even save one person.

"Hey Marissa," she called.

I turned.

"You watch yourself, too." Spoken begrudgingly, but aloud.

Joy welled up inside me. Ashley had asserted herself, and if only for a moment, had won out over Old Man Gloom.

But then she broke the spell with a mix of bewilderment and disgust at my reaction.

Of course she'd think I'd lost my mind. She had no clue what the stakes included.

Without further adieu, I hurried to my car. Getting fired for leaving earlier than I'd requested would be the least terrible thing that could happen today.

With the familiar blues riff, my cell signaled a text. I slid into the SUV and slammed the door. "All right, Zelda."

But Ray's name appeared in the display. I swiped the screen and read:

—*Be careful. I'll see you soon.*—

All the nervousness and anxiety that had been seeping under my skin stopped. Until then, I hadn't realized the overflow of everyone else's bad moods was infecting me.

One message from Ray was enough to re-center myself. I beamed as I texted him to be careful, too, then whispered, "Thanks, Sunshine."

I plastered a smile on my face like a shield and drove across town.

****

Zelda's hawk-like gaze followed me as I approached, camera in hand. I wielded it like another shield against her and lined up my picture, capturing the excitement on the kids' faces. Or so I thought. When I paid closer attention to their expressions, they mirrored the adults' disapproval and anger. One girl of about seven caught sight of the camera pointed at her, fully faced me, and stuck out her tongue. I took the shot, and she mouthed, *Asshole.*

My mouth dropped open. I knew if I let her get to me, a flood of bad vibes would follow, so I put up my best defense. I laughed. Then I pointed the lens in another direction. Some shots would have to show people from the back rather than the front.

Zelda stood at the burning site, arms folded and rolling her eyes, calling out instructions to the other committee members. Various pieces of the effigy were spread across the ground, still unassembled.

"Shouldn't Señor Zozobra be upright by now?" I murmured to her.

"He will be. As soon as our colleagues stop bickering and work together." She spoke loudly enough for them to hear.

George and Tomas ignored her. Trisha Brock looked peevish as she whispered something to Peter River, then called, "Rather than criticizing, perhaps you'd like to actually help."

"Of course, we'll help." Zelda grasped my arm and tugged me into the fray. Without intending to, I resisted, my senses repulsed at having to actually touch any part of the effigy. My aunt shot me a look of warning before releasing me. I forced myself to follow her, but my body moved as slowly as if fighting a current of murky water. Over the next hour, as we worked in teams to attach the head and limbs to the torso, the urge to let myself sink into their hazy depths whispered to me. I slowly quashed its siren call by repeating in my head the chants that *Halmeoni* had taught me. I hummed to myself to reinforce the protection against the spirit's assault, the temptation to give in, give up. Only despair would follow. When we'd finished our task, I stepped back with renewed strength.

Her breaths labored, Trisha stretched her back. "What's that tune?"

"I'm practicing for tonight." And continued with greater concentration as George, Tomas, and Peter fastened cables to the hooks of the interior harness hidden beneath the fifty-foot effigy's robes. George's design had worked fine in previous years, but there was no telling what the spirit would do this year.

"Right," said Trisha, "you and your aunt."

Not wanting to break the rhythm, I merely nodded. They'd begun hoisting the effigy. People cheered, and children screamed in excitement. They gave a collective moan when a cable snagged on the frame.

George called, "Hold up." He shielded his eyes against the sun and peered from below. "I don't see anything. One more time. If it's still stuck, I'll need to climb up there."

No. The spirit would sabotage the ladder and hurt George. It would try anything to ruin the event. I chanted aloud, strong enough for my voice to carry.

Zelda slipped her hand in mine and her deep, rich tone joined mine.

With one pull, the cable slid over the frame, and Old Man Gloom jerked upward, head hung low. I gave my aunt's hand a squeeze, and we chanted together. The effigy jerked with each tug, arms swinging like a drunk in a bar fight.

The crowd jeered with each swing and sent up a rousing yell when the effigy fully stood alongside the frame. Another pull of the cables, and its enormous head lifted. Red lips drawn in a wide smile appeared more jagged and vicious than it had before. Tension filled the air and hung heavy above us. Old Man Gloom's head turned slowly, seemingly scanning the people below. They stared back in hushed silence. Whether they felt the anger leeching from the effigy or not, I couldn't tell, but mothers gathered their children to them, and the crowd began to scatter.

Zelda sent them off with a beauty queen wave. "See you tonight. The festival starts at eight o'clock."

Through immobile lips, I murmured, "Might be better if they stayed home this time."

"Do you believe that would make any difference?"

Michael had been at home. It had done him more ill than good. "No," I conceded, and walked aside my aunt toward the parking lot. "Where is Grandmother?"

"At home. We need to go there anyway, to eat and change, among other things." Zelda shifted her gaze from side to side, her expression morphing into unabashed glamour when greeting someone she knew.

Grandmother had already warned me our work would begin at home. Every step of the ritual was sacred, to be performed with utmost intention and concentration. The strain of such an effort on an elderly woman must be terrible, I thought. "I hope she's resting for tonight."

"Resting? She's been up since daybreak, lighting incense and chanting. The ritual isn't a performance art piece, you know."

"I understand." I also understood that if Zelda

didn't lighten up, she'd become another disgruntled Santa Fe citizen. "Aunt Zelda?"

"What?" Her tone was flat.

I set my mouth in as wide a smile as I could manage. "Do this."

She shoo'd at me with a wave. "I've no time for nonsense."

"Not to get all Deepak Choprah or anything, but this"—I pointed to my lips, which were already growing tired—"is an important weapon against Old Man Gloom."

"Don't repeat that to my mother," she deadpanned. "Or you may have to fend her off, too."

"It makes sense to send out good vibes to counteract the bad." At her half-hearted attempt, I added, "Haven't you noticed people are already aggravated? By tonight, we may have an unruly mob on our hands. The more we can calm them the better until we can kick the spirit's ass."

"Just what do you think I've been doing all morning?" she countered.

She was right. And I wasn't helping, I was unwittingly stirring up irritation. So I clamped my mouth shut, climbed into my SUV, and hummed to dispel whatever negativity had slipped past my defenses.

If the protections erected by our chanting faded that fast, we were in for a hell of a night.

Chapter Twenty-Three

Tonight, fire was a welcome sight. As Zelda, my grandmother, and I rode to Fort Marcy Park, candles burned in the windows of homes, but the darkness encasing the city was thick and heavy and restless. Old Man Gloom loved the dark, loved how it seemed to magnify people's troubles and encouraged despair. Any type of light was welcome, yet another weapon for our battle.

Riding in the back seat of my aunt's car, my nerves hummed, every part of me singing with life as never before. We had begun our private ritual at Zelda's house after lunch, pooling our energies together. Whether chanting together or readying ourselves in silent meditation, the preparations had cleansed my spirit. Free of the weight of any ill feelings, I was worthy of wearing the costume. And the three of us had forged a strong spiritual connection. I literally felt the essences of my aunt and grandmother like a live electric wire running between us.

I smoothed the red skirt of the costume. Almost certainly my mother had worn this same one at some point. I could sense her with me, too. Her strength flowed into me, and her love wrapped around me.

Zelda parked and we climbed out of the car in unison, our linked power choreographing our movements. Our invincibility shrunk in the presence of the effigy towering over us. Its glowing green eyes gave its white face an even more ghastly appearance. We proceeded in a solemn line to its base, to the side of the platform.

Tens of thousands of people had gathered on the field, the press of bodies a weight on my consciousness. There were certainly more than the usual fifty thousand. A veritable feast for the spirit to gorge upon, if we let him. And if a mass panic should ensue, the crush of bodies… No. That's why we were there. To prevent such occurrences.

Zelda skirted along the stage to the front and made a quick check-in with the other committee members and hurried back to us. "They're set to start."

Halmeoni clasped her hands in front of her. "Then we must begin as well."

We stepped onto the platform and positioned ourselves in the rear corner. In with a deep breath, we chanted as one. We bowed our heads and lowered our voices as a local girl shuffled to the stage and gave a shaky but passable rendition of the national anthem. We maintained the same softness as Trisha Brock scurried to the spotlight to welcome everyone to the centennial celebration of Zozobra, then announced the fire spirit dancer.

A figure in a red bodysuit whirled onto the platform, ribbons flowing from his arms like flames as he leapt and twirled to chase away the glooms gathered within the effigy. Whistling pops gave way to booms as fireworks burst behind the monstrous puppet. Light applause echoed through the crowd. The committee kept the light show brief, and to the slow beat of a drum, Trisha Brock returned to announce Judge Sparkio

Illumino.

Dressed in a black suit, Peter River strode to the microphone. "We have gathered here to mete out punishment to Señor Zozobra, also known as Old Man Gloom. Zozobra has been found guilty of many crimes against the good people of Santa Fe. Innumerable counts of frightening youngsters with his moaning and growling. An untold number of times, Zozobra has roamed our streets undetected and haunted our dreams."

A shudder ran through me at the reminder of Old Man Gloom terrifying me while I dreamt. I hoped *Halmeoni* was right that our ritual could banish him.

She caught my glance and pinned me with a look to shame the doubt from me. If we were to succeed, I must set aside my fears and put every ounce of faith into our private ceremony.

Santa Fe. Holy faith.

As the Judge, Peter went on condemning Old Man Gloom for various crimes, upsetting the peace of Santa Fe residents, for inspiring only sadness and anxiety. Then he called out, "Good people of Santa Fe, it is time for you to decide the fate of Señor Zozobra, whether he should face a fiery death? What say you?"

The angry cheer that rang out in the night chilled my blood. People pumped their fists in the air.

"Shall we burn him?" Peter hardly needed to incite them.

Everyone yelled in chorus, "Burn him! Burn him!"

A deep groan rose from the effigy, and it swayed, though there was no wind.

Peter raised his hand. "The people have decided. I, Judge Sparkio Illumino, sentence Señor Zozobra to death by fire. On this very night, the ogre known as Old

Man Gloom shall burn in a righteous ceremony. The execution of this monster Zozobra shall thereby release the gathered sorrows, troubles, heartaches, and sadnesses of our fair city. And all who bear witness tonight shall be liberated from their sufferings."

"I ask that everyone here—" Peter shot a glance over his shoulder.

The fifty-foot Old Man Gloom growled and moaned behind him. As it had this morning, the effigy seemed to glare at the people encircling him. This time, rather than staring back like sheep, their faces mirrored Old Man Gloom's. Eyebrows knit into slanted slashes. Eyes burned with smoldering anger. Lips snarled in jagged grimaces.

Bad vibes zigzagged in the air like heat rising off a summer blacktop.

Zelda grasped my hand, and my grandmother's. "Keep chanting, no matter what." Her deep voice rumbled with fear, and mine sounded shaky and weak. *Halmeoni* sang out clear and strong.

Peter called out, "Señor Zozobra must burn!" He gestured to Tomas and Trish, who raised the lit torches they held. In unison, they swung them down and touched the tips to the hem of Old Man Gloom's robes.

Zozobra threw back his huge head and lifted his hands, what should have been an impossible move. One of the wires snapped, freeing his arm. His deep sleeve grazed the platform as he reached out toward the people gathered around him.

A glance over my shoulder, and my heart skipped. *Ashley.*

Mesmerized, she stood at the front of the crowd. From her expression, she wasn't certain who or what she was seeing as she stared at the effigy. Then she reached out toward the enormous white-gloved hand hovering toward her.

"No!" I started to lunge toward her. My aunt and grandmother held me back. "I have to stop her."

"You must stay in the circle with us," *Halmeoni* said.

Despair tangled my thoughts. I'd already broken the chant, and a young couple were arguing. A mother snapped at her teenaged daughters. Anger rippled through the masses.

I held tight to my aunt and grandmother and focused on our ritual. My concentration wavered when I spotted Javi threading through the crowd. His instinct to protect people must have propelled him toward the threat, though he didn't understand the real danger. He managed to squeeze through to the front.

"Javi!" I yelled between choruses. I caught his eye and nodded toward Ashley. "Get her out of here."

He scrambled along the press of people and threw his arms around Ashley. She twisted from his embrace and slapped him. My voice hitched, but I kept chanting, willing Javi not to give up. He looped an arm around her waist and dragged her. She kicked and screamed. Another man blocked his path. Javi argued, and two more men formed a barrier.

No, no. Half-heartedly, I remained in unison with my aunt and grandmother, but I strained to see what was happening.

A blond-haired man broke into their midst. *Ray!* My excitement came through in my chants. He held up his hands, his expression pleasant as he pointed to Ashley and Javi, and then gestured toward the parking lot. Whatever he told them worked, and the men stepped aside. Javi and Ray guided Ashley away.

A breath of relief escaped between chants. She was safe, thanks to Javi and Ray.

A flash of heat swept over us. Fire climbed the white robes, and the effigy thrashed its arms from side to side and bellowed in agony. At the noise, a gauzy shadow flew out from his side like a magician's scarf. Within were dark shapes, each one screaming as it fluttered into the night. The chittering of the escaping shadows grew louder until the shrieks pierced my ears like a hot needle. I chanted louder but couldn't drown out the high-pitched sound, like a flock of frenzied birds.

The shadowy shapes flitted through the crowd. One by one, the expressions of those in the audience twisted in pain, their faces reflected in the firelight as Old Man Gloom burned in front of them. The black shapes landed on the people, sometimes only one shadow, sometimes an entire group of them. When the shadows landed, they disappeared, as if absorbed beneath each person's skin. I didn't trust my own eyes and wondered if the play of firelight on their skin made it appear that way. Until I realized what the shadows really were— the written troubles returning to the one who'd brought them to the effigy.

Old Man Gloom was refusing to carry the burden and was casting off all the troubles, sending them back one-hundred fold to whomever they belonged.

I turned to my family. "Zelda, *Halmeoni.* We have failed."

"You must not give up."

At Zelda's stern voice, I joined in the chanting

again.

Then I saw him, the younger man who'd been haunting me. He stood near the front of the stage, laughing at us.

My mind blanked with fury. "How dare you?" I broke the circle and rushed at him.

This time, he raised his chin in defiance and waited. Despite my anger, I was awed by his beauty. The deep slant of his furrowed brow over large, expressive eyes. The full mouth, even set in a smirk, was perfect. The wind played in his black hair.

One so strikingly handsome must have some good in him. "Stop this. Please, before it's too late."

He shook in a hearty laugh, his only response.

"Señor Zozobra, I implore you. The people don't understand what they've done. Don't make them suffer."

Hate glittered in his eyes as he looked out over the crowd, most of whom were growing more miserable by the minute. The black forms still emptied from the effigy's side and swarmed back to their owners.

The man's expression shifted, a subtle change but important. More than bitterness and hatred, he seemed sad. If he had any feelings, there was a chance for good to prevail.

He startled when I stepped closer and turned his glare on me.

I reached up to stroke his cheek. His skin looked smooth but was prickly to the touch. I kept stroking, hoping to soothe him.

With a hiss, he grabbed my wrist to stay my hand. His grasp was like hot coals singeing my skin, but I didn't flinch. I searched his eyes, and the green of his irises began to glow. My pulse thudded, but I mustered the courage to raise up on tiptoe and brush my lips against his. A tingle of electricity sparked on my mouth, thousands of tiny knives stabbing me. I closed my eyes to block the sight of him.

He remained perfectly still, so I steeled myself against the increasing shock and held the kiss. He gave so much to the people for one hundred years. I wanted to show him not everything in this world was terrible.

His hand cupped the back of my neck like a vise. Panic welled up when he pressed his lips harder against mine, barbs of electric pain stabbing my mouth. His tongue parted my lips, a hot poker probing me. Invisible fire danced along my limbs, sinking into my muscles, turning my bones into molten lava. The pain paralyzed me, and I cried out, but his mouth on mine stifled the sound. Hot tears streamed down my face, the wetness cooling my cheeks for only a moment before vanishing, my desperately thirsty skin drinking them in nearly as fast as I shed them. I twisted against his weight, but only battered myself more. He didn't budge.

So I held him closer. Beneath his clothes, he was all hard angles, his joints like awkward hinges on wooden boards cobbled together. The rough skin of his palm bruised me through the fabric.

The tiny dark forms flew at me, their chittering shrieks a tangible terror. Burrowing beneath my skin, shredding my spirit. One hundred years of troubles ate away at me, ravenous for redemption. I knew Zozobra was feeding on my suffering, but I felt powerless to stop him.

From a dark place in my head that seemed to

stretch into a black void, a small voice cried out, *"That's what he wants. Humiliation. Surrender. You must have faith."*

"Holy faith," my mother's voice whispered. *"Santa Fe."* The faith that my aunt and grandmother used as their foundation of strength. The faith that was the foundation of this city.

But I was weak. The parasites had left only a thin, tattered veil of my former being. If I did nothing, soon there would be nothing left to me.

I let my instincts go fluid, to float in the black void. I felt myself wilting, shrinking in upon myself, slipping down, melting into a formless puddle. Only a tiny spark at the center held my soul's light. I concentrated on that spark. Bound it with gratitude and fed it unconditional love.

A pulse, and the spark grew. Within the light, my form began to rise and take shape once again. A girl of five, pure of heart, my soul untarnished. I was filled with joy and wonder and love.

I raised my hands and offered that trinity of purity to him.

Uncertainty lingered behind his glare. I radiated love and acceptance toward him. *"Be at peace,"* I told him without speaking.

His face softened, and he reached a tentative hand out. *"Peace is not in my nature."*

"You can resist your basest nature. Overcome it."

His laugh was like thunder. *"No. People conjured me to be who I am. Called me up from a blissful nothingness to become their Old Man Gloom. I am made up of sorrow and anguish, a hateful vessel to carry their troubles."* Each word was sharper and louder than the last. Anger electrified the air between us.

His fury blazed higher when he saw Zelda and my grandmother rushing toward us. Struggling to run, yet they were barely covering any ground. The man's humorless smile signaled he was keeping them at bay. When he raised his hand, I knew he was going to hurt them. He couldn't help himself. It was his nature.

But I couldn't let him.

I chanted, summoning the forces that wildly spun around us. The atmosphere around me thickened in concentration. An aura of energy hummed and sparkled like tiny fireworks. The electrified force simultaneously slid across my skin and beneath it, both a protection against an unseen assault and a power that bound itself to me.

From somewhere buried within myself, I dredged up a reserve of energy. Deep as the ocean, with calm as its center, power awaited my command. I concentrated on harnessing that force, drawing it up my spine, its spiky cogs digging into each vertebra as it scaled higher. The heated mass gathered momentum as it climbed. Anger crested at the base of my skull. The buzz of energy built inside me, a pressure cooker with the lid jangling. It took everything I had to hold onto it. When it threatened to burst out uncontrolled, I focused on releasing it all at once. In my mind, I saw a spike of light shoot from the hollow of my throat and through my silver flame necklace. Instead, the energy poured from my fingertips, my eyes, my pores. The ends of my hair writhed like live wires.

I needed no flame pendant for a talisman. I alone controlled the power.

I aimed the burst at him. "No!"

The jolt of lightning flung him backward. He stumbled, backpedaling, then crumpled to the ground. He lay there, staring at me, his mouth gaping, the smile replaced by surprise.

I glared at him. *"I am Sioux-sister to Ptesan-Wi, White Buffalo Woman. Keeper of the eternal lightning."* The words came through me like the power—unbidden but unstoppable.

The same as in my vision, I felt White Buffalo Woman's presence behind me. But this time, we didn't join into one entity, and I didn't act through her. Whatever energy poured through me, I alone possessed.

Yet I was anything but alone. The spirit of Fire Eagle rose to my left, and on my right, my mother stood with me. I existed in two realms, that of the earth, and that of the spirit. Somewhere behind me, and above me, my brother's presence rose, a powerful shield between Zozobra and the people gathered around the effigy.

In the earthly world, my aunt and grandmother broke through the transparent barrier that the spirit had erected to keep them out.

I ran toward the young Zozobra, and at the same time extended my hand to my aunt and grandmother. "Hurry."

They hurried up behind me on either side, grabbed my hands and we rushed toward him.

The spirit-man realized too late what we meant to do. Behind the stage, towering over us, the monstrous effigy yowled. Bits of embers broke from its burning body and rained down around us, scorching the ground.

Zelda and *Halmeoni* and I quickly formed a circle around the man, linked by our hands. We chanted. My aunt's voice, smoke over gravel, underscored my grandmother's high-pitched and my mid-range tone. We were in perfect synchronization and harmony.

Echoed by the burning effigy, the young Zozobra's groans issued through the air, loud as thunder. A dark cyclone whirled around him. Its winds whipped at us like a cat o' nine tails. His features were blurred behind the whirlwind, which grew thicker with each turn.

A powerful energy zinged through my body, remnants left behind by the lightning instilled in me during the first ritual. Afraid that my family would be harmed, I spun a web of binding light around the spirit-man. Sparks ignited through my body as I summoned the electricity embedded within me. Flashes jabbed the air around me, a charged aura ready to burst. Rather than merely channeling it, I became the lightning. I was the electric fire with the power to parse the spirit from its sheltered haven within the effigy.

Directing a laser of concentration upon him, I burned open the shell housing the essence of Zozobra. He twisted and turned, trying to shield himself, but was helpless against the searing force that stripped away the protective layers, exposing him so that the fire could do the most important work of all: freeing the spirit.

Trouble by trouble, year by year, I incised with razor precision, feeling my way intuitively around the edges fastening the spirit to the effigy. Each newly shredded strip of black fell from him, embers fading into cold nothingness. Each loss robbed him of more power. Stole more of his essence until finally, only a wisp remained. Not black, as I'd expected, but white. Flames surrounded him, the very fire required to finally sever the spirit from its encasement.

"Marissa…" someone called, his voice sounding as if through a long tunnel.

At the jolt to my consciousness, I nearly lost my hold on the spirit. I glanced away long enough to spot Ray along the outer edge of the circle wrapped around my aunt, grandmother, and me. I couldn't answer the question in his eyes, not right now.

But when he looked at the place where we'd trapped Old Man Gloom, his gaze intensified.

He sees. The thought interrupted the flow of lightning energy, but I quickly reinforced it and sealed the opening so Zozobra could not escape before we'd completed our ritual.

Behind us, I clearly heard Ray this time. "Do it. Hurry!" Whatever distance had existed between us, he'd somehow bridged it. His presence was as palpable as *Ptesan-Wi*'s.

The ground beneath the whittled spirit of Old Man Gloom opened up into a pit of blackness with no bottom. My stomach churned as I fought the familiar horror of falling endlessly through nothing, an endless abyss. Zelda and my grandmother squeezed my hands tight and chanted louder. So did I.

With Ray behind us, and Fire Eagle and my mother above us, our trio had expanded into a mandala of power.

Trembles shook the ground, the tremors climbing my legs, but I stood fast and strong. Even when my teeth threatened to rattle from my head, I chanted along with my family.

I sensed rather than the saw the shadowed bits soaring down into the pit after the spirit. The black rain shrieked past me into the midst of our circle, pelting us like a shower of stones. My aunt and grandmother tightened their grasps on my hands, and I did the same. Their echoing sound faded as the dark bits fell into the vast well of nothingness.

Like a burrowing rodent, the spirit and his swarming entourage of troubles tunneled underground in the direction of the Sangre de Cristo Mountains. We had severed the spirit from his century-old fortress.

After what might have been moments or minutes, the tremors gradually eased. The cyclone died down to a mere breeze, then the air stilled. The abyss in the earth crumbled and groaned as it knit its edges together until once again solid ground sat beneath our feet. Zelda and my grandmother continued to chant, and I followed their lead. With our hands clasped tightly together, we finished the ritual to the end, and then we, too, fell silent.

The quiet of the night was more eerie than Zozobra's growls. Was the spirit truly gone? Listening for any sign, my shallow breaths scraped in and out. My flesh smoldered, slowly cooling from the extreme heat. The back of my neck burned to the touch.

"Leave that be," *Halmeoni* said in a hush, then gestured Zelda to look. "The lightning left its mark upon her."

Awe washed over my aunt's face. "You did it, didn't you? You severed the spirit from its connection to the effigy." No taunt sounded in her tone, no dig at my grandmother, who'd tried many times before, and failed.

But had I really succeeded?

"Did we banish him?" I whispered, afraid to look anywhere but at my grandmother. I wouldn't claim to have accomplished such a feat on my own. Without my family—both alive and in spirit—the outcome would have been far different.

Halmeoni's eyes were brightly glowing coals in the darkness. "Are we not *mudang*?"

A laugh burst from me. "The best in town."

"In town," *Halmeoni* murmured with a shake of her head, then fluttered a theatrical hand. "In the world." She grasped my shoulders. "From this day forward, Marissa, you need never fear again."

Had she heard what I'd told the spirit, that I was a Sioux-sister to White Buffalo Woman?

"What about them?" I searched the faces of those people nearest to us and was buoyed by their cheerfulness. Their troubles had fled into the pit with the man. *No, not a man*, I reminded myself. A vengeful spirit personified, and now vanquished.

Only one man's face registered worry as he stepped inside the circle of burnt ground. "Marissa?"

"Ray." He was safe. A flood of relief nearly made me blubber his name.

"What the hell was that?" He let out a stilted breath. "The spirit of Old Man Gloom? How did you defeat him?"

"You saw." I hadn't imagined it.

"Yes. No one else seemed to, but…" He shook his head. "The lightning, the fire…that was not for show. And those tremors weren't a normal earthquake. You risked your lives, going up against Old Man Gloom like that."

"He's gone." So had the lightning retreated, to somewhere deep inside. All that remained were tiny sparks in my bones. Waiting for the next time I summoned them.

Halmeoni's nod was solemn. "He is indeed. For now."

I squeezed her hand. So long as the effigy had a name, the spirit would return each year. But at least we'd relieved the burden from him. For now.

No one should have to carry one hundred years' worth of troubles.

"Are you all right?" He brushed his hand across my cheek, the back of my neck.

My skin sizzled along the path of his fingertips. I curled against the heat and drew in a different sort of energy. It traveled through his touch, yet also radiated from all over his body.

"You were part of it, too." The ground hadn't split apart until Ray stood with us. If he hadn't come along when he did, would we have been able to defeat the spirit?

I'd never know. All I knew for certain was that I didn't want to lose Ray.

Then I saw him with new eyes and understood that I was not the only one who had yet to explore undiscovered powers. Whether he understood it or not, he possessed an innate gift, a strength beyond mere muscles, that had reinforced ours.

"Me? I didn't do anything."

"Just by standing beside us, you lent me your strength." Ray had become a firefighter out of a sense of duty and honor. Beneath that was another calling, a more primitive one that urged him to act without thought to his own welfare. Some ancient heritage that had been passed down through generation after generation. It had touched Rusty, but fully infused Ray.

He had yet to fully explore and exercise his powers.

But the heat he ignited in me was a different sort of fire. It set sparks dancing in my flesh. It was the kind of blaze that cried out for more, that wanted to dance into a frenzy of passion, to be consumed by its own flame, and then rise again, a phoenix of desire.

Was that why the spirit of Old Man Gloom worked so hard to keep us apart? Together, we generated a powerful force. One the spirit could never overcome, because it was the most positive thing in the universe, the one force not even time could extinguish.

Love.

Chapter Twenty-Four

Nothing remained of Zozobra, either the effigy or the spirit. A heap of charred ashes sat beneath the metal stand used to maneuver the puppet. The last of the smoke had dissipated from the sky, and stars shone crisp and clear above Fort Marcy Park.

Around us, people had stopped cheering and wore somewhat dazed expressions.

One older woman shook her head. "I feel like I'm waking up from a bad dream."

"You too?" the elderly man beside her asked. "I thought it was just me."

"Yes," the woman said, "but I could swear I'm ten pounds lighter, like a weight's been lifted from me."

"I haven't felt this good in years." The man grasped her hand. "Let's go get a drink and celebrate."

Joy lifted my spirit, too. I turned to Ray, and he took my hand in his. The connection between us was immediate and more solid than I'd ever known.

We watched as the throngs began to break up, couples and families strolling off. Relief showed on some faces, and weariness on others, but beneath an unmistakable glow of serenity.

Old Man Gloom had tried to curse everyone as they had cursed him, by making them carry their own troubles, times one hundred. Our ritual had cleansed that burden from those who had gathered.

"They have been granted peace."

My grandmother spoke my thought. The buzz of irritation and unpleasantness that had infested the city since I'd arrived had dissipated, broken apart, and receded like a storm. Even now, the last remnants of the disturbance were ebbing, returning to their source at the pulsing heart of the mountain, there to be held until called upon again.

Zelda herded us toward the debris, where a dozen volunteers were assisting the other committee members with cleanup. "One final task. Let's get this over with."

Ray worked alongside us, raking burnt linen and wood into piles, then he shoveled them into tin garbage cans. George and Peter hauled away the filled containers and loaded them onto the back of a pickup. Trisha doused what remained of the fires with water, and then she scooped the wet mess into recycled plastic containers.

Finished with our duty, we stood back to survey the area and make certain nothing had been left undone. Volunteers had disassembled the stage platform and the frame to which the effigy had been strapped. Only a few blackened patches of ground marred Fort Marcy Park.

"Thank you, everyone," Zelda called.

Ray turned to me. "Anything else you need me to do?"

The hopeful tone filled me with such yearning, I wanted to take him in my arms and float off like a Chagall painting. "No. We couldn't have done it without you."

"Please don't thank me."

I knew what he meant, that he didn't want me to

312

treat him like a stranger. I had no intention. I rested a hand on his chest and kissed his cheek. "I'm going back to my aunt's to change."

He made no challenge, no excuses. Only calm acceptance shone in his face. "I'll call you later."

"Yes." Yes, he understood my need to spend time with family. Yes, he wanted me to have what I needed. Yes, I knew how rare and precious he was. He glanced back at me a few times as he walked away. Each time, the connection between us strengthened rather than weakened and stayed strong after he faded into the darkness.

A moan, and my grandmother nudged me. "I need *sansachun*." She leaned closer to clarify, "Medicine alcohol."

I laughed. "A glass, or a bottle?"

"I planned for the worst case scenario and told my daughter to buy three bottles." She turned to Zelda. "You did buy three bottles."

"Yes, *Eomeoni.*"

Grandmother linked arms with me, and with Zelda, and we headed for the car like Dorothy, the Tinman, and the Lion heading down the Yellow Brick Road. "We will wing it."

"I doubt you've ever winged anything in your life."

"You don't know as much as you think," *Halmeoni* said good-naturedly.

"I'm hoping you'll teach me." I matched her pleasantness but meant every word. I opened the passenger door for her.

She climbed inside, graceful as a long-limbed heron, and gathered up her skirt to keep it from getting crushed.

As I sat on the back seat, I wondered if my grandmother did everything with such purpose. I envied the way she lived in each moment with intention, clear in her surety of what must be done.

My admiration wavered after we reached my aunt's house and my grandmother poured three rounds of the alcohol she'd demanded Zelda buy in advance of her visit. When I lifted the glass to my lips, the rank odor caused me to jerk my head back. "Is *sansachun* supposed to smell so terrible?"

"Like ripe cheese?" Zelda tucked her legs beneath her on the sofa. "Yes." She tilted the glass to her lips.

Halmeoni gulped a good portion. "You get used to it. Drink."

I held my breath and sipped. A fruity flavor sloshed over my palate. "Oh, this is nice." I tasted it again. Already, the scent bothered me less.

Grandmother pointed at me. "Careful, it will sneak up on you."

"Like everything else in my life." I gulped.

Zelda eyed me. "Raymond seems very fond of you."

The mere mention of his name sent a buzz through me. "He's a good guy."

"Almost as handsome as his grandfather," *Halmeoni* said. "If I hadn't been married, I might have ruined my reputation with him."

"Rusty?" I asked at the same time Zelda burst out yelling, "Mother!"

I leaned forward, eager to hear more.

She didn't disappoint. A dreaminess in her face matched her story, and she told it like a fairy tale with a Shakespearean twist, A Midsummer Night's Dream entwined with Sleeping Beauty. She'd never thought of herself as beautiful until he'd looked in her eyes, never thought herself capable of more than being a mother and wife. He'd taught her to believe in herself, in the unique spirit she embodied. She loved her husband, but Rusty had worked some sort of magic on her, brought the best in her to the surface. Though they never so much as held hands, their bond had grown as deep.

"We are soul mates. Not in the way of lovers. In the way of two souls meeting at a time in our lives when we needed each other."

Lost in our own thoughts, we fell silent. The haze surrounding us might have been wistfulness, or maybe the *sansachun* kicking in.

My grandmother rose. It registered on my consciousness like seaweed flowing up through the water to the surface.

She shuffled to the kitchen. "We will need hangover stew."

"Ugh," I groaned. "Stew? For hangovers?"

"Koreans know the best remedies. With this stew, I will be able to get on the plane tomorrow with a clear head."

"You're leaving tomorrow?" When had she made reservations? Zelda wore the same expression of surprise that I probably had.

"It is time." She rummaged through the pantry. "I suppose you have no congealed ox blood?"

"I ran out last week." Zelda winked at me.

A small gesture, but an undeniable sign of inclusion. Belonging.

"I will make do." My grandmother softly sang what sounded like a Korean tune, and Phoebe joined in.

I watched them with a mix of incredulity and humor. "Phoebe has to be the strangest parrot ever. Where did you find her, anyway?" We'd had a cat when I was growing up, one we'd brought along when we moved, but after that, no pets.

"She found us."

"A stray?" A hiccup erupted, and I pressed fingers to my lips, to no effect. "'Scuse me."

"You can't hold your liquor." Zelda, on the other hand, appeared the same as always.

"*Sansachun*," which I could no longer pronounce, "agrees with you." I squinted to get a better view of her. "You're practically glowing." It was true. An aura of light pulsed around her, and I doubted the alcohol had anything to do with it.

"As does my mother." Zelda inclined her head toward *Halmeoni*. "And you, though yours is stronger than ours."

I turned a hand in front of me. "I do?" Had some of White Buffalo Woman's gift of lightning lingered in my system?

Halmeoni yawned. "I need to rest. So do you. My plane is at ten o'clock. We will need to leave for the airport no later than seven thirty."

My movements sloppy, I took my grandmother in my arms, once again struck by the tensile strength in her tall, slim frame.

Zelda held up a finger to me. "You're sleeping on the sofa." She fetched blankets and a pillow and made up the couch. I settled gratefully onto the soft cushions.

Zelda leaned over and kissed my cheek. "Sleep well."

"You, too," I murmured, more content than I'd felt

in a long time. The medicinal alcohol not only healed our frayed nerves, it was helping to heal my family.

Silence nestled throughout the house. Rather than falling into a slumber as I'd expected, I was wide awake. When my cell chimed, I knew why. I'd been waiting for Ray to call, and he hadn't disappointed me. The sound of his voice through the phone calmed me more than the *sansachun*.

"I didn't wake you, I hope." He sounded sleepy himself, as if reclined on his bed.

I wished I could nestle into him, absorb his warmth.

"No, I'm drunk," I admitted with a chuckle. "My grandmother's a bad influence."

"You didn't drive home like that? I could have picked you up."

"You are the sweetest man," I said, not caring if I gushed. "I'm camping out at my aunt's for tonight. My grandmother's leaving in the morning, and I want to see her off."

"She's leaving already?"

"That's what I said. But I'm going to visit her in Texas soon."

"Good, so you won't lose touch with her."

"Never again," I said sleepily.

"You sound tired. I'll let you go. I just wanted to make sure you were all right. And I'm glad you're with your family. I didn't want you to be alone tonight."

All the responses that came to mind probably wouldn't come out right in my alcoholic state. "I'm glad you care enough to check in."

"I'm glad you're glad."

I could hear his smile through the phone, and my

embarrassment faded. "Talk to you tomorrow."

"Tomorrow. Good. Yes."

"Yes," I repeated, and that bubble of effervescence encased me. Who needed a black star? I now had happiness to shield me.

I stared into the darkness, and scenes of the night replayed in my head. Surreal. No wonder my mother never told me about this part of her life. I'd never have believed her. But now there was no other explanation for the strange occurrences I'd experienced.

Next year, we'd once again summon Old Man Gloom to act as a vessel for everyone's troubles. But next year, the flames would consume him along with the rest and release him from the effigy. Like the phoenix, the spirit would turn to ash and rise again, renewed. The cycle would continue year after year.

So long as someone was there to tend to the flames, to gather the deadened ashes that no one else could see and blow them away until my breath brushed against the empty skin of my palm.

Until my dying breath, that someone would be me. I was exactly where I was supposed to be. Home.

Chapter Twenty-Five

If the previous night lasted an eternity, the next few days breezed by. *Halmeoni* Bong-Cha was gone like the crane woman, folding her long legs aboard the Delta 787. Our goodbye was tearful but full of love. I promised I'd visit soon and bring Zelda along.

My obligation to the festival had ended with the burning of Zozobra, but curiosity drew me to the streets. La Fiesta de Santa Fe offered more events, and I wanted to be certain that no ill will lingered in the city.

Grandparents and parents gathered for The Children's Pet Parade, which proved as loud and boisterous as I'd expected. Kids led leashed dogs, cats, even a goat, an iguana sporting a bandanna, and a llama along the streets. The family members beamed as they waved and took pictures.

Everything appeared to be back to normal. My overabundance of caution was a good thing, probably, but unnecessary. I turned to stroll through the plaza, where every outdoor table was occupied. Couples sat on the ground, wrapped in their own worlds. One blonde sat close to a buff dark-haired man. Recognition stopped me in my tracks.

"Javi?" With Ashley. Oh, what had I cursed him with?

They both looked up. Ashley said, "Hey."

"Sorry, I didn't mean to intrude." All I wanted to

do now was get away.

But Javi gestured to an empty spot on the ground. "Hey, Mar. Have a seat."

"Only for a minute. I have to…" No excuse sprang to mind, so I crossed my legs as I sat. "What are you guys up to?" How awkward.

Javi turned his easy grin to me. "Just taking a lunch break. Want something from the food truck? I'm going for another water."

"Coffee would be great. Thanks."

He hopped to his feet and left Ashley and me to avoid each other's gaze.

My first thought slipped from my mouth. "I'm surprised to see you two together."

Her polite smile relaxed into a more natural one but held a secret. "I was on my way to the festival last night and ran into your cousin."

She didn't remember him dragging her away from Zozobra? "Oh." Afraid to say the wrong thing, I said no more.

Breaking from her private thoughts, she said, "Sorry I missed the event. Did it go well?"

"Yes. Very well. But you didn't miss much."

She stretched out her legs, not bothering to shield her heels from the dirt. "I suppose it was the same old, same old. And it's so funny, but Javi and I spent the whole night talking."

"The whole night," I repeated.

Turning her face up to the sun, she closed her eyes. "Yeah. It was nice. He's a great guy."

"He really is." Too bad I sounded less than enthusiastic.

One slitted eye peered at me. "He was a perfect

gentleman, if you're worried." Then she lifted her chin and appeared so at ease, she might have been sleeping.

"I wasn't." Not about her.

Javi appeared at my side and handed me a cup.

Ashley leaned close to him as he sat next to her. "I was just telling Marissa what a great listener you are."

His face flushed, and he looked about ten years old, innocent and happy. "Anytime you want to talk, I'm here for you."

"You're sweet." She ducked her head, and they exchanged a glance that spoke volumes without saying a single word.

My cue to leave. "I'd better go."

Ashley checked her watch. "Me, too. Some of us have work today."

A dig? "I put in for a vacation day long ago."

"I'm just joking. Lighten up." She sounded pleasant—and sincere. "See you around."

Javi watched her walk away. "She dodged a big one last night, didn't she?" His narrowed eyes dared me to bullshit him.

"She did. But I think she'll be fine."

"Go easy on her. She needs friends."

"Don't we all?" I raised my cup to Javi. "Thanks for the coffee. You're a good guy, Javi Furtado."

"Yeah, yeah. Say hi to Ray for me." He gave my shoulder a gentle squeeze.

My cell signaled a text. Sure enough, Ray's name showed in the display. "Are you psychic?"

"He said he wasn't taking no for an answer anymore."

"No is such a negative word anyway." The last few weeks had put a damper on what we'd started, but I had no pressing obligations anymore. I intended to be the essence of positivity.

"*Hasta la vista.*" A grin, and Javi turned and strode off.

I read the message:

—*How are you feeling after your big night?*—

Feeling? There was no way to express them. As for how I was, the answer was as equally complex as it was simple: I was changed forever. One text could never convey it all, only a slow unveiling. One that would last years, I hoped.

One word encapsulated how I felt.

—*Good.*—

A call from Ashley interrupted, and curiosity got the better of me. "Hey, what's up?"

"An assignment. I thought you might want to cover the story instead."

"What story?"

"Luis Valdez is home. If you don't want to, I'll—"

Luis had come home? "I do." I was nearly sprinting toward my SUV already.

"I'll send a photographer to meet you there."

Questions were already lining up in my mind. Where had Luis gone? And why? "Thanks, Ashley. I owe you one."

"Two," she corrected.

She hadn't forgotten I'd scooped her story about the fire. Nor did I blame her. "Two," I agreed as I climbed into the driver's seat. The extra traffic from the festival slowed me down, making the drive to the Valdez residence twice as long as it should have been. Larsen leaned against his car, parked in the street, so I pulled up behind him and clambered out.

He shouldered his digital camera bag. "Thought Stirling was covering this one."

"She gave me her blessing," I assured him, and hurried to the front door.

Mrs. Valdez answered and ushered us in, dabbing at her eyes. She spoke excitedly in a mix of Spanish and English and gestured to the front room.

At seeing me, Luis rose slowly from the sofa. The change in him was immediately evident—no more hunched shoulders, no averting his gaze. Everything about him appeared more open.

"Ms. Tahy." Luis spoke first. No more murmuring, either.

"Luis, I'm so glad you're back." I extended my hand, wishing I could hug him instead, but that would cross a line. "May I sit?"

"Yes, please," Mr. Valdez urged, his arm flung around the boy's shoulder.

Luis waited for me to take a seat before reclaiming his spot on the sofa.

Bill busied himself setting up and looking for the angle with the best lighting.

No longer cluttered, the tidy home lent a cozy atmosphere. Mrs. Valdez fluttered between us, offering an array of refreshments. Her constant smile was a lovely alternative to the harsh expression she wore last time. But of course, she was happy. Her son had returned.

"This is amazing, Luis. You look very healthy, so I'm assuming that no one forced you to leave Santa Fe?"

He glanced uncertainly at his father, then his mother. Maybe something, or someone, had compelled

C. A. Masterson

him, but he couldn't identify it.

I simplified the question. "You weren't abducted, correct?"

"No. We were fighting every day, about the smallest things. Everyone was so angry. I couldn't take it anymore. I felt like if I didn't get away, I'd explode."

Temporary madness. We'd all been infected with some degree of insanity these past few months. Luis had the good sense to get away from the source: the spirit of Zozobra.

I spoke softly, not wanting to appear judgmental. "Where were you all this time, Luis?"

"California. For some reason, waiting another year to graduate high school became unbearable."

His mother dabbed a tissue to her eyes.

"I needed to get away from this city," Luis went on, "and start my future now. Such a stupid thing to do. I made a terrible mistake." The last, he said to his father, as if seeking absolution.

His father didn't hesitate. He drew him close and kissed his head.

Adjusting the digital camera, Bill clicked away, capturing the intense emotions. Readers would love this feel-good feature story. I was feeling pretty great about it myself. Luis had managed to escape great danger unscathed.

I hated to interrupt their reunion, but the sooner I finished, the sooner they could celebrate privately. "Where were you staying?"

Luis shrugged. "Shelters, mostly. I didn't have a lot of money, so I wandered the streets a lot."

"When did you decide to come home?"

He furrowed his brows. "I suddenly missed my

324

family, so bad it was like someone had cut a hole in me. I caught the first bus home on Thursday night."

Thursday night. The night Old Man Gloom burned. When we'd released the spirit from the effigy, the spirit had released its hold on Luis.

I nodded. "So you decided on the spot? Just like that?"

Perplexed, he shook his head. "I can't explain, except it was like someone had been Tasering me over and over, and then bam, it stopped. My mind cleared, and I knew what I had to do."

"So you came home." I sent him an encouraging smile. "That's wonderful. I'm sure your parents are thrilled." I looked to them for affirmation.

Mrs. Valdez sobbed. "We were out of our minds with worry."

Luis clasped his mother's hand. "I'm sorry for any pain I caused my family. And I appreciate the city's efforts to find me." Without prompting, Luis offered more. "I decided that, after I graduate college, I'm going to return to New Mexico, and eventually establish a practice in Santa Fe."

"That's a fantastic way to give back to your community."

"They've done so much for me. It's the least I can do."

"I'm sure I can speak for everyone when I say how happy we are to have you back safe and sound." I rose. "I'm grateful you welcomed us into your home at such an emotional time."

The family walked us outside, and we shook hands. Bill got one last shot, the three of them in front of their house, the door open. Their happy faces said more than my article could convey.

****

Everyone in the newsroom was surprised to see me. Except Ashley. After a breezy hello, she went back to work on her computer, and I got to work writing the article.

Spotting me from his office, Weller scowled as he approached. "Thought you were off today."

"I am. I'll be gone as soon as I wrap this story."

A grunt, and he left me alone. With a satisfied sigh, I submitted the article and shut down the computer. I still had time to catch part of the *Entrada,* the re-enactment of when Don Diego de Vargas returned to reclaim the city he'd conquered after the Pueblo Revolt. Or maybe I'd skip that event. I'd rather not have any more visions from that time period in the history of Santa Fe. The City Different. Different even from yesterday. What a relief that was true.

On my way out, I stopped by Ashley's desk. "Hey, thanks again for handing over that story. It was really great to see Luis."

"How is the kid?"

"Great." How nice to be able to say that with no hesitation. "Have a great weekend."

"Hey, Marissa. Wait. 'I wanted to apologize."

"For what?"

"You were right. That guy turned out to be a jerk. I should have listened to you."

"I'm glad you're all right." More than simply all right. She was being genuine, not acting out of despair or anger.

"And your cousin's a great guy, but I'm not seeing him, just so you know. He helped me through a rough night, and I appreciate that."

She must think of me as a judgmental jerk. "Ashley—"

"It's okay. I had to get that off my chest. I'm not going to see anyone for a while. It's time I reconnect with myself." She grinned. "And the next Happy Hour, beer's on me."

I gave a nod. "Okay then. See you Monday."

"Have a good one." She sounded sincere.

"Yeah, you too." In the parking lot, I checked my cell. Three texts from Ray, each shorter than the last. I responded:

—*Got caught up in work, sorry.*—

His answer came immediately.

—*Thought I'd lost you.*—

Warmth spread through me, as if he'd wrapped his arms around me.

—*Never.*—

—*I was hoping you'd say that. What are you doing for dinner?*—

—*I have some Korean recipes I want to try out on you.*—

—*Korean? Cool.*—

—*Yeah, my grandmother taught me a few.*—

Among other things I wouldn't mention. I intended to not only acknowledge my heritage but celebrate it. Our family's odd mix of cultures was rich and ready to be explored. So what if we didn't fit any particular mold? What was normal anyway?

Another blues riff, and I read Ray's text.

—*What time should I come over?*—

Without the slightest hesitation, I typed:

—*Anytime after three. I have some errands to*

run.—

One in particular, I wasn't looking forward to doing. But I'd avoided the old Mission Road lot long enough. It was time to make peace with the site, with all the memories it held. Not all of them were horrible. Except for that one terrible night, my family had been happy there.

My false bravado abandoned me once I'd finished the other tasks on my To Do list, and only the last stop remained. I'd put it off till last as a matter of practicality, I told myself, because it was only a few blocks from the apartment.

I pulled the SUV into where the old driveway had been, the lane barely discernible among the overgrown weeds. A few patches of overturned dirt appeared fresher than the last time I'd been here, more than three months ago.

Seemed more like a lifetime.

When I stepped out and stood on the lot, I braced for an onslaught of horrific memories. Nothing hit me except a gentle breeze. The early September sun warmed my skin. Everything was…peaceful. Settled.

The neighborhood looked much the same as I'd remembered, the adobe and stucco homes, wood trimmed in cozy Santa Fe styles, all well maintained. The stand of trees across the road were in full leaf glory, their green a welcome contrast to the earthy tans and browns of the houses.

I picked my way across the ground and stopped about where I guessed our house had stood. I crouched, ran my fingers across the gritty dirt. No screams sounded in my head. I sifted some through my fingers. A low-level energy hummed beneath the surface, steady and tranquil. Like Michael's presence. I could almost hear him say, "Hey, who cares about them? You and me, we're *thiwahe*. And family *akiksiza.*"

In my mind's eye, I saw him at the window. Heard his voice repeating those words. Now I finally knew what he meant.

"Yes," I said aloud. "We protect each other. We refuse to surrender."

Michael had been as much a part of the ritual as any of us. More than the rest of us. He had literally been on the front line of defense, his very remains part of the metallic laden clay that composed the black stars. Because of his sacrifice that night, and his great love for all of us, he'd protected us. Even *Ptesan-Wi*'s blessing couldn't have made the stars any purer, or any more powerful.

I rose and looked out over the Sangre de Cristo Mountains. The afternoon sun lit their peaks in a glorious display, yet serene. Like Michael, the spirit was at rest.

A word about the author…

Award-winning author C. A. Masterson loves stories of any genre. Multi-published in contemporary to historical, fantasy/dark fantasy to paranormal/speculative, she sometimes mashes genres.

Visit her at:

http://paintingfirewithwords.blogspot.com

and in strange nooks and far-flung corners of the web.